point of retreat

Also by Colleen Hoover

Slammed

point of retreat

Colleen Hoover

London · New York · Sydney · Toronto · New Delhi

First published in Great Britain in 2012 by Simon & Schuster UK Ltd

13

Simon & Schuster UK Ltd
1st Floor
222 Gray's Inn Road
London WC1X 8HB

www.simonandschuster.co.uk

Simon & Schuster Australia, Sydney
Simon & Schuster India, New Delhi

A CIP catalogue copy for this book
is available from the British Library.

Paperback ISBN: 978-1-47112-568-3
Ebook ISBN: 978-1-47112-556-0

Printed and bound by CPI Group (UK) Ltd, Croydon, CR0 4YY

This book is dedicated to everyone who read Slammed *and encouraged me to continue telling the story of Layken and Will.*

point of retreat

prologue

DECEMBER 31

"Resolutions"

I'm confident this will be our year. Lake's and my year.

The last few years have definitely not been in our favor. It was over three years ago when my parents both passed away unexpectedly, leaving me to raise my little brother all on my own. It didn't help that Vaughn decided to end our two-year relationship on the heels of their death. To top it off, I ended up having to drop my scholarship. Leaving the university and moving back to Ypsilanti to become Caulder's guardian was one of the hardest decisions I've ever made . . . but also one of the best decisions.

I spent every single day of the next year learning how to

adjust. How to adjust to heartbreak, how to adjust to having no parents, how to adjust to essentially becoming a parent myself and the sole provider of a family. Looking back on it, I don't think I could have made it without Caulder. He's the only thing that kept me going.

I don't even remember the entire first half of last year. Last year didn't start for me until September 22, the day I first laid eyes on Lake. Of course, last year turned out to be just as difficult as the previous years, but in a completely different way. I'd never felt more alive than when I was with her—but considering our circumstances, I couldn't be with her. So I guess I didn't spend a lot of time feeling alive.

This year has been better, in its own way. A lot of falling in love, a lot of grief, a lot of healing, and even more adjusting. Julia passed away in September. I didn't expect her death to be as hard on me as it was. It was almost like losing my mother all over again.

I miss my mother. And I miss Julia. Thank God I have Lake.

Like me, my father loved to write. He always used to tell me that writing down his daily thoughts was therapeutic for his soul. Maybe one of the reasons I've had such a difficult time adjusting over the past three years is that I didn't take his advice. I assumed slamming a few times a year was enough "therapy" for me. Maybe I was wrong. I want the upcoming year to be everything I've planned for it to be: perfect. With all that said (or written), writing is my resolution. Even if it's just one word a day, I'm going to write it down . . . get it out of me.

part one

1.

THURSDAY, JANUARY 5

I registered for classes today. Didn't get the days I wanted, but I only have two semesters left, so it's getting harder to be picky about my schedule. I'm thinking about applying to local schools for another teaching job after next semester. Hopefully, by this time next year, I'll be teaching again. For right now, though, I'm living off student loans. Luckily, my grandparents have been supportive while I work on my master's degree. I wouldn't be able to do it without them, that's for sure.

We're having dinner with Gavin and Eddie tonight. I think I'll make cheeseburgers. Cheeseburgers sound good. That's all I really have to say right now . . .

"IS LAYKEN OVER HERE OR OVER THERE?" EDDIE asks, peering in the front door.

"Over there," I say from the kitchen.

Is there a sign on my house instructing people *not* to knock? Lake never knocks anymore, but her comfort here apparently extends to Eddie as well. Eddie heads across the street to Lake's house, and Gavin walks inside, tapping his knuckles against the front door. It's not an official knock, but at least he's making an attempt.

"What are we eating?" he asks. He slips his shoes off at the door and makes his way into the kitchen.

"Burgers." I hand him a spatula and point to the stove, instructing him to flip the burgers while I pull the fries out of the oven.

"Will, do you ever notice how we somehow always get stuck cooking?"

"It's probably not a bad thing," I say as I loosen the fries from the pan. "Remember Eddie's Alfredo?"

He grimaces when he remembers the Alfredo. "Good point," he says.

I call Kel and Caulder into the kitchen to have them set the table. For the past year, since Lake and I have been together, Gavin and Eddie have been eating with us at least twice a week. I finally had to invest in a dining room table because the bar was getting a little too crowded.

"Hey, Gavin," Kel says. He walks into the kitchen and grabs a stack of cups out of the cabinet.

"Hey," Gavin responds. "You decide where we're having your party next week?"

Kel shrugs. "I don't know. Maybe bowling. Or we could just do something here."

Caulder walks into the kitchen and starts setting places at the table. I glance behind me and notice them setting an extra place. "We expecting company?" I ask.

"Kel invited Kiersten," Caulder says teasingly.

Kiersten moved into a house on our street about a month ago, and Kel seems to have developed a slight crush on her. He won't admit it. He's just now about to turn eleven, so Lake and I expected this to happen. Kiersten's a few months older than he is, and a lot taller. Girls hit puberty faster than boys, so maybe he'll eventually catch up.

"Next time you guys invite someone else, let me

know. Now I need to make another burger." I walk to the refrigerator and take out one of the extra patties.

"She doesn't eat meat," Kel says. "She's a vegetarian."

Figures. I put the meat back in the fridge. "I don't have any fake meat. What's she gonna do? Eat bread?"

"Bread's fine," Kiersten says as she walks through the front door—without knocking. "I like bread. French fries, too. I just don't eat things that are a result of unjustified animal homicide." Kiersten walks to the table and grabs the roll of paper towels and starts tearing them off, laying one beside each plate. Her self-assurance reminds me a little of Eddie's.

"Who's she?" Gavin asks, watching Kiersten make herself at home. She's never eaten with us before, but you wouldn't know that by how she's taking command.

"She's the eleven-year-old neighbor I was telling you about. The one I think is an imposter based on the things that come out of her mouth. I'm beginning to suspect she's really a tiny adult posing as a little redheaded child."

"Oh, the one Kel's crushing on?" Gavin smiles, and I can see his wheels turning. He's already thinking of ways to embarrass Kel at dinner. Tonight should be interesting.

Gavin and I have become pretty close this past year. It's good, I guess, considering how close Eddie and Lake are. Kel and Caulder really like them, too. It's nice. I like the setup we all have. I hope it stays this way.

Eddie and Lake finally walk in as we're all sitting down at the table. Lake has her wet hair pulled up in a knot on top of her head. She's wearing house shoes, sweatpants, and a T-shirt. I love that about her, the fact that she's so comfortable here. She takes the seat next to mine and leans in and kisses me on the cheek.

"Thanks, babe. Sorry it took me so long. I was trying to register online for Statistics, but the class is full. Guess I'll have to go sweet-talk someone at the admin office tomorrow."

"Why are you taking Statistics?" Gavin asks. He grabs the ketchup and squirts it on his plate.

"I took Algebra Two in the winter mini-mester. I'm trying to knock out all my math in the first year, since I hate it so much." Lake grabs the ketchup out of Gavin's hands and squirts some on my plate, then on her own.

"What's your hurry? You've already got more credits than Eddie and I do, put together," he says. Eddie nods in agreement as she takes a bite of her burger.

Lake nudges her head toward Kel and Caulder. "I've already got more *kids* than you and Eddie put together. *That's* my hurry."

"What's your major?" Kiersten asks Lake.

Eddie glances toward Kiersten, finally noticing the extra person seated at the table. "Who are you?"

Kiersten looks at Eddie and smiles. "I'm Kiersten. I live diagonal to Will and Caulder, parallel to Layken and Kel. We moved here from Detroit right before Christmas. Mom says we needed to get out of the city before the city got out of us . . . whatever that means. I'm eleven. I've been eleven since eleven-eleven-eleven. It was a pretty big day, you know. Not many people can say they turned eleven on eleven-eleven-eleven. I'm a little bummed that I was born at three o'clock in the afternoon. If I would have been born at eleven-eleven, I'm pretty sure I could have got on the news or something. I could have recorded the segment and used it someday for my portfolio. I'm gonna be an actress when I grow up."

Eddie, along with the rest of us, stares at Kiersten without responding. Kiersten is oblivious, turning to Lake to repeat her question. "What's your major, Layken?"

Lake lays her burger down on her plate and clears her throat. I know how much she hates this question. She tries to answer confidently. "I haven't decided yet."

Kiersten looks at her with pity. "I see. The proverbial undecided. My oldest brother has been a sophomore in college for three years. He's got enough credits to have five majors by now. I think he stays undecided because he'd rather sleep until noon every day, sit in class for three hours, and go out every night, than actually graduate and get a real job. Mom says that's not true—she says it's because he's trying to 'discover his full potential' by examining all of his interests. If you ask me, I think it's bullshit."

I cough when the sip I just swallowed tries to make its way back up with my laugh.

"You just said 'bullshit'!" Kel says.

"Kel, don't say 'bullshit'!" Lake says.

"But she said 'bullshit' first," Caulder says, defending Kel.

"Caulder, don't say 'bullshit'!" I yell.

"Sorry," Kiersten says to Lake and me. "Mom says the FCC is responsible for inventing cuss words just for media shock value. She says if everyone would just use them enough, they wouldn't be considered cuss words anymore, and no one would ever be offended by them."

This kid is hard to keep up with!

"Your mother *encourages* you to cuss?" Gavin says.

Kiersten nods. "I don't see it that way. It's more like she's encouraging us to undermine a system flawed through overuse of words that are made out to be harmful, when in fact they're just letters, mixed together like every other word. That's all they are, mixed-up letters. Like, take the word 'butterfly,' for example. What if someone decided one day that 'butterfly' is a cuss word? People would eventually start using the word 'butterfly' as an insult and to emphasize things in a negative way. The actual *word* doesn't mean anything. It's the negative association people give these words that make them cuss words. So, if we all just decided to keep saying 'butterfly' all the time, people would stop caring. The shock value would subside, and it would become just another word again. Same with every other so-called bad word.

If we would all start saying them all the time, they wouldn't be bad anymore. That's what my mom says, anyway." She smiles and takes a french fry and dips it in ketchup.

I often wonder, when Kiersten's visiting, how she turned out the way she did. I have yet to meet her mother, but from what I've gathered, she's definitely not ordinary. Kiersten is obviously smarter than most kids her age, even if it is in a strange way. The things that come out of her mouth make Kel and Caulder seem somewhat normal.

"Kiersten?" Eddie says. "Will you be my new best friend?"

Lake grabs a french fry off her plate and throws it at Eddie, hitting her in the face with it. "That's bullshit," Lake says.

"Oh, go *butterfly* yourself," Eddie says. She returns a fry in Lake's direction.

I intercept the french fry, hoping it won't result in another food fight, like last week. I'm still finding broccoli everywhere. "Stop," I say, dropping the french fry on the table. "If you two have another food fight in my house, I'm kicking *both* of your butterflies!"

Lake can see I'm serious. She squeezes my leg under the table and changes the subject. "Suck-and-sweet time," she says.

"Suck-and-sweet time?" Kiersten asks, confused.

Kel fills her in. "It's where you have to say your suck and your sweet of the day. The good and the bad. The high and the low. We do it every night at supper."

Kiersten nods as though she understands.

"I'll go first," Eddie says. "My suck today was registration. I got stuck in Monday, Wednesday, Friday classes. Tuesday and Thursdays were full."

Everyone wants the Tuesday/Thursday schedules. The classes are longer, but it's a fair trade, having to go only twice a week rather than three times.

"My *sweet* is meeting Kiersten, my new best friend," Eddie says, glaring at Lake.

Lake grabs another french fry and throws it at Eddie. Eddie ducks, and the fry goes over her head. I take Lake's plate and scoot it to the other side of me, out of her reach.

Lake shrugs and smiles at me. "Sorry." She grabs a fry off my plate and puts it in her mouth.

"Your turn, Mr. Cooper," Eddie says. She still calls me

that, usually when she's trying to point out that I'm being a "bore."

"My suck was definitely registration, too. I got Monday, Wednesday, Friday."

Lake turns to me, upset. "What? I thought we were both doing Tuesday/Thursday classes."

"I tried, babe. They don't offer my level of courses on those days. I texted you."

She pouts. "Man, that really is a suck," she says. "And I didn't get your text. I can't find my phone again."

She's always losing her phone.

"What's your sweet?" Eddie asks me.

That's easy. "My sweet is right now," I say as I kiss Lake on the forehead.

Kel and Caulder both groan. "Will, that's your sweet *every* night," Caulder says, annoyed.

"My turn," Lake says. "Registration was actually my sweet. I haven't figured out Statistics yet, but my other four classes were exactly what I wanted." She looks at Eddie and continues. "My suck was losing my best friend to an eleven-year-old."

Eddie laughs.

"I wanna go," Kiersten says. No one objects. "My

suck was having bread for dinner," she says, eyeing her plate.

She's ballsy. I toss another slice of bread on her plate. "Maybe next time you show up uninvited to a carnivore's house, you should bring your own fake meat."

She ignores my comment. "My sweet was three o'clock."

"What happened at three o'clock?" Gavin asks.

Kiersten shrugs. "School let out. I butterflying *hate* school."

All three kids glance at one another, as if there's an unspoken agreement. I make a mental note to talk to Caulder about it later. Lake nudges me with her elbow and shoots me a questioning glance, letting me know she's thinking the same thing.

"Your turn, whatever your name is," Kiersten says to Gavin.

"It's Gavin. And my suck would have to be the fact that an eleven-year-old has a larger vocabulary than me," he says, smiling at Kiersten. "My sweet today is sort of a surprise." He looks at Eddie and waits for her response.

"What?" Eddie says.

"Yeah, what?" Lake adds.

I'm curious, too. Gavin just leans back in his seat with a smile, waiting for us to guess.

Eddie gives him a shove. "Tell us!" she says.

He leans forward in his chair and slaps his hands on the table. "I got a job! At Getty's, delivering pizza!" He looks happy, for some reason.

"*That's* your sweet? You're a pizza delivery guy?" Eddie asks. "That's more like a suck."

"You know I've been looking for a job. And it's Getty's. We love Getty's!"

Eddie rolls her eyes. "Well, congratulations," she says unconvincingly.

"Do we get free pizza?" Kel asks.

"No, but we get a discount," Gavin replies.

"That's my sweet, then," Kel says. "Cheap pizza!" Gavin looks pleased that someone is excited for him. "My suck today was Principal Brill," Kel says.

"Oh Lord, what'd she do?" Lake asks him. "Or better yet, what did *you* do?"

"It wasn't just me," Kel says.

Caulder puts his elbow on the table and tries to hide his face from my line of sight.

"What did you do, Caulder?" I ask him. He brings his hand down and looks up at Gavin. Gavin puts his elbow on the table and shields his face from my line of sight as well. He continues to eat as he ignores my glare. "Gavin? What prank did you tell them about this time?"

Gavin grabs two fries and throws them at Kel and Caulder. "No more! I'm not telling you any more stories. You two get me in trouble every time!" Kel and Caulder laugh and throw the fries back at him.

"I'll tell on them, I don't mind," Kiersten says. "They got in trouble at lunch. Mrs. Brill was on the other side of the cafeteria, and they were thinking of a way to get her to run. Everyone says she waddles like a duck when she runs, and we wanted to see it. So Kel pretended he was choking, and Caulder made a huge spectacle and got behind him and started beating on his back, pretending to give him the Heimlich maneuver. It freaked Mrs. Brill out! When she got to our table, Kel said he was all better. He told Mrs. Brill that Caulder saved his life. It would have been fine, but she had already told someone to call 911. Within minutes, two ambulances and a fire truck showed up at the school.

One of the boys at the next table told Mrs. Brill they were faking the whole thing, so Kel got called to the office."

Lake leans forward and glares at Kel. "Please tell me this is a joke."

Kel looks up with an innocent expression. "It was a joke. I really didn't think anyone would call 911. Now I have to spend all next week in detention."

"Why didn't Mrs. Brill call me?" Lake asks him.

"I'm pretty sure she did," he says. "You can't find your phone, remember?"

"Ugh! If she calls me in for another conference, you're grounded!"

I look at Caulder, who's attempting to avoid my gaze. "Caulder, what about you? Why didn't Mrs. Brill try to call me?"

He turns toward me and gives me a mischievous grin. "Kel lied for me. He told her that I really thought he was choking and I was trying to save his life," he says. "Which brings me to my sweet for the day. I was rewarded for my heroic behavior. Mrs. Brill gave me two free study hall passes."

Only Caulder could find a way to avoid detention and

get rewarded instead. "You two need to cut that crap out," I say to them. "And Gavin, no more prank stories."

"Yes, Mr. Cooper," Gavin says sarcastically. "But I have to know," he says, looking at the kids, "does she really waddle?"

"Yeah." Kiersten laughs. "She's a waddler, all right." She looks at Caulder. "What was your suck, Caulder?"

Caulder gets serious. "My best friend almost choked to death today. He could have *died.*"

We all laugh. As much as Lake and I try to do the responsible thing, sometimes it's hard to draw the line between being the rule enforcer and being the sibling. We choose which battles to pick with the boys, and Lake says it's important that we don't choose very many. I look at her and see she's laughing, so I assume this isn't one she wants to fight.

"Can I finish my food now?" Lake says, pointing to her plate, still on the other side of me, out of her reach. I scoot the plate back in front of her. "Thank you, Mr. Cooper," she says.

I knee her under the table. She knows I hate it when she calls me that. I don't know why it bothers me so much. Probably because when I actually was her teacher, it was absolute torture. Our connection progressed so quickly that first night I took her out. I'd never met anyone I had so much fun just being myself with. I spent the entire weekend thinking about her. The moment I walked around the corner and saw her standing in the hallway in front of my classroom, I felt like my heart had been ripped right out of my chest. I knew immediately what she was doing there, even though it took her a little longer to figure it out. When she realized I was a teacher, the look in her eyes absolutely devastated me. She was hurt. Heartbroken. Just like me. One thing I know for sure, I never want to see that look in her eyes again.

Kiersten stands up and takes her plate to the sink. "I have to go. Thanks for the bread, Will," she says sarcastically. "It was delicious."

"I'm leaving, too. I'll walk you home," Kel says. He jumps out of his seat and follows her to the door. I look at Lake, and she rolls her eyes. It bothers her that Kel has developed his first crush. Lake doesn't like to think that we're about to have to deal with teenage hormones.

Caulder gets up from the table. "I'm gonna watch TV in my room," he says. "See you later, Kel. Bye, Kiersten." They both tell him goodbye as they leave.

"I really like that girl," Eddie says after Kiersten leaves. "I hope Kel asks her to be his girlfriend. I hope they grow up and get married and have lots of weird babies. I hope she's in our family forever."

"Shut up, Eddie," Lake says. "He's only ten. He's too young for a girlfriend."

"Not really, he'll be eleven in eight days," Gavin says. "Eleven is the prime age for first girlfriends."

Lake takes an entire handful of fries and throws them toward Gavin's face.

I just sigh. She's impossible to control. "You're cleaning up tonight," I say to her. "You, too," I say to Eddie. "Gavin, let's go watch some football, like real men, while the women do their job."

Gavin scoots his glass toward Eddie. "Refill this glass, woman. I'm watching some football."

While Eddie and Lake clean the kitchen, I take the opportunity to ask Gavin for a favor. Lake and I haven't had any alone time in weeks due to always having the boys. I really need alone time with her.

"Do you think you and Eddie could take Kel and Caulder to a movie tomorrow night?"

He doesn't answer right away, which makes me feel guilty for even asking. Maybe they had plans already.

"It depends," he finally responds. "Do we have to take Kiersten, too?"

I laugh. "That's up to your girl. She's her new best friend."

Gavin rolls his eyes at the thought. "It's fine; we had plans to watch a movie anyway. What time? How long do you want us to keep them?"

"Doesn't matter. We aren't going anywhere. I just need a couple of hours alone with Lake. There's something I need to give her."

"Oh ... I see," he says. "Just text me when you're through 'giving it to her,' and we'll bring the boys home."

I shake my head at his assumption and laugh. I like Gavin. What I hate, however, is the fact that everything that happens between me and Lake, and Gavin and Eddie ... we all seem to *know* about. That's the drawback of dating best friends: there are no secrets.

"Let's go," Eddie says as she pulls Gavin up off the

couch. "Thanks for supper, Will. Joel wants you guys to come over next weekend. He said he'd make tamales."

I don't turn down tamales. "We're there," I say.

After Eddie and Gavin leave, Lake comes to the living room and sits on the couch, curling her legs under her as she snuggles against me. I put my arm around her and pull her closer.

"I'm bummed," she says. "I was hoping we'd at least get the same days this semester. We never get any alone time with all these butterflying kids running around."

You would think, with our living across the street from each other, that we would have all the time in the world together. That's not the case. Last semester she went to school Monday, Wednesday, and Friday, and I went all five days. Weekends we spent a lot of time doing homework but mostly stayed busy with Kel's and Caulder's sports. When Julia passed away in September, that put even more on Lake's plate. It's been an adjustment, to say the least. The only place we seem to be lacking is getting quality alone time. It's kind of awkward, if the boys are at one house, to go to the other house to be alone. They almost always seem to follow us whenever we do.

"We'll get through it," I say. "We always do."

She pulls my face toward hers and kisses me. I've been kissing her every day for over a year, and it somehow gets better every time.

"I better go," she says at last. "I have to get up early and go to the college to finish registration. I also need to make sure Kel's not outside making out with Kiersten."

We laugh about it now, but in a matter of years it'll be our reality. We won't even be twenty-five, and we'll be raising teenagers. It's a scary thought.

"Hold on. Before you leave . . . what are your plans tomorrow night?"

She rolls her eyes. "What kind of question is that? You're my plan. You're always my only plan."

"Good. Eddie and Gavin are taking the boys. Meet me at seven?"

She perks up and smiles. "Are you asking me out on a real, live date?"

I nod.

"Well, you suck at it, you know. You always have. Sometimes girls like to be *asked* and not *told.*"

She's trying to play hard to get, which is pointless,

since I've already got her. I play her game anyway. I kneel on the floor in front of her and look into her eyes. "Lake, will you do me the honor of accompanying me on a date tomorrow night?"

She leans back into the couch and looks away. "I don't know, I'm sort of busy," she says. "I'll check my schedule and let you know." She tries to look put out, but a smile breaks out on her face. She leans forward and hugs me; I lose my balance, and we end up on the floor. I roll her onto her back, and she stares up at me and laughs. "Fine. Pick me up at seven."

I brush her hair out of her eyes and run my finger along the edge of her cheek. "I love you, Lake."

"Say it again," she says.

I kiss her forehead and repeat, "I love you, Lake."

"One more time."

"I." I kiss her lips. "And love." I kiss them again. "And you."

"I love you, too."

I ease my body on top of hers and interlock my fingers with hers. I bring our hands above her head and press them into the floor, then lean in as if I'm going to kiss her, but I don't. I like to tease her when we're in this position. I barely touch my lips to hers until she closes her eyes, then I slowly pull away. She opens her eyes, and I smile at her, then lean in again. As soon as her eyes are closed, I pull away again.

"Dammit, Will! Butterflying kiss me already!"

She grabs my face and pulls my mouth to hers. We continue kissing until we get to the "point of retreat," as Lake likes to call it. She climbs out from under me and sits up on her knees as I roll onto my back and remain on the floor. We don't like to get carried away when we aren't alone in the house. It's so easy to do. When we catch ourselves taking things too far, one of us always calls retreat.

Before Julia passed away, we made the mistake of taking things too far, too soon—a crucial mistake on my part. It was just two weeks after we started officially dating, and Caulder was spending the night at Kel's house. Lake and I came back to my place after a movie. We started making out on the couch, and one thing led to another, neither of us willing to stop it. We weren't having sex, but we would have eventually if Julia hadn't walked in when she did. She completely flipped out. We were mortified. She grounded Lake and wouldn't let me see her for two weeks. I apologized probably a million times in those two weeks.

Julia sat us down together and made us swear we would wait at least a year. She made Lake get on the pill and made me look her in the eyes and give her my word. She wasn't upset about the fact that her eighteen-year-old daughter almost had sex. Julia was fairly reasonable and knew it would happen at some point. What hurt her was that I was so willing to take that from Lake after only two weeks of dating. It made me feel incredibly guilty, so I agreed to the promise. She also wanted us to set a good example for Kel and Caulder; she asked us not to spend the night at each other's houses during that year, either. After Julia passed away, we've stuck to our word. More out of respect for Julia than anything. Lord knows it's difficult sometimes. A lot of times.

We haven't discussed it, but last week was exactly a year since we made that promise to Julia. I don't want to rush Lake into anything; I want it to be completely up to her, so I haven't brought it up. Neither has she. Then again, we haven't really been alone.

"Point of retreat," she says, and stands up. "I'll see you tomorrow night. Seven o'clock. Don't be late."

"Go find your phone and text me good night," I tell her.

She opens the door and faces me as she backs out of the house, slowly pulling the door shut. "One more time?" she says.

"I love you, Lake."

2.

FRIDAY, JANUARY 6

I'm giving Lake her present in a little while. I'm not even sure what it is, since it's not something I picked out. I can't write any more right now, my hands are shaking. How the hell do these dates still make me nervous? I'm so pathetic.

"BOYS, NO BACKWARD TONIGHT. YOU KNOW GAVIN can't keep up when you guys talk backward." I wave goodbye and shut the door behind them.

It's almost seven. I go to the bathroom and brush my teeth, then grab my keys and jacket and head to my car. I can see Lake watching from the window. She probably doesn't realize it, but I could always see her watching from the window. Especially in the months before we were officially dating. Every day I would come home and see her shadow. It's what gave me hope that one day we would be able to be together: the fact that she still thought about me. After our fight in the laundry room, though, she stopped watching from the window. I thought I'd screwed everything up for good.

I back out of the driveway and straight into hers. I leave the car running and walk around to open the door for her. When I get back inside the car, I get a whiff of her perfume. It's the vanilla one, my favorite.

"Where are we going?" she asks.

"You'll see. It's a surprise," I say as I pull out of her driveway. Rather than turn onto the street, I pull right into my own driveway. I kill the ignition and run around to her side of the car and open the door.

"What are you doing, Will?"

I take her hand and pull her out of the car. "We're here." I love the look of confusion on her face, so I spare the details.

"You asked me out on a date to your house? I got dressed up, Will! I want to go somewhere."

She's whining. I laugh and take her hand and walk her inside. "No, *you* made me ask you out on a date. I never said we were going anywhere. I just asked if you had plans."

I've already cooked pasta, so I walk into the kitchen and get our plates. Rather than setting the table, I take the plates to the coffee table in the living room. She pulls off her jacket, seeming a little disappointed. I continue to elude her while I make our drinks and then take a seat on the floor with her.

"I'm not trying to seem ungrateful," she says around a mouthful of food. "It's just that we never get to go anywhere anymore. I was looking forward to doing something different."

I take a drink and wipe my mouth. "Babe, I know what you mean. But tonight has sort of already been planned out for us." I toss another bread stick on her plate.

"What do you mean, *planned out* for us? I'm not following," she says.

I don't respond. I just continue eating.

"Will, tell me what's going on, your evasiveness is making me nervous."

I grin at her and take a drink. "I'm not trying to make you nervous. I'm doing what I was told."

She can tell I'm enjoying this. She gives up trying to get anything out of me and takes another bite. "The pasta's good, at least," she says.

"So is the view."

She smiles and winks at me and continues to eat.

She's wearing her hair down tonight. I love it when she wears her hair down. I also love it when she wears it up. In fact, I don't think she's ever worn it in a way that made me not love it. She's so incredibly beautiful, especially when she's not trying to be. I realize I've been staring at her, lost in thought. I've eaten barely half my food, and she's almost finished.

"Will?" She wipes her mouth with her napkin. "Does this have anything to do with my mom?" she asks quietly. "You know . . . with our promise to her?"

I know what she's asking me. I immediately feel guilty that I haven't considered what she would think my intentions were tonight. I don't want her to feel like I expect anything at all from her.

"Not in that way, babe." I reach across and take her hand. "That's not what tonight's about. I'm sorry if you thought that. That's for another time . . . when you're ready."

She smiles at me. "Well, I wasn't gonna object if it was."

Her comment catches me off guard. I've gotten so used to the fact that one of us always calls retreat; I haven't entertained the possibility of the alternative for tonight.

She looks embarrassed by her forwardness and diverts her attention back down to her plate. She tears off a piece of bread and dips it in the sauce. When she's finished chewing, she takes a drink and looks back up at me.

"Before," she whispers unsteadily, "when I asked if this had anything to do with my mom, you said, 'Not in that way.' What'd you mean by that? Are you saying tonight has something to do with her in a different way?"

I nod, then stand and take her hand and pull her up. I wrap my arms around her, and she leans against my chest and clasps her hands behind my back. "It does have to do with her." She pulls her face away from my chest and looks up at me while I explain, "She gave me something else . . . besides the letters."

Julia made me promise not to tell Lake about the letters and the gift until it was time. Lake and Kel have already opened the letters; the gift was meant for Lake and me. It was intended to be a Christmas gift for us to open together, but this is the first chance we've had to be alone.

"Come to my bedroom." I release my hold on her and grab her hand. She follows until we get to my room, where the box Julia gave me is sitting on the bed.

Lake walks over to it and runs her hand across the wrapping paper. She fingers the red velvet bow and sighs. "Is it really from her?" she asks quietly.

I sit on the bed and motion for her to sit with me. We pull our legs up and sit with the gift between us. There's a card taped to the top of it with our names on it, along with clear instructions not to read the card until after we open the gift.

"Will, why didn't you tell me there was something else? Is this the last one?" I can see the tears forming in her eyes. She always tries so hard to conceal them. I don't know why she hates it so much when she cries.

I run my finger across her cheek and wipe away a tear. "Last one, I swear," I say. "She wanted us to open it together."

She straightens up and does her best to regain her composure. "Do you want to do the honors, or should I?"

"That's a dumb question," I say.

"There's no such thing as a dumb question," she says. "You should know that, Mr. Cooper." She leans forward and kisses me, then pulls back and starts to loosen the edge of the package. I watch as she tears it open, revealing a cardboard box wrapped in duct tape.

"My God, there must be six layers of duct tape on here," she says sarcastically. "Kind of like your car." She looks up and gives me a sly grin.

"Funny," I say. I stroke her knee and watch her poke through the tape with her thumbnail. Just when she breaks through the final edge, she pauses.

"Thank you for doing this for her," she says. "For keeping the gift." She looks back down at it and holds it without opening it. "Do you know what it is?" she asks.

"No clue. I'm hoping it's not a puppy—it's been under my bed for four months."

She laughs. "I'm nervous," she says. "I really don't want to cry again." She hesitates before she opens the top of the box and folds the flaps back. She pulls the contents out as I pull the cardboard away. She tears the tissue off and reveals a clear glass vase, full to the brim with geometrical stars in a variety of colors. It looks like origami. Hundreds of thumbnail-sized 3-D paper stars.

"What is it?" I ask Lake.

"I don't know, but it's beautiful," she says. We continue to stare at the gift, trying to make sense of it. She opens the card and looks at it. "I can't read it, Will. You'll have to do it." She places it in my hands.

I open it and read aloud.

Will and Lake,

Love is the most beautiful thing in the world. Unfortunately, it's also one of the hardest things in the world to hold on to, and one of the easiest things to throw away.

Neither of you has a mother or a father to go to for relationship advice anymore. Neither of you has anyone to go to for a shoulder to cry on when things get tough, and they will get tough. Neither of you has someone to go to when you just want to share the funny, or the happy, or the heartache. You are both at a disadvantage when it comes to this aspect of love. You both only have each other, and because of this, you will have to work harder at building a strong foundation for your future together. You are not only each other's love; you are also each other's sole confidant.

I handwrote some things onto strips of paper and folded them into stars. It might be an inspirational quote, an inspiring lyric, or just some downright good parental advice. I don't want you to open one and read it until you feel you truly need it. If you have a bad day, if the two of you fight, or if you need something to lift your spirits . . . that's what these are for. You can open one together; you can open one alone. I just want there to be something both of you can go to if and when you ever need it.

Will . . . thank you. Thank you for coming into our lives. So much of the pain and worry I've been feeling has been alleviated by the mere fact that I know my daughter is loved by you.

Lake takes my hand when I pause. I wasn't expecting Julia to address me personally. Lake wipes away a tear. I do my best to fight back my own tears. I take a deep breath and clear my throat, then finish reading the letter.

You are a wonderful man, and you've been a wonderful friend to me. I thank you from the bottom of my heart for loving my daughter like you do. You respect her, you don't need to change for her, and you inspire her. You can never know how grateful I have been for you, and how much peace you have brought my soul.

And Lake, this is me nudging your shoulder, giving you my approval. You couldn't have picked anyone better to love if I'd hand-picked him myself. Also, thank you for being so determined to keep our family together. You were right about Kel needing to be with you. Thank you for helping me see that. And remember, when things get tough for him, please teach him how to stop carving pumpkins . . .

I love you both and wish you a lifetime of happiness together.

—Julia

"*And all around my memories, you dance . . .*"

—The Avett Brothers

I put the card back in the envelope and watch as Lake runs her fingers along the rim of the vase, spinning it around to view it from all angles. "I saw her making these once. When I walked into her room, she was folding strips of paper, and she stopped and put them aside as we talked. I forgot about it. I forgot all about it. This must have taken her forever."

She stares at the stars, and I stare at her. She wipes more tears from her eyes with the back of her hand. She's holding it together well, all things considered.

"I want to read them all, but at the same time, I hope we never need to read them at *all*," she says.

I lean forward and give her a quick kiss. "You are as amazing as your mother." I take the vase and set it down on the dresser. Lake shoves the wrapping paper inside the box and sets it on the floor. She puts the card on the table, then lies back on the bed. I lie down beside her, turn toward her, and rest my arm over her waist. "You okay?" I ask. I can't tell whether she's sad.

She looks at me and smiles. "I thought it would hurt to hear her words again, but it didn't. It actually made me happy," she says.

"Me, too," I say. "I was really worried it was a puppy."

She laughs and lays her head on my arm. We lie there in silence, watching each other. I run my hand up her arm and trace her face and neck with my fingertips. I love watching her think.

She eventually lifts her head off my arm and slides on top of me, placing her hands on the back of my neck. She leans in and slowly parts my lips with hers. I become quickly consumed by the taste of her lips and the feel of her warm hands. I wrap my arms around her and run my fingers through her hair as I return her kiss. It's been so long since we've been alone together without the possibility of being interrupted. I hate being in this predicament, but I love being in this predicament. Her skin is so soft; her lips are perfect. It gets harder and harder to retreat.

She runs her hands underneath my shirt and lightly teases my neck with her mouth. She knows this drives me crazy, yet she's been doing it more and more lately. I think she likes pushing her boundaries. One of us needs to retreat, and I don't know if I can bring myself to do it. Apparently, neither can she.

"How much time do we have?" she whispers. She lifts up my shirt and kisses her way down my chest.

“Time?” I say weakly.

“Until the boys get home.” She slowly kisses her way back up to my neck. “How long do we have until they get home?” She brings her face back to mine and looks at me. I can see by the look in her eyes that she’s telling me she’s not retreating.

I bring my arm over my face and cover my eyes. I try to talk myself down. This isn’t how I want it to be for her. Think about something else, Will. Think about college, homework, puppies in cardboard boxes . . . anything.

She pulls my arm away from my face so she can look me in the eyes. “Will . . . it’s been a year. I want to.”

I roll her onto her back and prop my head up on my elbow and lean in toward her, stroking her face with my other hand. “Lake, believe me, I’m ready, too. But not here. Not right now. You’ll have to go home in an hour when the boys get back, and I don’t think I could take it.” I kiss her on the forehead. “In two weeks we get a three-day weekend. We’ll go away together. Just the two of us. I’ll see if my grandparents will watch the boys, and we can spend the whole weekend together.”

She kicks her legs up and down on the bed, frustrated.

"I can't wait two more weeks! We've been waiting fifty-seven weeks already!"

I laugh at her childishness and lean in, planting a kiss on her cheek. "If *I* can wait, you can *definitely* wait," I assure her.

She rolls her eyes. "God, you're such a bore," she teases.

"Oh, I'm a bore?" I say. "You want me to throw you in the shower again? Cool you off? I will if that's what you need."

"Only if you get in with me," she says. Her eyes grow wide, and she sits up and pushes me flat on my back, leaning over me. "Will!" she says excitedly as a realization dawns on her. "Does that mean we can take showers together? On our getaway?"

Her eagerness surprises me. Everything she does surprises me. "You aren't nervous?" I ask her.

"No, not at all." She smiles and leans in closer. "I know I'll be in good hands."

"You will definitely be in good hands," I say, pulling her to me. Just when I'm about to kiss her again, my phone vibrates. She reaches into my pocket and pulls it out.

"Gavin," she says. She hands the phone to me and rolls off.

I read the text. "Great, Kel threw up. They think he has a stomach bug, so they're bringing them home."

She groans and gets off the bed. "Ugh! I hate vomit! Caulder's probably gonna get it, too, the way they pass crap back and forth."

"I'll text him and tell him to take Kel to your house. You go home and wait; I'll run to the store and get him some medicine." I pull my shirt back on and grab the vase that Julia made us so I can put it on the bookshelf in the living room. We exit the bedroom in parent mode.

"Get some soup, too. For tomorrow. And some Sprite," she says.

When I set the vase down in the living room, she reaches her hand inside and grabs a star. She sees me eyeing her and grins. "There might be a good tip in here. For vomit," she says.

"We've got a long road ahead of us; you better not waste those." When we walk outside, I grab her arm and pull her to me and hug her good night. "You want me to drive you home?"

She laughs and hugs me back. "Thanks for our date. It was one of my favorites."

"The best is yet to come," I say, hinting at our upcoming getaway.

"I'm holding you to that." She backs away and then turns and starts walking toward her house. I've opened the car door when she yells from across the street.

"Will! One more time?"

"I love you, Lake!"

3.

JANUARY 7

I butterflying hate cheeseburgers.

HELL. PURE HELL IS THE BEST WAY I CAN DESCRIBE the last twenty-four hours. By the time Gavin and Eddie made it home with the boys, it was apparent that Kel didn't have a stomach bug after all. Gavin didn't knock when he ran through the front door and headed straight for the bathroom. Caulder was next, then Lake and Eddie. I was the last to feel the effects of the food poisoning. Caulder and I have done nothing but lie on the couch, taking turns in the bathroom since midnight last night.

I can't help but envy Kiersten. I should have just had bread, too. About the time that thought crosses my mind, there's a knock at the front door. I don't get up. I don't even speak. No one I know extends the courtesy of knocking, so I don't know who could be at the door. I guess I won't find out, either, because I'm not moving.

I'm facing away from the door, but I hear it slowly open and can feel the cold air circulate as a female voice I don't recognize calls my name.

I still don't care who it is. At this point, I'm wishing it's someone here to finish me off, put me out of my misery. It takes all the energy I have to just raise my hand in the air to let whoever it is know that I'm here.

"Oh, you poor thing," she says. She shuts the door behind her and walks around to the front of the couch and stares down at me. I glance up at her and realize I have absolutely no idea who this woman is. She's probably in her forties; her short black hair is traced with gray. She's petite, shorter than Lake. I try to smile, but I don't think I do. She frowns and glances over to Caulder, who is passed out on the other couch. I notice a bottle in her hands when she passes through the living room into the kitchen. I hear her opening drawers, and she comes back with a spoon.

"This will help. Layken said you guys were sick, too." She pours some of the liquid into a spoon and bends down, handing it to me.

I take it. I'll take anything at this point. I swallow the medicine and cough when it burns my throat. I reach for a glass of water and take a sip. I don't want to drink too much; it's just been coming right back up. "What the hell is that?" I ask.

She looks disappointed at my reaction. "I made it. I make my own medicine. It'll help, I promise." She walks over to Caulder and shakes him awake. He accepts the medicine as I did, without question, then closes his eyes again.

"I'm Sherry, by the way. Kiersten's mother. She said you guys ate some rancid meat." She makes a face when she says the word "meat."

I don't want to think about it, so I close my eyes and try to put it out of my mind. I guess she sees the nausea building behind my expression, because she says, "Sorry. This is why we're vegetarian."

"Thanks, Sherry," I say, hoping she's finished. She's not.

"I started a load of laundry over at Layken's house. If you want, I'll wash some of yours, too." She doesn't wait for me to respond. She walks down the hallway and starts gathering clothes, then takes them into the laundry room. I hear the washer start, followed by noise in the kitchen. She's cleaning. This woman I don't know is cleaning my house. I'm too tired to object. I'm even too tired to be pleased about it.

"Will?" She walks back through the living room. I open my eyes, but barely. "I'll be back in an hour to put the clothes in the dryer. I'll bring some minestrone, too."

I just nod. Or at least I think I nod.

IT HASN'T BEEN an hour yet, but whatever Sherry gave me already has me feeling a little better. Caulder manages to make it to his room and passes out on his bed. I've gotten into the kitchen and poured myself a glass of Sprite when the front door opens. It's Lake. She looks as rough as I do, but still beautiful.

"Hey, babe." She shuffles into the kitchen and wraps her arms around me. She's in her pajamas and house shoes. They aren't the Darth Vader ones, but they're still sexy. "How's Caulder feeling?" she asks.

"Better, I guess. Whatever Sherry gave us worked."

"Yeah, it did." She rests her head against my chest and takes a deep breath. "I wish we had enough couches in one house so we could all be sick together."

We've brought up the subject of living together before. It makes economic sense; our bills would be cut in half. She's only nineteen, though, and she seems to like having her alone time. The thought of taking such a huge leap makes us both a little apprehensive, so we agreed to wait on that step until we're certain about it.

"I wish we did, too," I say. I naturally lean in to kiss her, but she shakes her head and backs away.

"Nuh-uh," she says. "We're not kissing for at least twenty-four more hours."

I laugh and kiss her on top of her head instead.

"I guess I'll go back now. I just wanted to check on you." She kisses me on the arm.

"You two are so cute!" Sherry says. She walks through the dining room and places a container of soup in the fridge, then turns and heads into the laundry room. I never even heard her open the front door, much less knock.

"Thanks for the medicine, Sherry. It really helped," Lake says.

"No problem," Sherry says. "That concoction can knock the shit out of anything. You two let me know if you need more."

Lake looks at me and rolls her eyes. "See you later. Love you."

"Love you, too. Let me know when Kel feels better, and we'll come over."

Lake leaves, and I take a seat at the table and slowly sip my drink. I still don't trust ingesting anything.

Sherry pulls out the chair across the table from me and takes a seat. "So, what's your story?" she asks.

I'm not sure what story she's referring to, so I raise my eyebrows at her as I take another sip and wait for her to elaborate.

"With the two of you. And Kel and Caulder. It's a little strange, from a mother's point of view. I've got an eleven-year-old daughter who seems to enjoy spending time with all you guys, so I feel it's my duty as a mom to know your story. You and Lake are both practically children, raising children."

She's very blunt. However, the way she says it comes off as appropriate, somehow. She's easy to like. I see why Kiersten is the way she is.

I set my Sprite down on the table and wipe the condensation off the glass with my thumbs. "My parents died three years ago." I continue to stare at the glass, avoiding her gaze. I don't want to see the pity. "Lake's father died over a year ago, and her mother passed away in September. So . . . here we are, raising our brothers."

Sherry leans back in her chair and folds her arms across her chest. "I'll be damned."

I nod and give her a half smile. At least she didn't say how sorry she is for us. I hate pity more than anything.

"How long have the two of you been dating?"

"Officially? Since December eighteenth, a little over a year ago."

"What about *un*officially?" she says.

I shift in my seat. Why did I even specify "officially"?

"December eighteenth, a little over a year ago," I say again, and smile. I'm not getting any more detailed than that. "What's *your* story, Sherry?"

She laughs and stands up. "Will, has anyone ever told you it's rude to be nosy?" She makes her way to the front door. "Let me know if you need anything. You know where we live."

THE FOUR OF us spend the entire day Sunday watching movies and being sore. We're all a little queasy, so we skip the junk food. Monday it's back to reality. I drop Kel and Caulder off at their school and head to the college. Three of my four classes are in the same building: one of the benefits of being in grad school. Once your course of study is set, all the classes are similar and usually taught in the same area. The first of my four classes, however, is halfway across campus. It's a graduate-level elective called Death and Dying. I thought it would be interesting, since I'm more than experienced in the subject. I also didn't have a choice. There wasn't another graduate elective that I could take during the eight o'clock block, so I'm stuck with this one if I want all my credits to count.

When I walk in, students are seated sporadically around the room. It's an auditorium-style room set up with tables for two. I walk up the stairs and take a seat in the back of the room. It's different, being the student rather than the teacher. I got so used to being at the head of the classroom. The role reversal has taken some getting used to.

All twenty tables fill up fairly quickly, other than an empty seat next to me. It's the first day of the semester, so it will probably be the only day that people show up early. That's usually how it is; the newness wears off by day two. It's rare for a professor to have the entire roll show up after day two.

My phone vibrates inside my pocket. I take it out and slide my finger across the screen. It's a text from Lake.

Finally found my phone. Hope you like your classes. I love you and I'll see you tonight.

The professor starts calling roll. I send Lake a quick reply text that states, "Thx. Love you, too," then put the phone back in my pocket.

"Will Cooper?" the professor says. I raise my hand, and he looks up at me and nods, then marks his form. I glance around the room to see if I recognize anyone.

There were a couple of people from high school in my elective last semester, but I don't usually see many familiar faces. Most of my high school classmates graduated from college last May, and not many of them decided on grad school.

I notice a girl with blond hair in the front row turned completely around in her seat. When I meet her gaze, my heart sinks. She smiles and waves when she sees that I've recognized her. She gathers her things, then stands and makes her way up the stairs.

No. She's coming toward me. She's about to sit with me.

"Will! Oh my God, what are the chances? It's been so long," she says.

I do my best to smile at her, trying to figure out if what I'm feeling is anger or guilt. "Hey, Vaughn." I try to sound pleased to see her.

She takes the seat next to me and leans in and hugs me. "How are you?" she whispers. "How's Caulder?"

"He's good," I say. "Growing up. He'll be eleven in two months."

"Eleven? Wow," she says, shaking her head in dis belief.

We haven't seen each other in almost three years. We parted on bad terms, to put it mildly, yet she's acting genuinely excited to see me. I wish I could say the same.

"How's Ethan?" I ask her. Ethan is her older brother. He and I were pretty good friends while Vaughn and I dated, but we haven't spoken since the breakup.

"He's good. He's really good. He's married now, with a baby on the way."

"Good for him. Tell him I said so."

"I will," she says.

"Vaughn Gibson?" the professor calls.

She raises her hand. "Up here." She brings her attention back to me. "What about you? You married?"

I shake my head.

"Me, neither." She smiles.

I don't like how she's looking at me. We dated for over two years, so I know her pretty well. And right now her intentions aren't good for me.

"I'm not married, but I am dating someone," I clarify. I see the slight shift in her expression, though she attempts to mask it with a smile.

"Good for you," she says. "Is it serious?" She's digging for hints about my relationship, so I make it clear to her.

"Very."

When the professor starts explaining the semester requirements and going over the syllabus, we both face forward and don't speak much, other than occasional comments from her regarding the class. When the professor dismisses us, I quickly stand up.

"It's really good seeing you, Will," she says. "I'm excited about this class now. We have a lot of catching up to do."

I smile at her without agreeing. She gives me another quick hug and turns away. I gather my things and head to my second class as I think of a way to break this news to Lake.

Lake has never asked about my past relationships. She says there isn't anything good that can come from discussing them. I'm not sure she knows about Vaughn. She knows I had a pretty serious relationship in high school, and she knows I've had sex; we talked about that. I don't know how she'll take this. I'd hate to upset her, though I don't want to hide anything.

But what would I be hiding? Is it necessary to tell her about all the students in my classes? We've never discussed it before, so why do I feel the need to now? If I tell her, it will just cause her to worry unnecessarily. If I don't tell her, what harm is it doing? Lake's not in my class, she's not even in school on the same days I am. I've made it clear to Vaughn that I'm in a relationship. That should be good enough.

By the end of my last class, I've convinced myself that Lake doesn't need to know.

WHEN I PULL up at the elementary school, Kel and Caulder are seated outside on a bench, away from the rest of the students. Mrs. Brill is standing right behind them, waiting.

"Great," I mumble to myself. I've heard the horror stories about her, but I've never had to deal with her. I kill the engine and get out. It's obvious what she's expecting me to do.

"You must be Will," she says, extending her hand. "I don't believe we've met before."

"Good to meet you." I glance at the boys, who aren't making eye contact with me. When I look back at Mrs. Brill, she nods to the left, indicating that she would like to talk to me out of their earshot.

"There was an incident with Kel last week in the cafeteria," Mrs. Brill says as we walk down the sidewalk, away from the crowd. "I'm not sure what the relationship is between Kel and you, but I wasn't able to get in touch with his sister."

"We're aware of what happened," I say. "Layken misplaced her phone. Do I need to let her know to contact you?"

"No, that isn't why I want to talk to you," she says. "I just wanted to be sure both of you were aware of last week's incident and that it was handled appropriately."

"It was. We took care of it," I say. I don't know what she means by "handled appropriately," but I doubt she expects that the punishment was laughing about it at the dinner table. Oh well.

"I wanted to talk to you about a different matter. There's a new student here who seems to have taken to Kel and Caulder. Kiersten?" She waits for me to acknowledge that. I nod. "There was an incident today involving her and a few of the other students," she says.

I stop walking and turn toward her, becoming more

vested in the conversation. If it has anything to do with how the kids acted at the dinner table the other night, I want to know about it.

"She's being picked on. Some of the other students find that her personality doesn't mesh well with theirs. Kel and Caulder found out about a couple of the older boys saying some things to her, so they decided to take matters into their own hands." She pauses and glances back at Kel and Caulder, who are still seated in the same positions.

"What'd they do?" I ask nervously.

"It's not what they did, really. It's what they said . . . in a note." She takes a piece of paper out of her pocket and hands it to me.

I unfold it and look at it. My mouth gapes open. It's a picture of a bloody knife with "*You will die, asswipe!*" written across the top.

"Kel and Caulder wrote this?" I ask, embarrassed.

She nods. "They've already admitted to it. You're a teacher, so you know the significance of this kind of threat on campus. It can't be taken lightly, Will. I hope you understand. They'll be suspended for the rest of the week."

"Suspended? For an entire week? But they were defending someone who was being bullied."

"I understand that, and those boys have been punished as well. But I can't condone bad behavior in the defense of more bad behavior."

I know where she's coming from. I look down at the note again and sigh. "I'll tell Lake. Is there anything else? They're free to come back on Monday?"

She nods. I thank her and walk back to the car and get in. The boys climb into the backseat, and we drive home in silence. I'm too pissed at them to say anything. Or at least I *think* I'm pissed. I'm supposed to be, right?

LAKE IS SEATED at the bar when I walk through her front door. Kel and Caulder follow behind me, and I sternly instruct them to take a seat. Lake shoots me a confused look when I walk through the living room and motion for her to follow me to her bedroom. I shut the door for privacy and explain everything that happened, showing her the note.

She stares at it for a while, then covers her mouth and tries to hide her laugh. She thinks it's funny. I feel relieved, because the more thought I gave it on the way home, the funnier I thought it was. When we make eye contact, we start laughing.

"I know, Lake! From a sibling standpoint, it's really funny," I say. "But what are we supposed to do from a *parent* standpoint?"

She shakes her head. "I don't know. I'm sort of proud of them for taking up for Kiersten." She sits down on her bed and throws the note aside. "Poor Kiersten."

I sit down beside her. "Well, we have to act mad. They really can't do crap like this."

Lake nods in agreement. "What do you think their punishment should be?"

I shrug. "I don't know. Being suspended seems kind of like a reward. What kid wouldn't want to get a week off from school?"

"I know, right?" she says. "I guess we could ground them from their video games while they're home," she suggests.

"If we do that, they'll just annoy us the entire time out of boredom," I say. She groans at the thought. I think back on my own punishments as a child and try to come up with a solution. "We could make them write 'I will not write threatening notes' a thousand times."

She shakes her head in disagreement. "Kel loves to write. He would consider that another reward, just like the suspension." We both think for a while, but neither of us comes up with any more ideas for punishment.

"I guess it's a good thing we have different schedules this semester," she says. "That way, every time they get suspended, at least one of us will be home."

I smile at her and hope she's wrong. This better be their first and last suspension. Lake doesn't know it, but she's made my life with Caulder so much easier. Before I met her, I agonized over every single parenting decision I had to make. Now that we make a lot of those choices together, I'm not as hard on myself. We seem to agree on most aspects of how the boys should be raised. It also doesn't hurt having her maternal instincts in the picture. It's in moments like these, when we're required to join forces, that it's almost unbearable for me to take things slowly. If I left my head out of it and followed my heart, I'd marry her today.

I push her back on the bed and kiss her. Due to the weekend from hell, I haven't been able to kiss her since Friday. I've missed kissing her. From the way she kisses me back, it's obvious she's missed kissing me, too.

"Have you talked to your grandparents about next weekend?" she asks.

My lips move from her mouth, down her cheek, and to her ear. "I'll call them tonight," I whisper. "Have you thought about where you want to go?" Goose bumps break out on her skin, so I continue kissing down her neck.

"We could stay here at my house, for all I care. I'm just looking forward to being with you for three whole days. And finally getting to spend the night together . . . in the same bed, at least."

I'm trying not to come off too eager, but next weekend is all I've been thinking about. She doesn't need to know that I've got an internal countdown going. Ten days and twenty-one more hours.

"Why don't we do that?" I stop kissing her neck and look at her. "Let's just stay here. Kel and Caulder will be in Detroit. We can lie to Eddie and Gavin and tell them we're going away, so they won't stop by. We'll pull the shades down and lock the doors and hole up for three whole days, right here in this bed. And in the shower, too, of course."

"Sounds bemazing," she says. She likes to smoosh words together for emphasis. I'm pretty sure "bemazing" is "beautiful" and "amazing." I think it's cute.

"Now back to the punishment," she says. "What would our parents do?"

I honestly have no clue what my parents would do. If I did have a clue, it wouldn't be so hard to come up with solutions to all the problems that come along with raising kids.

"I know," I say. "Let's scare the butterfly out of them."

"How?" she says.

"Act like you're trying to calm me down, like I'm really pissed off. We can make them sit out there and sweat for a while."

She laughs. "You're so bad." She stands up and walks closer to the door. "Will! Calm down!" she yells.

I walk over to the door and hit it. "I will not calm down! I'm *pissed*!"

Lake throws herself onto the bed and pulls a pillow

over her face to stifle her giggles before she continues. "No, stop it! You can't go out there yet! You need to calm down, Will! You might *kill* them!"

I glare at her. "*Kill* them?" I whisper. "*Really?*" She laughs as I hop back on the bed with her. "Lake, you suck at this."

"Will, no! Not the belt!" she yells dramatically.

I clasp my hand over her mouth. "Shut up!" I say, laughing.

We give ourselves a few minutes to regain composure before we exit the bedroom. When we walk down the hallway, I do my best to look intimidating. The boys are watching us with fear in their eyes as we take our seats across the bar from them.

"I'll talk," Lake says to them. "Will is entirely too upset right now to speak to either of you."

I stare at them and don't speak, putting on my best display of anger. I wonder if this is how parenting is with real parents. A bunch of pretending to be responsible grown-ups.

"First of all," Lake says in a superbly faked motherly tone, "we would like to commend you for defending your friend. However, you went about it all wrong. You should have spoken to someone about it. Violence is never the answer to violence."

I couldn't have said it better if I'd been reading from a parenting handbook.

"You are both grounded for two weeks. And don't think your suspension will be fun, either. We're giving you each a list of chores to do every day. Including Saturday and Sunday."

I tap my knee against hers under the bar, letting her know that was a nice touch.

"Do either of you have anything to say?" she asks.

Kel raises his hand. "What about my birthday on Friday?"

Lake looks at me, and I shrug. She turns back to Kel. "You don't have to be grounded on your birthday. But you'll get an extra day of grounding at the end. Any more questions?"

Neither of them says anything.

"Good. Go to your room, Kel. No hanging out with Caulder or Kiersten while you're grounded. Caulder, same goes for you. Go to your house and to your room."

The boys get up from the bar and go to their

respective bedrooms. When Kel has disappeared down the hallway and Caulder has disappeared out the front door, I give Lake a high five.

"Well played," I tell her. "You almost had me convinced."

"You, too. You really seemed pissed!" she says. She heads to the living room and sits down to fold a pile of laundry. "So? How were your classes?"

"Good," I reply. I spare her the details of first period. "I do have a lot of homework I need to get started on, though. Are we eating together tonight?"

She shakes her head. "I promised Eddie we could have some girl time tonight. Gavin started his job at Getty's. But tomorrow I'm all yours."

I kiss her on top of the head. "You two have fun. Text me good night," I say. "You do know where your phone is, right?"

She nods and pulls it out of her pocket to show me. "Love you," she says.

"Love you, too," I say as I leave.

When I shut the door behind me, I feel like I left a moment too soon. When I walk back in, she's facing the other way, folding a towel. I turn her around and take the towel out of her hands. I wrap my arms around her and kiss her again, but better this time. “I love you,” I say again.

She sighs and leans in to me. “I can’t wait until next weekend, Will. I wish it would just hurry up and get here.”

“You and me both.”

4.

TUESDAY, JANUARY 10

If I were a carpenter, I would build you a window to my soul.
But I would leave that window shut and locked,
so that every time you tried to look through it . . . all you would
see is your own reflection.
You would see that my soul
is a reflection of you . . .

LAKE HAS ALREADY LEFT FOR SCHOOL BY THE TIME I wake up. Kel is asleep on the couch. She must have sent him over before she left. It's trash day, so I slip my shoes on and head outside to take the can to the curb. I have to knock almost a foot of snow off the lid before I can get it to budge. Lake forgot, so I walk to her house and pull hers to the curb as well.

"Hey, Will," Sherry says. She and Kiersten are making their way outside.

"Morning," I say to them.

"What happened with Kel and Caulder yesterday? Are they in lots of trouble?" Kiersten asks.

"Suspended. They can't go back until Monday."

"Suspended for what?" Sherry asks. I can tell by her tone that Kiersten must not have told her.

Kiersten turns toward her mother. "They threatened those boys the school called you about. They wrote them a note, threatening their life. Called them ass-wipes," she says matter-of-factly.

"Aww, how sweet," Sherry says. "They defended you." She turns to me before she gets in her car. "Will, tell them thank you. That's too sweet, defending my baby girl like that."

I laugh and shake my head as I watch them drive away. When I get back inside, Kel and Caulder are sitting on the couch watching TV. "Morning," I say to them.

"Are we allowed to watch TV, at least?" Caulder asks.

I shrug. "Whatever. Do what you want. Just don't threaten to kill anyone today." I should probably be stricter, but it's too early in the morning to care.

"They were really mean to her, Will," Kel says. "They've been being mean to her since she moved here. She hasn't done anything to them."

I sit down on the other couch and kick off my shoes. "Not everyone is gonna be nice, Kel. There are a lot of cruel people in the world, unfortunately. What kinds of things are they doing to her?"

Caulder answers me. "One of the sixth-grade boys asked her to be his girlfriend about a week after she moved here, but she told him no. He's kind of a bully. She said she was a vegetarian and couldn't date *meat*-heads. It made him really mad, so he's been spreading rumors about her since then. A lot of kids are scared of him because he's a dickhead, so now other kids are being mean to her, too."

"Don't say 'dickhead,' Caulder. And I think you guys are doing the right thing by defending her. Lake and I aren't mad about that; we're actually a little proud. We just wish you would use your heads before you make some of the choices you do. This is two weeks in a row you guys have done something stupid at school. This time you got suspended because of it. We all have enough on our plates as it is . . . we don't need the added stress."

"Sorry," Kel says.

"Yeah. Sorry, Will," Caulder says.

"As for Kiersten, you two keep doing what you're doing, sticking by her. She's a good kid and doesn't deserve to be treated like that. Is anyone being nice to her other than you two? She doesn't have any other friends?"

"She's got Abby," Caulder says.

Kel smiles. "She's not the only one who has Abby."

"Shut up, Kel!" Caulder hits him on the arm.

"Whoa! What's this? Who's Abby? Caulder, do you have a girlfriend?" I tease.

"She's not my girlfriend," Caulder says defensively.

"Only because he's too shy to ask her," Kel says.

"You're one to talk," I say to Kel. "You've been crushing on Kiersten since the day she moved in. Why haven't you asked *her* to be your girlfriend?"

Kel blushes and tries to hide his smile. He reminds me

of Lake when he does this. "I already asked her. She *is* my girlfriend," he says.

I'm impressed. He's got more nerve than I thought.

"You better not tell Layken!" he says. "She'll embarrass me."

"I won't say anything," I say. "But your birthday party is this Friday. Tell Kiersten not to be kissing you in front of Lake if you don't want her finding out."

"Shut up, Will! I'm not kissing her," Kel says with a disgusted look.

"Caulder, you should invite Abby to Kel's party," I say.

Caulder gets the same embarrassed look Kel had. "He already did," Kel says. Caulder hits him on the arm again.

I stand up. It's obvious my advice isn't needed here. "Well, you two have it all figured out. What do you need me for?"

"Someone has to pay for the pizza," Caulder says.

I walk to the front door and grab their jackets and toss them in their laps.

"Punishment time," I say. They groan and roll their eyes. "You guys get to shovel driveways today."

"Drive*ways*? As in plural? More than *one*?" Caulder asks.

"Yep," I say. "Do mine and Lake's, and when you're done, do Sherry's, too. While you're at it, go ahead and do Bob and Melinda's."

Neither of them moves from the couch.

"Go!"

MY STOMACH IS in knots Wednesday morning. I really don't want to see Vaughn today. I try to leave a few minutes sooner, hoping I can make it to class early enough to pick a seat next to someone else. Unfortunately, I'm the first to arrive. I take a seat in the back again, hoping she won't want to make the trek to the back of the room.

She does. Arriving almost immediately after me, she smiles and runs up the steps, throwing her bag down on the table. "Morning," she says. "I brought you a coffee. Two sugars, no cream, just like you like it." She sets the coffee down in front of me.

"Thanks," I say. She's got her hair pulled back in a bun. I know exactly what she's doing. I told her once that

I loved it when she wore her hair like that. It's no coincidence that she's wearing it like that today.

"So, I was thinking we should catch up. Maybe I could come by your house sometime. I miss Caulder; I'd like to see him."

Absolutely not! Hell no! That's what I really want to say. "Vaughn, I don't think that's a good idea," is what I actually say.

"Oh," she says quietly. "Okay."

I can tell I've offended her. "Look, I'm not trying to be rude. It's just . . . you know, we have a lot of history. It wouldn't be fair to Lake."

She cocks her head at me. "*Lake?* Your girlfriend's name is *Lake*?"

I don't like her tone. "Her name is Layken. I call her Lake."

She puts her hand on my arm. "Will, I'm not trying to cause trouble. If Layken is the jealous type, just say so. It's not a big deal."

She grazes her thumb across my arm, and I look down at her hand. I hate how she's trying to undermine my relationship with a snide comment. She always used to do this. She hasn't changed at all. I pull my arm away from her and face the front of the room. "Vaughn, stop. I know what you're doing, and it's not gonna happen."

She huffs and focuses her attention on the front of the room. She's pissed. Good, maybe she got the not so subtle hint.

I really don't understand where she's coming from. I never imagined I would see her again, much less have to practically fight her off. It's strange how I had so much love for her then but feel nothing for her now. I don't regret what I went through with her, though. We did have a pretty good relationship, and I honestly think I would have married her had my parents not passed away. But only because I was naive about what a relationship should be. What *love* should be.

We met when we were freshmen but didn't start dating until our junior year. We hung out at a party I went to with my best friend, Reece. Vaughn and I went out a few times, then agreed to make the relationship exclusive. We dated for about six months before we had sex for the first time. We both still lived at home with our parents, so it ended up being in the backseat of her car. It was awkward, to say the least. We were cramped, it was cold, and it was probably the most unromantic atmosphere a girl could want in that moment. Of course, it got much better over the next year and a half, but I'll always regret that being our first time. Maybe that's why I want Lake's first time to be perfect. Not just another spur-of-the-moment kind of thing like Vaughn and I had.

I was grieving and going through a lot of emotional issues after my relationship with Vaughn ended. Raising Caulder and doubling up on classes didn't leave me any time to date. Vaughn was the last relationship I had up until I met Lake. And after only one date with Lake, I knew the connection between us was something more than I'd had with Vaughn, more than I ever thought I could have with anyone.

At the time Vaughn broke up with me, I thought she was making a huge mistake, telling me she wasn't ready to be a mom to Caulder. She admitted she wasn't ready for that kind of responsibility and I resented her for it. I'm past the resentment now. Seeing how things may have turned out differently had she not made that decision, I'll be forever grateful to her for calling off our relationship when she did.

*

FRIDAY IS MUCH better. Vaughn doesn't show up to class, so it makes the rest of the day a lot easier. I stop by the store after my last class and grab Kel's birthday present, then head home to get ready for his party.

The only two people Kel and Caulder invited to the party were Kiersten and Abby. Sherry and Kiersten went to pick up Abby while Lake and Eddie left to go get the cake. Gavin showed up with pizza at the same time I pulled into the driveway. It's his night off, but I had him pick it up, since he gets a discount now.

"You nervous?" I ask Caulder as I unstack the pizzas on the counter. I know he's barely eleven, but I remember having my first crush.

"Stop it, Will. You're gonna make tonight my suck if you keep it up," he says.

"Fair enough, I'll drop it. But first I need to lay down some rules. No holding hands until you're at least eleven and a half. No kissing until you're thirteen. And no tongue until you're fourteen. I mean fifteen. Once you get to that point, we'll revisit the rules. Until then, you stick to those."

Caulder rolls his eyes and walks away.

That went well, I guess. Our first official "sex" talk. I

think the one I really need to be having the talk with is Kel. He seems a little bit more girl-crazy than Caulder does.

"Who placed the order for this cake?" Lake asks as she walks through the front door carrying it. She doesn't look pleased.

"I let Kel and Caulder order it when we were grocery shopping the other day. Why? What's wrong with it?"

She walks over to the bar and sets the cake down. She opens the lid and stands back so I can see it. "Oh," I say.

The cake is covered in white buttercream frosting. The writing across the top is done in blue.

Happy Butterflying Birthday, Kel

"Well, it's not *really* a bad word," I say.

Lake sighs. "I hate that they're so damn funny," she says. "It's just gonna get harder, you know. We really need to start beating them now, before it's too late." She closes the lid and walks the cake to the refrigerator.

"Tomorrow," I say as I wrap my arms around her from

behind. “We can’t beat Kel on his birthday.” I lean in and kiss her ear.

“Fine.” She leans her head to the side, allowing me easier access. “But I get the first punch.”

“Stop it!” Kel yells. “You guys can’t do that crap tonight. It’s my birthday, and I don’t want to have to watch y’all make out!”

I let go of Lake and pick Kel up and throw him over my shoulder. “This is for the butterflying cake,” I say. I turn his backside toward Layken. “Birthday beating, here’s your chance.”

Lake starts counting off birthday spankings while Kel fights to get out of my grasp. He’s getting stronger. “Put me down, Will!” He’s punching me in the back, trying to break free.

I put him down after Lake finishes with the beating. Kel laughs and tries to shove me, but I don’t budge.

“I can’t wait until I’m bigger than you! I’m gonna kick your butterfly!” He gives up and runs down the hallway to Caulder’s room.

Lake is staring down the hallway with a serious expression. “Should we be letting them say that?”

I laugh. “Say what? Butterfly?”

She nods. "Yeah. I mean, it seems like it's already a bad word."

"Would you rather him say 'ass'?" Kiersten says, passing between Lake and me. Again, she's here, and I didn't even hear her knock.

"Hey, Kiersten," Lake says.

There's a young girl following closely behind Kiersten. She looks at Lake and smiles.

"You must be Abby," Lake says. "I'm Layken, this is Will."

Abby gives us a slight wave but doesn't say anything.

"Abby's shy. Give her time, she'll warm up to you," Kiersten says. They make their way to the table in the kitchen.

"Is Sherry coming?" Lake says.

"No, probably not. She wants me to bring her some cake, though."

Kel and Caulder run into the kitchen. "There they are," Kiersten says. "How was your week off school, lucky butts?"

"Abby, come here," Caulder says. "I want to show you my room."

After Abby follows Caulder out of the room, I look at

Lake, a little concerned. She sees the worry in my eyes and laughs. "Relax, Will. They're only ten. I'm sure he just wants to show her his toys."

Regardless, I walk down the hallway and spy.

"I'm the guest, dork. I should get to be player one," I hear Abby say.

Sure enough, they're just being ten. I go back into the kitchen and wink at Lake.

AFTER THE PARTY is over, Eddie and Gavin agree to take Abby home. Kel and Caulder retreat to Caulder's room to play Kel's new video games. Lake and I are alone in the living room. She's lying on the couch with her feet in my lap. I rub her feet, massaging the tension away. She's been going nonstop all day, getting everything prepared for Kel's party. She's lying with her eyes closed, enjoying the relaxation.

"I have a confession to make," I say, still rubbing her feet.

She reluctantly opens her eyes. "What?"

"I've been counting down the hours in my head until next weekend."

She grins at me, relieved that this is my confession. “So have I. One hundred and sixty-three.”

I lean back against the couch and smile at her. “Good, I don’t feel so pathetic now.”

“It doesn’t make you any less pathetic,” she says. “It just means we’re both pathetic.” She sits up and grabs my shirt, pulling me to her. Her lips brush against mine and she whispers, “What are your plans for the next hour or so?”

Her words cause my pulse to race and chills to run down my arms. She touches her cheek to mine and whispers in my ear. “Let’s go to my house for a little while. I’ll give you a little preview of next weekend.”

She doesn’t have to ask twice. I pull away from her and jump over the back of the couch and run to the front door. “Boys, we’ll be back in a little while! Don’t leave!” Lake is still sitting on the couch, so I go over and grab her hands, pulling her up. “Come on, we don’t have much time!”

When we get to her house, she shuts the door behind us. I don’t even wait until we get to the bedroom. I shove her against the front door and start kissing her. “One hundred and sixty-two,” I say between kisses.

"Let's go to the bedroom," she says. "I'll lock the front door. That way, if they come over here, they'll have to knock first." She turns around and latches the dead bolt.

"Good idea," I say. We continue to kiss as we make our way down the hallway. We can't seem to make it very far without one of us ending up against a wall. By the time we get to the bedroom, my shirt's already off.

"Let's do that thing again where the first person to call retreat is the loser," she says. She's kicking off her shoes, so I do the same.

"You're about to lose, then, 'cause I'm not retreating," I say. She knows I'll lose. I always do.

"Neither am I," she says, shaking her head. She pulls her legs up and scoots back onto the bed. I stand at the edge of the bed and take in the view. Sometimes, when I watch her, it seems surreal that she's mine. That she really loves me back. She blows a strand of hair out of her face, then tucks her hair behind her ears and positions herself against the pillow. I slide on top of her and slip my hand behind her neck, gently pulling her lips to mine.

I move slowly as I kiss her, trying to savor every

second. We hardly ever get to make out; I don't want to rush it. "I love you so much," I whisper.

She wraps her legs around my waist and tightens her arms around my back in an attempt to pull me in closer. "Spend the night with me, Will. Please? You can come over after the boys go to sleep. They'll never know."

"Lake, it's just one more week. We can make it."

"I don't mean for *that.* We can wait until next weekend. I just want you in my bed tonight. I miss you. Please?"

I continue kissing her neck without responding. I can't say no, so I don't respond at all.

"Don't make me beg, Will. You're so damn responsible sometimes, it makes me feel weak."

I laugh at the thought that she believes *she's* weak. I kiss my way down to the collar of her shirt. "If I spend the night . . . what are you gonna wear?" I slowly unbutton the top button of her shirt and press my lips to her skin.

"Oh my God," she breathes. "I'll wear whatever the hell you *want* me to wear."

I unbutton the next button and move my lips a little lower. "I don't like this shirt. I definitely don't want you to wear this shirt," I say. "In fact, it's a really ugly shirt. I think you should take it off and throw it away." I unbutton the third button, waiting for her to call retreat. I know I'm about to win.

When she doesn't, I continue kissing lower and lower as I unbutton the fourth button, then the fifth button, then the last button. She still doesn't call retreat. She's testing me. I slowly bring my lips back to her mouth, and she rolls me onto my back and straddles me, then slides her shirt off and tosses it aside.

I run my hands up her arms and over the curves of her chest. Her hair has gotten a lot longer since I met her. It's hanging loosely around her face as she leans over me. I tuck it behind her ears so I can see her face better. It's dark in the room, but I can still make out her smile and the amazing emerald hue of her eyes. I slide my hands back up to her shoulders and trace the outline of her bra. "Wear this tonight." I slide my fingers under the straps. "I like this."

"So does that mean you're staying the night?" she asks. Her tone is more serious. Not so playful.

"If you wear this," I say, being just as serious. She presses her body against mine, our bare skin meeting for the first time in months. I'm definitely not calling retreat. I can't. I'm not usually so weak; I don't know what it is about her right now that's making me so weak.

"Lake." I break my lips apart from hers, though she continues kissing the edges as I speak, short of breath. "It's just a matter of hours until next weekend. It's coming up so fast, in fact, that this weekend can be considered part of the upcoming week. And the upcoming week is part of next weekend. So technically, next weekend is sort of occurring right now ... this very second."

She grabs my face and positions me so that she can look straight in my eyes. "Will? You better not be saying this because you think I'm about to call retreat, because I'm not. Not this time."

She's serious. I gently roll her onto her back and ease myself on top of her. I stroke her cheek with my thumb. "You're not? Are you positive you're ready to *not* call retreat? Right now?"

"Positive," she whispers. She wraps her legs tightly around my thighs, and we completely give in to our need for each other. I grab the back of her head and press her mouth into mine even harder. I can feel my pulse rushing through my entire body as we both begin to gasp for air between each kiss, as if we suddenly forgot how to breathe. We're both desperate, doing our best to get past the moment when one of us usually calls retreat. We pass that moment pretty quickly. I reach around to her back until I find the clasp on her bra, and I unhook it while she frantically tugs at the button on my pants. I've pulled the straps of her bra down over her arms to slide it off when the worst thing in the world happens. Someone knocks on the damn door.

"Christ!" I say. My head is spinning so fast, I have to take a moment to calm down. I press my forehead into the pillow next to her, and we try to catch our breath.

She slides out from under me and stands up. "Will, I can't find my shirt," she says with panic in her voice.

I roll onto my back and pull her shirt out from beneath me and toss it to her. "Here's your ugly shirt," I tease.

The boys are beating on the door now, so I hop out of the bed and go down the hallway to find my own shirt before opening the front door for them.

"What took you so long?" Kel asks as they shove their way past me.

"We were watching a movie," I lie. "We were at a really good part and didn't want to pause it."

"Yeah," Lake agrees, emerging from the hallway. "A *really* good part."

Kel and Caulder walk to the kitchen, and Kel flips the light on. "Can Caulder stay here tonight?" he asks.

"I don't know why you guys even bother asking anymore," Lake says.

"Because we're grounded. Remember?" Caulder says.

Lake looks to me for assistance.

"It's your birthday, Kel. The grounding can resume tomorrow night," I say. They go to the living room and turn on the TV.

I reach out to Lake. "Walk me home?" Lake grabs my hand, and we head out the front door.

"Are you coming back over later?" she asks.

Now that I've had the chance to cool off, I can see that coming back might not be a good idea. "Lake, maybe I shouldn't. We got really carried away just now. How do you expect me to sleep in the same bed with you after that?"

I expect her to object, but she doesn't.

"You're right, like always. It'd be weird, anyway, with

our brothers in the house." She wraps her arms around me when we reach my front door. It's incredibly cold outside, but she doesn't seem to care as we stand there. "Or maybe you're wrong," she says. "Maybe you should come back in an hour. I'll wear the ugliest pajamas I can find, and I won't even brush my teeth. You won't want to touch me. All we'll do is sleep."

I laugh at her absurd plan. "You could go a week without brushing your teeth or changing clothes, and I still wouldn't be able to keep my hands off you."

"I'm serious, Will. Come back in an hour. I just want to cuddle with you. I'll make sure the boys are in their room, and you can sneak in like we're in high school."

She doesn't have to do much convincing. "Fine. I'll be back in an hour. But all we're doing is sleeping, okay? No tempting me."

"No tempting, I promise," she says with a grin.

I cup her chin in my hand and lower my voice. "Lake, I'm serious. I want this to be perfect for you, and I get really carried away when I'm with you. We only have a week left. I want to stay the night with you, but I need you to promise me you won't put me in that position again for at least a hundred and sixty-two more hours."

"One hundred sixty-one and a half," she says.

I shake my head and laugh. "Go put those boys to bed. I'll see you in a little while."

She kisses me goodbye, and I head into the house and take a shower. A *cold* shower.

When I get to her house an hour later, all the lights are off. I lock the door behind me and ease down the hallway and into her bedroom. She left the bedside lamp on for me. She's lying in bed with her back toward me, so I climb in behind her and slide my arm under her head. I expect her to respond, but she's out. She's actually snoring. I brush her hair behind her ear and kiss the back of her head as I pull the covers around us both and close my eyes.

5.

SATURDAY, JANUARY 14

I love being with you so bad
When we aren't together, I miss you so bad
One of these days, I'm going to marry you so bad
And it'll be
so
so
good.

LAKE WAS UPSET WHEN SHE WOKE UP SATURDAY morning and I was already gone. She says it wasn't fair that she slept through our entire first sleepover. Regardless, I enjoyed it. I watched her sleep for a while before I went back home.

We didn't get into any more situations like the one in her bedroom Friday night. I think we were both surprised by how intense things got, so we're trying to keep it from happening again. Until this coming weekend, anyway. Saturday, we spent the evening at Joel's with Eddie and Gavin. Sunday, Lake and I did homework together. Pretty typical weekend.

Now I'm sitting here in Death and Dying, being stared down by the only person I've ever had sex with. It's awkward. The way Vaughn is acting, I feel like I really *am* hiding something from Lake. But telling her about Vaughn now would just prove that I wasn't being completely honest the first week of school. The last thing I want to do before this weekend is upset Lake, so I decide to wait another week before I bring it up.

"Vaughn, the professor is up there," I say, pointing to the front of the room.

Vaughn continues to stare at me. "Will, you're being a snob," she whispers. "I don't understand why you won't just talk to me. If you were really over what happened between us, it wouldn't bother you this much."

I can't believe she honestly thinks I'm not over us. I've been over us since the day I first laid eyes on Lake. "I'm over us, Vaughn. It's been three years. You're over us, too. You just always want what you can't have, and it's pissing you off. It's got nothing to do with me."

She folds her arms across her chest and sits back in her chair. "You think I *want* you?" She glares at me, then turns her attention to the front of the room. "Has anyone ever told you that you're an asshole?" she whispers.

I laugh. "As a matter of fact, yes. More than once."

TODAY HAS BEEN Kel and Caulder's first day back to school since their suspension. After school, they climb in the car with defeated expressions. I eye the books spilling out of their backpacks and realize it's going to be a night full of catching up on homework for the two of them. "I guess you guys learned your lesson," I say.

Lake is walking out of my house when the boys and I get out of the car. It doesn't bother me at all that she's at my house when I'm not home, but I'm a little curious about what she was doing. She sees the confusion on my face as she walks toward me. She holds out her hand and reveals one of the stars that her mother made, resting in her palm.

"Don't judge me," she says. She rolls the star around in her hand. "I just miss her today."

The look on her face makes me sad for her. I give her a quick hug, then watch her walk across the street and go back inside her house. She's in need of alone time, so I give it to her. "Kel, stay over here for a while. I'll help you guys with all your homework."

It takes us a couple of hours to finish the assignments that piled up while the boys were suspended. Gavin and Eddie are supposed to come over for dinner tonight, so I head to the kitchen to start cooking. We're not having burgers tonight. I'm sure we'll never have burgers again. I debate whether or not I want to make basagna but decide against it. Honestly, I don't feel like cooking. I go to the fridge and slide the Chinese menu out from under the magnet.

Half an hour later, Eddie and Gavin show up, followed a minute later by Lake, then the Chinese delivery guy. I set the containers in the middle of the table, and we all start filling our plates.

"We're in the middle of a game. Can we eat in my room tonight?" Caulder asks.

"Sure," I say.

"I thought they were grounded," Gavin says.

"They are," Lake replies.

Gavin takes a bite of his egg roll. "They're playing video games. What exactly are they grounded from, then?"

Lake looks to me for assistance. I don't know the answer, but I try anyway. "Gavin, are you questioning our parenting skills?" I ask.

"Nope," Gavin says. "Not at all."

There's a weird vibe tonight. Eddie is extremely quiet as she picks at her food. Gavin and I try to make small talk, but that doesn't last long. Lake seems to be in her own little world, not paying much attention to what's going on. I try to break the tension. "Suck-and-sweet time," I say. Almost simultaneously, all three of them object.

"What's going on?" I ask. "What's with all the depression tonight?" No one answers me. Eddie and Gavin look at each other. Eddie looks like she's about to cry, so Gavin kisses her on the forehead. I look over at Lake, who's just staring down at her plate, twirling her noodles around. "What about you, babe? What's wrong?" I say to her.

"Nothing. Really, it's nothing," she says, unsuccessfully trying to convince me she's fine. She smiles at me and grabs both of our glasses and goes to the kitchen to refill them.

"Sorry, Will," Gavin says. "Eddie and I aren't trying to be rude. We've just got a lot on our minds lately."

"No problem," I say. "Anything I can do to help?"

They shake their heads. "You going to the slam Thursday night?" Gavin asks, changing the subject.

We haven't been in a few weeks. Since before Christmas, I think. "I don't know, I guess we could." I turn to Lake. "You want to?"

She shrugs. "Sounds fun. We'll have to see if someone can watch Kel and Caulder, though."

Eddie clears the table while Gavin puts his jacket on. "We'll see you there, then. Thanks for supper. We won't suck so much next time."

"It's fine," I say. "Everyone's entitled to a bad day every now and then."

After they leave, I close the take-out containers and

put them in the refrigerator while Lake washes our dishes. I walk over to her and hug her. "You sure you're okay?" I ask.

She turns around and hugs me back, laying her head against my chest. "I'm fine, Will. It's just . . ."

I lift her face to mine and see that she's trying to hold back tears. I place my hand on the back of her head and pull her to me. "What's wrong?"

She quietly cries into my shirt. I can tell she's trying to stop herself. I wish she wouldn't be so hard on herself when she gets sad.

"It's just today," she says. "It's their anniversary."

I realize she's talking about her mom and dad, so I don't say anything. I just hug her tighter and kiss the top of her head.

"I know it's silly that I'm upset. I'm mostly upset about the fact that it's making me so upset," she says.

I place my hands on her cheeks and pull her gaze to mine. "It's not silly, Lake. It's okay to cry sometimes."

She smiles and kisses me, then breaks away. "I'm going shopping with Eddie tomorrow night. Wednesday night I have a study group, so I won't see you until Thursday. Are you getting a sitter, or should I?"

"Do you really think they need one? Kel's eleven now, and Caulder will be eleven in two months. Don't you think they can stay home by themselves for a few hours?"

She nods. "I guess so. Maybe I'll ask Sherry if she'll at least feed them supper and check on them. I could give her some money."

"I like that idea," I say.

She calls for Kel after she gets her jacket and shoes on, then walks back to the kitchen and puts her arms around me. "Ninety-three more hours," she says, planting a kiss on my neck. "I love you."

"Listen to me," I say as I look her intently in the eyes. "It's okay to be sad, Lake. Quit trying to carve so many pumpkins. And I love you, too." I kiss her one last time and lock the door behind them when they leave.

Tonight was really strange. The whole vibe seemed off. Since we're going to the slam, I decide to try to put my thoughts down on paper. I'll surprise Lake and do one for her this week. Maybe it'll help her feel better.

*

point of retreat

FOR REASONS BEYOND my comprehension, Vaughn sits next to me again on Wednesday. You would think after our little tiff on Monday that she would have given up. I was hoping she would have, anyway.

She pulls out her notebook and opens her textbook to where we left off Monday. She doesn't stare at me this time. In fact, she doesn't speak at all during the entire class period. I'm happy she's not talking to me, but at the same time I feel a little guilty for being so rude to her. Not guilty enough to apologize about it. She did deserve it.

As we're packing up our things up, still not speaking, she slides something across the table to me, then walks out. I debate throwing the note in the trash without reading it, but my curiosity gets the better of me. I wait until I'm seated in my next class to open it.

Will,

You may not want to hear this, but I need to say it. I'm really sorry. Breaking up with you is one of my biggest regrets in life so far. Especially breaking up with you when I did. It wasn't fair to you, I realize that now—but I was young and I was scared.

You can't act like what we had between us was nothing. I loved you, and I know you loved me. You at least owe me the courtesy of talking to me. I just want the chance to apologize to you in person. I can't seem to let go of how things ended between us. Let me apologize.

Vaughn

I fold the note and put it in my pocket, then lay my head down on the desk and sigh. She's not going to let it go. I don't want to think about it right now, so I don't. I'll worry about it later.

THE NEXT NIGHT, I don't think about anything other than Lake.

I'm picking her up in an hour, so I rush through my homework and head to the shower. I walk past Caulder's bedroom on my way. He and Kel are playing video games.

"Why can't we go with you? You said yourself there wasn't an age limit," Kel says.

I pause and back-step to their doorway. "You guys actually want to go? You realize it's poetry, right?"

"I like poetry," Caulder says.

"Not me," Kel says. "I just want to go 'cause we never get to go anywhere."

"Fine, let me make sure it's okay with Lake first." I head out the front door and across the street. When I open the door to her house, she screams.

"Will! Turn around!" I turn around, but not before I see her. She must have just gotten out of the shower, because she's standing in the living room completely naked. "Oh my God, I thought I locked the door. Doesn't anyone knock?"

I laugh. "Welcome to my world."

"You can turn around now," she says.

When I turn around, she's wrapped in a towel. I wrap my arms around her waist, pick her up off the floor, and spin her around. "Twenty-four more hours," I say as her feet touch the floor again. "You nervous yet?"

"Nope, not at all. Like I said before, I'm in good hands."

I want to kiss her, but I don't. The towel is too much, so I back away and ask what I came here to ask her. "Kel and Caulder want to know if it's okay if they go with us tonight. They're curious."

"Really? That's weird . . . but I don't care if you don't care," she says.

"Okay, then. I'll tell them." I head toward the door. "And Lake? Thanks for giving me another preview."

She looks slightly embarrassed, so I wink at her and shut her front door behind me. This is about to be the longest twenty-four hours of my life.

WE TAKE A seat in the back of the club with Gavin and Eddie. It's the same booth where Lake and I sat on our first date. Kiersten wanted to come, too, so it's a tight fit.

Sherry must trust us a lot, although she did ask a lot of questions before she agreed to let Kiersten come. By the end of the question/answer session, Sherry was intrigued. She said it would be good for Kiersten to see a slam. Kiersten said doing a slam would be good for her portfolio, so she brought a pen and a notebook to take notes.

"All right, who's thirsty?" I take drink orders and head to the bar before the sacrifice is brought onstage to perform. I explained the rules to all the kids on the way here, so I think they have a pretty good understanding. I haven't told them I'm performing, though. I want it to be a surprise. Lake doesn't know, either, so before I take the drinks back to the table, I go pay my fee.

"This is so cool," Kiersten says when I get back to the booth. "You guys are the coolest parents ever."

"No, they aren't," Kel says. "They don't let us cuss."

Lake hushes them as the first performer steps up to the microphone. I recognize the guy; I've seen him perform here a lot. He's really good. I put my arm around Lake, and he begins his poem.

"My name is Edmund Davis-Quinn, and this is a piece I wrote called 'Write Poorly.' "

Write poorly.
Suck
Write ***awful***
Terribly
Frightfully
Don't ***care***
Turn off the inner editor
Let yourself ***write***
Let it ***flow***
Let yourself ***fail***
Do something ***crazy***
Write fifty thousand words in the
month of November.

I did it.

It was ***fun***, it was ***insane***, it was ***one thousand six hundred and sixty-seven words a day.***

It was ***possible.***

But you have to turn off your inner critic.

Off completely.

Just ***write.***

Quickly.

In ***bursts.***

With ***joy.***

If you can't write, run away for a few.

Come ***back.***

Write ***again.***

Writing is like anything else.

You won't get good at it immediately.

It's a craft, you have to keep getting better.

You don't get to Juilliard unless you practice.

If you want to get to Carnegie Hall,

practice, practice, practice.

. . . Or give them a lot of money.

Like anything else, it takes ten thousand hours to get to mastery.

Just like Malcolm Gladwell says.

So ***write.***

Fail.

Get your ***thoughts*** down.

Let it ***rest.***

Let it ***marinate.***

Then edit.

But don't edit as you type,

that just slows the brain down.

Find a daily practice,

for me it's blogging every day.

And it's ***fun.***

The ***more*** you write, the ***easier*** it gets. The more it is a ***flow,*** the less a ***worry.*** It's not for ***school,*** it's not for a ***grade,*** it's just to get your thoughts ***out there.***

You ***know*** they want to come ***out.***

So ***keep at it.*** Make it a practice. And write ***poorly,*** write ***awfully,*** write with ***abandon*** and it may end up being

really

really

good.

When the crowd starts cheering, I glance at Kiersten and the boys. They're just staring at the stage. "Holy shit," Kiersten says. "This is awesome. That was incredible."

"Why are you only now bringing us here, Will? This is so cool!" Caulder says.

I'm surprised they all seem to like it as much as they do. They're relatively quiet the rest of the night as they watch the performers. Kiersten keeps writing in her notebook. I'm not sure what kind of notes she's taking, but I can see she's really into it. I make a mental note to give her some of my older poems later.

"Next up, Will Cooper," the emcee says. Everyone at the table looks at me, surprised.

"Are you doing one?" Lake says. I smile at her and nod as I stand and walk away from the table.

I used to get nervous when I performed. A small part of me still does, but I think it's more the adrenaline rush than anything. The first time I ever came here was with my father. He was very into the arts. Music, poetry, painting, reading, writing, all of it. I saw him perform here the first time when I was fifteen. I've been hooked since. I hate that Caulder never got to know that side of him. I've kept as much of our dad's writings as I could find, even a couple of old paintings. Someday I'll give them all to Caulder. Someday when he's old enough to appreciate them.

I take the stage and adjust the microphone. My poem isn't going to make sense to anyone besides Lake. This one's just for her.

"My piece is called 'Point of Retreat,' " I say into the microphone. The spotlight is bright, so I can't see her from up here, but I have a pretty good idea that she's smiling. I don't rush the poem. I perform slowly so she can take in every word.

Twenty-two hours and our war ***begins.***
Our war of ***limbs***
and ***lips***
and ***hands*** . . .
The point of ***retreat***
Is no longer a ***factor***
When both sides of the line
Agree to ***surrender.***
I can't ***tell*** you how many times I've ***lost*** . . .
Or is it how many times you've ***won***?
This game we've been playing for fifty-nine weeks

I'd say the score
is
none
to
none.
Twenty-two hours and our war ***begins***
Our war of ***limbs***
and ***lips***
and ***hands*** . . .
The best part of finally
Not calling retreat?
The ***showers*** above us
Raining down on our feet
Before the ***bombs explode*** and the ***guns*** fire
their ***rounds.*** Before the ***two*** of us ***collapse*** to the
ground. Before the ***battle,*** before the ***war*** . . .
You need to ***know***
I'd go fifty-nine ***more.***
Whatever it ***takes*** to let you ***win.***
I'd retreat ***all over***
and ***all over***
and ***over***
again.

I back away from the microphone and find the stairs. I'm not even halfway back to the booth when Lake throws her arms around my neck and kisses me. "Thank you," she whispers in my ear.

When I slide into the booth, Caulder rolls his eyes. "You could have warned us, Will. We would have hidden in the bathroom."

"I thought it was beautiful," Kiersten says.

It's after nine when round two gets under way. "Come on, kids, you guys have school tomorrow. We need to go," I say. They whine as they slide out of the booth one by one.

ONCE WE GET home, the kids head into the houses, and Lake and I linger in the driveway, hugging. It's getting harder and harder to separate from her at night, knowing she's just yards away. It's become a nightly struggle not to text her and beg her to come crawl in bed with me. Now that our promise to Julia has been fulfilled, I have a feeling nothing will stop us after tomorrow night. Well, other than the fact that we're trying to set a good example for Kel and Caulder. But there are ways to sneak around that.

I slide my hands up the back of her shirt to warm them. She begins to squirm, trying to get out of my grasp. "Your hands are freezing!" she says, laughing.

I just squeeze her tighter. "I know. That's why you need to be still, so I can warm them up." I rub them against her skin, attempting to keep the images of tomorrow night from overtaking my thoughts. They're distracting, so I remove my hands from her shirt and wrap my arms around her.

"Do you want the good news or the bad news first?" I ask her.

She shoots me a dirty look. "Do you want me to punch you in the face or the nuts?"

I laugh but prepare to defend myself just in case. "My grandparents are worried the boys will get bored at their house, so they want to keep them at my house instead. The good news is, we can't stay at your house now, so I booked two nights at a hotel in Detroit."

"That's not bad news. Don't scare me like that," she says.

"I just thought you would be a little apprehensive about seeing my grandmother. I know how you feel about her."

She looks at me and frowns. "Don't, Will. You know good and well it's not how *I* feel about *her*. She hates me!"

"She doesn't hate you," I say. "She's just protective of me." I try to push the thought out of her mind by kissing her ear.

"It's your fault she hates me, anyway."

I pull back and look at her. "My fault? How is it my fault?"

She rolls her eyes. "Your graduation? You don't remember what you said the first night I met her?"

I don't remember. I don't know what she's talking about. Nothing comes to mind.

"Will, we were all *over* each other. After your graduation, when we all went out to eat, you could barely talk, you were kissing me so much. It was making your grandmother really uncomfortable. When she asked you how long we'd been dating, you told her eighteen hours! How do you think that made me look?"

I remember now. That dinner was really fun. It felt great not to be ethically bound from putting my hands all over her, so that was all I did all night long.

"But it's sort of true," I say. "We were only officially dating for eighteen hours."

Lake hits me on the arm. "She thinks I'm a slut, Will! It's embarrassing!"

I touch my lips against her ear again. "Not yet you're not," I tease.

She pushes me away and points to herself. "You aren't getting any more of this for twenty-four hours." She laughs and starts to walk backward up her driveway.

"Twenty-one," I correct her.

She reaches the front door and turns and goes inside without so much as a good-night kiss. What a tease! She's not getting the upper hand tonight. I run up the driveway and open her front door and pull her back outside. I push her against the brick wall of the entryway and look her in the eyes as I press my body against hers. She's trying to look mad, but I can see the corner of her mouth break into a smile. Our hands interlock, and I bring them over her head and press them against the wall. "Listen to me very carefully," I whisper. I continue to stare into her eyes. She listens. She likes it when I try to intimidate her. "I don't want you to pack a damn thing. I want you to wear exactly what you were wearing last Friday night. Do you still have that ugly shirt?"

She smiles and nods. I'm not sure she could speak right now if she wanted to.

"Good. What you're wearing when we leave tomorrow night is the only thing you're allowed to bring. No pajamas, no extra clothes. Nothing. I want you to meet me at my house at seven o'clock tomorrow night. Do you understand?"

She nods again. Her pulse is racing against my chest, and I can tell from the look in her eyes that she needs me to kiss her. My hands remain clasped with hers against the wall as I move my mouth closer to her lips. I hesitate at the last minute and decide not to kiss her. I slowly drop her hands and back away from her, then head to my house. When I reach the front door, I turn around. She's still leaning against the brick in the same position. Good. I got the upper hand this time.

6.

FRIDAY, JANUARY 20

Lake will never read my journal, so I should say what's really on my mind, right? Even if she does read this, it'll be after I'm dead, when she's sorting through my things. So technically, maybe one day she will read this. But it won't matter by then, 'cause I'll be dead.

So, Lake . . . if you're reading this . . . I'm sorry I'm dead.

But for right now, in this moment, I am so alive. So very much alive. Tonight is the night. It's been worth the wait. All fifty-nine weeks of it. (Over seventy if you count from our first date.)

I'll just say what's on my mind, okay?

Sex.

Sex, sex, sex. I'm having sex tonight. Making love. Butterflying. Whatever you want to call it, we'll be doing it.

And I can't freaking wait.

I WANT TODAY TO BE PERFECT, SO I DECIDE TO SKIP school, clean the house, and finalize the plans before my grandparents arrive. I can't believe how nervous I am. Or maybe it's excitement; I don't know what it is. I just know I want the day to hurry the hell up.

On the way home from picking the boys up at school, we stop at the store to get a few things for dinner. Lake and I don't have plans to leave until seven, so I text my grandfather and tell them I'm making basagna. Julia said to wait for a good day to make it again, and it's definitely a good day. I'm running behind when I see their headlights through the living room window. I haven't even showered yet, and I still need to cook the bread sticks.

"Caulder, Grandma and Grandpa are here, go open the door!"

He doesn't need to—they open the door anyway. Without knocking, of course. My grandmother walks through the door first, so I go over and kiss her on the cheek.

"Hi, sweetie," she says. "What smells so good?"

"Basagna." I walk to my grandfather and give him a hug.

"*Basagna?*" she says.

I shake my head and laugh. "Lasagna, I mean."

My grandmother smiles, and it reminds me of my mom. She and my grandfather are both tall and thin, just like my mom. A lot of people find my grandmother intimidating, but I find it hard to be intimidated by her. I've spent so much time with her, I sometimes feel like she's my own mother.

My grandfather sets their bags down by the front door, and they follow me into the kitchen. "Will, have you heard of this *Twitter*?" He brings his glasses to the edge of his nose and looks down at his phone.

My grandmother looks at me and shakes her head. "He got one of those intelligent phones. Now he's trying to twit the president."

"Smart phones," I correct her. "And it's tweet, not twit."

"He follows me," my grandfather says defensively.

"I'm not kidding, he really does! I got a message yesterday that said, 'The president is now following you.' "

"That's cool, Grandpa. But no, I don't tweet."

"Well, you should. A young man your age needs to stay ahead of the game when it comes to the social media."

"I'll be fine," I assure him. I put the bread sticks in the oven and start to grab plates out of the cabinet.

"Let me do that, Will," my grandmother says, pulling the plates out of my hands.

"Hey, Grandma, hey, Grandpa," Caulder says, running into the kitchen to hug them. "Grandpa, do you remember the game we played last time you were here?"

My grandfather nods. "You mean the one where I killed twenty-six enemy soldiers?"

"Yeah, that one. Kel got the newest one for his birthday. You want to play it with us?"

"You bet I do!" he says, following Caulder to his bedroom.

The funny thing is, my grandfather isn't being overdramatic for Caulder's benefit. He genuinely wants to play.

My grandmother pulls a stack of glasses out of the

cabinet and turns to me. “He’s getting worse, you know,” she says.

“How so?”

“He bought himself one of those game thingies. He’s getting all into this technology stuff. Now he’s on the Twitter!” She shakes her head. “He’s always telling me things he twitted to people. I don’t get it, Will. It’s like some sort of midlife crisis, twenty years too late.”

“It’s tweeted. And I think it’s cool. It gives him and Caulder a way to relate.”

She fills the glasses with ice and walks back to the bar. “Should I set a place for Layken, too?” she says flatly. I can tell by her tone that she’s hoping I’ll say no.

“Yes, you should,” I say sternly.

She darts a look in my direction. “Will, I’m just going to say it.”

Oh boy, here we go.

“It’s not appropriate, the two of you running off for the weekend like this. You aren’t even engaged yet, much less married. I just think you two have rushed into things so quickly. It makes me nervous.”

I put my hands on my grandmother’s shoulders and smile reassuringly at her. “Grandma, we aren’t rushing into things, believe me. And you need to give her a chance; she's amazing. Promise me you'll at least pretend to like her when she gets here. And be nice!"

She sighs. "It's not that I don't like her, Will. It just makes me uncomfortable, the way you two act together. It seems like you're . . . I don't know . . . too in love."

"If your only complaint is that we're too in love, I guess I'll take it."

She brings an extra place setting to the table for Lake.

"I still need to jump in the shower, it won't take long," I say. "The bread sticks should be done in a few minutes, if you'll take them out."

She agrees, and I head to my room to pack a few things before going to shower. I reach under the bed to grab my bag and set it on the comforter. When I zip it open, I notice my hands are shaking. Why the hell am I so nervous? It's not like I've never done this before. Then again, it's *Lake.* I realize as I'm shoving the last of my clothes into the bag that I'm grinning like a complete idiot.

I've grabbed my change of clothes and headed to the bathroom when I hear a knock on the front door. I smile. Lake is trying to impress my grandmother, so she's knocked this time. It's cute. She's making an effort.

"Oh my God! Look who it is!" I hear my grandmother squeal after she opens the front door. "Paul! Come look who's here!"

I roll my eyes. I know I asked her to be polite to Lake, but I didn't expect her to make a spectacle. I open the door and head for the living room. Lake will be pissed if I leave her to fend for herself while I shower.

Shit! Shit, shit, shit! What the hell is she doing here?

She's hugging my grandfather when she sees me standing in the hallway. "Hey, Will." She smiles.

I don't smile back.

"Vaughn, we haven't seen you in years," my grandmother says. "Stay for dinner, it's almost ready. I'll make you a plate."

"No!" I yell, probably a little too angrily.

My grandmother turns toward me and frowns. "Will, that's not very nice," she says.

I ignore her. "Vaughn? Can I talk to you, please?" I motion for her to join me in the bedroom. I need to get rid of her now. "What are you doing here?"

She sits down on the edge of the bed. "I told you, I

just need to talk to you." She's got her blond hair pulled back in a bun again. She's looking at me all doe-eyed, trying to gain my sympathy.

"Vaughn, it's really not a good time."

She folds her arms over her chest and shakes her head. "I'm not leaving until you talk to me. All you've done is avoid me."

"I can't talk right now, I'm leaving in half an hour. I've got a lot I need to get done, and I won't be back until Monday. I'll talk to you after class on Wednesday. Just please *leave*."

She doesn't move. She looks down at her hands and starts crying. Good God, she's crying! I throw my hands up in frustration and walk over to the bed and sit beside her. This is horrible. This is so bad.

We're in almost the same predicament that we were three years ago. We were sitting on this very bed when she broke up with me. She said she couldn't imagine being nineteen and raising a child and having such big responsibilities. I was so upset with her for leaving me during the lowest point in my life. I'm almost as upset with her now, but this time it's because she *won't* leave.

"Will, I miss you. I miss Caulder. Since I saw you the

first day of class, I've done nothing but think about you and how we ended things. I was wrong. Please hear me out."

I sigh and throw myself back on the bed and cover my eyes with my arms. She could not have picked a worse time. Lake's going to be here in less than fifteen minutes. "Fine, talk. Make it quick," I say.

She clears her throat and wipes her eyes. It's odd how I don't care that she's crying. How can I love someone so much for so long, then have absolutely no sympathy for her whatsoever?

"I know you have a girlfriend. But I also know that you haven't been dating her nearly as long as you and I dated. And I know about her parents and that she's raising her brother. People talk, Will."

"What's your point?" I say.

"I think maybe you're with her for all the wrong reasons. Maybe you feel sorry for her since she's going through what you went through with your family. It's not fair to her if that's why you're with her. I think you owe it to her to give you and me another shot. To see where your heart really is."

I sit up on the bed. I want to yell at her, but I take a deep breath and calm myself down. I feel sorry for her. "Vaughn, listen. You're right, I did love you. 'Did' being the key word here. I'm in love with Lake. I would never do anything to hurt her. And you being here, it would hurt her. That's why I want you to leave. I'm sorry, I know this isn't what you want to hear. But you made your choice, and I've moved on from that choice. Now you need to move on, too. Please do us both a favor and just go."

I stand beside the bedroom door and wait for her to do the same. She stands, but rather than following me to the door, she starts to cry again. I roll my head and walk over to her. "Vaughn, stop. Stop crying. I'm sorry," I say, putting my arms around her. Maybe I've been too hard on her. I know it took a lot for her to come here and apologize. If she does still love me, I shouldn't be acting like such a jerk due to her bad timing.

She pulls away. "It's fine, Will. I'm okay with it. I shouldn't be putting you in this predicament. I just hated how I hurt you, and I wanted to say I'm sorry in person. I'll go," she says. "And … I really do want you to be happy. You deserve to be happy."

I can tell by her tone of voice and the look in her eyes that she's being genuine. Finally. I know she's a good person; otherwise, I wouldn't have spent two years of my life with her. But I also know the selfish side of her, and I'm thankful that side didn't win tonight.

I brush the hair away from her face and wipe the tears from her cheeks. "Thank you, Vaughn."

She smiles and hugs me goodbye. I'll admit, it feels good having closure between us. I feel like I've had my own closure for a while, but maybe this is what she needs. Maybe being in class with her won't be so unbearable now. I give her a quick peck on the forehead when we separate, and I turn to the door.

And that's when it happens: My whole world comes crashing down around me.

Lake is standing in the doorway watching us, her mouth open as if she's about to say something but can't. Caulder brushes past her when he sees Vaughn standing behind me. "Vaughn!" he says excitedly, rushing to her and hugging her.

Lake looks into my eyes, and I see it—I see her heart breaking.

I can't find words. Lake slowly shakes her head, clearly trying to make sense of what she's seeing. She pulls her gaze away from mine and turns and leaves. I run after her, but she's already out the front door. I slip my shoes on and swing the door open.

"Lake!" I yell as soon as I'm outside. I reach her as she makes it to the street. I grab her arm and turn her to face me. I don't know what to say. What can I say?

She's crying. I try to pull her to me, but she fights. She shoves me backward and starts hitting me in the chest without saying a word. I grab her hands and pull her to me, but she continues to try to hit me. I keep holding her until she grows weaker in my arms and starts to fall to the ground. Rather than hold her up, I melt to the snow-covered street with her and hold her as she cries.

"Lake, it's nothing. I swear. It's nothing."

"I *saw* you, Will. I saw you hugging her. It wasn't nothing," she cries. "You kissed her on the forehead! Why would you *do* that?" She isn't trying to hold back her tears this time.

"I'm sorry, Lake. I'm so sorry. It didn't mean anything. I was asking her to leave."

She pulls away from me and stands and walks toward her house. I follow her. "Lake, let me explain. *Please.*"

She continues inside the house and slams the door in my face . . . and locks it. I place my hands on both sides of the doorframe and hang my head. I've screwed up again. I've really screwed up this time.

"Will, I'm so sorry," Vaughn says from behind me. "I didn't mean to cause problems."

I don't turn around when I respond. "Vaughn, just go. Please."

"Okay," she says. "One more thing, though. I know you don't want to hear this right now, but you weren't in class today. He assigned our first test for Wednesday. I copied my notes for you and put them on your coffee table. I'll see you on Wednesday." I hear the crunch of the snow beneath her feet fading as she walks back to her car.

The lock unlatches, and Lake slowly opens her front door. She pulls it open just far enough so that I can see her face when she looks me in the eyes. "She's in your *class*?" she says quietly.

I don't respond. My whole body flinches when she slams the door in my face. She doesn't only lock it this time, she dead bolts it and turns off the outside light. I lean against the door and close my eyes, doing my best to hold back my own tears.

*

"HONEY, IT'S FINE. We're taking the box with us; that way they won't be bored. We don't mind, really," my grandmother says as they pack their things in the car.

"It's not a box, Grandma, it's an Xbox," Caulder says. He and Kel climb into the backseat.

"Now, you go get some rest. You've had enough stress for one night," she says to me. She leans in and kisses me on the cheek. "You can pick them up on Monday."

My grandfather hugs me before he gets in the car. "If you need to talk, you can tweet me," he says.

I watch as they drive away. Rather than go inside and get some rest, I walk back to Lake's house and knock on the door, hoping she's ready to talk. I knock for five minutes, until I see her bedroom light turn off. I give up for the night and go back to my house. I leave the front light on and the door unlocked, in case she changes her mind and wants to talk. I also decide to sleep on the couch instead of in my bedroom. If she knocks, I want to be able to hear it. I lie there for half an hour, cussing myself. I can't believe this is happening right now. This isn't how I'd envisioned falling asleep tonight at all. I blame the damn basagna.

I jerk up when the front door opens and she walks in. She doesn't look at me as she continues across the living room. She stops at the bookshelf and reaches inside the vase and pulls out a star, then turns and goes back to the front door.

"Lake, wait," I plead. She slams the door behind her. I get off the couch and run outside after her. "Please let me come over. Let me explain everything." We cross the street. She keeps walking until she gets to her front door, then turns to face me.

"How are you going to explain it?" she says. Her cheeks are streaked with mascara. She's heartbroken, and it's all my fault. "The one girl you've had sex with has been sitting in class with you every day for over two weeks! Why haven't you explained *that*? And the very night I'm about to leave with you . . . to make *love* to you . . . I find you in your bedroom with her? And you're kissing her on the freaking forehead!"

She starts crying again, so I hug her. I have to; I can't watch her cry and not hug her. She doesn't hug me back. She pulls away from me and looks up at me with pain in her eyes.

"That's the one kiss of yours that I love the most, and you gave it to her," she says. "You took that from me and gave it to *her*! Thank you for allowing me to see the *real* you before making the biggest mistake of my life!" She slams the door, then opens it again. "And where the *hell* is my brother?"

"In Detroit," I whisper. "He'll be back Monday."

She slams the door again.

I've turned to head back to my house when Sherry appears out of nowhere. "Is everything okay? I heard Layken yelling."

I pass her without responding and slam my own door. I don't do it hard enough, so I open it and slam it again. I do this two or three more times until I realize I'll have to pay for it when it breaks. I shut the door and punch it. I am an asshole. I'm an asshole, a jerk, a bastard, a dickhead . . . I give up and throw myself on the couch.

When Lake cries, it breaks my heart. But the fact that her tears are because of me? That my own actions are responsible for her heart breaking? That's a whole new emotion for me. One I don't know how to deal with. I don't know what to do. I don't know what I can say to her. If she would just let me explain. But that wouldn't help at this point. She's right. She didn't accuse me of anything I didn't actually do. God, I need my dad right now. I need his advice so bad.

Advice! I go to the vase and pull out one of the stars. I sit down on the couch and unfold it and read the words handwritten across it.

> *Sometimes two people have to fall apart to realize how much they need to fall back together.*
>
> —AUTHOR UNKNOWN

I fold the star and place it back inside the vase on the very top. I'm hoping Lake picks this one next.

7.

SATURDAY, JANUARY 21

FML.

I DIDN'T GET ANY SLEEP AT ALL LAST NIGHT. EVERY single noise I heard bolted me right off the couch in the hope that it was Lake. It never was.

I put on a pot of coffee and walk to the window. Her house is quiet; the shades are all drawn. Her car is in the driveway, so I know she's home. I'm so used to seeing the gnomes lining the driveway next to her car. They aren't there anymore. After her mother died, Lake gathered all the gnomes and threw them in the trash. She doesn't know it, but I dug one out and kept it. The one with the broken red hat.

I remember walking out of my house the morning after they moved here and seeing Lake dart out the front door with no jacket, in house shoes. I knew as soon as those shoes hit the pavement, she was going to bust her butt. Sure enough, she did. I couldn't help but laugh. Southerners seem to underestimate the power of cold weather.

I hated that she had cut herself when she landed on the gnome, but I was so happy to have the excuse to spend those few minutes with her. After I put the bandage on her and she left, I spent the entire day at work in a daze. I couldn't stop thinking about her. I was so nervous that my life and responsibilities would scare her off before I got the chance to know her. I didn't want to tell her everything right away, but the night of our first date, I knew I had to. There was something about her that was so much more than all the other girls I'd known. She had this resiliency and confidence.

I wanted to be sure Lake knew what my life was about that night. I wanted her to know about my parents, about Caulder, about my passion. I needed her to know the real me and understand who I was before we took it any further. When she watched her first performance that night, I couldn't take my eyes off her. I saw the passion and depth as she watched the stage, and I fell in love with her. I've loved her every second since.

Which is why I refuse to let her give up.

I'M ON MY fourth cup of coffee when Kiersten walks in. She doesn't check to see if Caulder is here, she just walks straight to the couch and plops down beside me. "Hey," she says flatly.

"Hey."

"What's going on with you and Layken?" she asks. She looks at me like she deserves an answer.

"Kiersten? Hasn't your mother ever told you it's rude to be nosy?"

She shakes her head. "No, she says the only way to get the facts is to ask the questions."

"Well, you can ask as many questions as you want. That doesn't mean I have to answer them."

"Fine," she says, standing up. "I'll go ask Layken."

"Good luck getting her to open the door."

Kiersten leaves, and I jump up and go to the window. She gets halfway down my driveway before she comes back. When she passes my window, she looks up with pity and slowly shakes her head. She opens the front door and comes back inside. "Is there anything in particular you want me to ask her? I can report back to you."

I love this kid. "Yeah, good idea, Kiersten." I think for a second. "I don't know, just gauge her mood. Is she crying? Is she mad? Act like you don't know we're fighting and ask her about me. See what she says."

Kiersten nods and starts to shut the front door.

"Wait—one more thing. I want to know what she's wearing."

Kiersten eyes me curiously.

"Just her shirt. I want to know which shirt she has on."

I wait by the window and watch as Kiersten walks across the street and knocks on the door. Why does she knock on Lake's door and not mine? The door opens almost immediately. Kiersten walks inside, and the door closes behind her.

I pace the living room and drink another cup of

coffee, watching out the window, waiting for Kiersten to emerge. A half hour goes by before the front door opens. Kiersten heads to her house rather than coming back across the street.

I give her a while. Maybe she had to go home to eat lunch. After an hour passes, I can't wait any longer. I make a beeline to Kiersten's house and knock on the door.

"Hey, Will, come on in," Sherry says. She steps aside. Kiersten's watching TV in the living room.

Before bombarding Kiersten, I turn to Sherry. "Last night . . . I'm sorry. I wasn't trying to be rude."

"Oh, stop it. I was just being nosy," she says. "You want something to drink?"

"No, I'm good. I just need to talk to Kiersten."

Kiersten gives me a dirty look. "You're a jerk, Will," she says.

I guess Lake's not over it. I sit down on the couch and put my hands between my knees. "Will you at least tell me what she said?" This is so pathetic. I'm entrusting my relationship to an eleven-year-old.

"Are you sure you want to know? I should probably warn you, I have an excellent memory. Mom says I've been able to quote entire conversations verbatim since I was three years old."

"Positive. I want to know everything she said."

Kiersten sighs and pulls her legs up on the couch. "She thinks you're a jerk. She said you were an asshole, a dickhead, a bas—"

"A bastard. I know, I get it. What else did she say?"

"She didn't tell me why she was mad at you, but she's *really* mad at you. I don't know what you did, but she's at her house right now, cleaning like a psycho. When she opened the door, she had hundreds of index cards all over the living room floor. It looked like recipes or something."

"Oh God, she's alphabetizing," I say. It's worse than I thought. "Kiersten, she won't answer the door if I go over there. Will you knock so she'll open the door and I can slip inside? I really need to talk to her."

Kiersten presses her lips together. "You're asking me to trick her? To basically *lie* to her?"

I shrug and nod.

"Let me get my coat."

Sherry comes from the kitchen and holds out her hand. I hold open my palm, and she puts something in it and folds my fingers over it. "If it doesn't go the way you're hoping, take these with some water. You look like shit." She can see my hesitation and smiles. "Don't worry, I made them. They're completely legal."

I DON'T HAVE a plan of attack. I'm hiding against the wall in front of Lake's house when Kiersten knocks. My heart is beating so fast, I feel like I'm about to commit a robbery. I take a deep breath when I hear the door open. Kiersten steps aside, and I brush past her and slip inside Lake's house faster than she can realize what happened.

"Get out, Will," she says as she holds the door open and points outside.

"I'm not leaving until you talk to me," I say. I back farther into the living room.

"Get out! Get out, get out, get out!"

I do what any sane male would do in this situation: I run down the hallway and lock myself in her bedroom. I realize I still don't have a plan. I don't know how I can talk to her if I'm locked in her bedroom. But at least she can't kick me out of her house. I'll stay here all day if I have to.

I hear the front door slam, and within seconds she's standing outside the bedroom door. I wait for her to say something or to yell at me, but she doesn't. I watch the shadow of her feet disappear as she walks away.

What now? If I open the door, she'll just try to kick me out again. Why didn't I formulate a better plan? I'm an idiot. I'm a freaking idiot! Think, Will. Think.

I see the shadow of her feet reappear in front of her bedroom door.

"Will? Open the door. I'll talk to you."

She doesn't sound angry. My idiotic plan actually worked? I unlock the door to her bedroom, and as soon as I open it all the way, I'm completely drenched in water. She just threw water on me! She threw an entire pitcher of water in my face!

"Oh," she says. "You look a little wet, Will. You better go home and change before you get sick." She calmly turns and walks away.

I'm an idiot, and she's not ready to give in. I make the walk of shame down her hallway, out the front door, and across the street to my house. It's freezing. She didn't even bother warming the water. I take off my clothes and get in the shower. A hot shower this time.

*

THE SHOWER DIDN'T help at all. I feel like complete crap. Five cups of coffee and no sleep on an empty stomach doesn't make for a great start to the day. It's almost two o'clock in the afternoon. I wonder what Lake and I would be doing right now if I weren't such an idiot. Who am I kidding? I know what we'd be doing right now. My reflection on the turn of events over the past twenty-four hours causes my head to hurt. I pick my pants up off the bedroom floor and reach inside the pocket, pulling out whatever it is that Sherry gave me. I walk to the kitchen and down the medicine with an entire glass of water before going to the couch.

IT'S DARK WHEN I wake up. I don't even remember lying down. I sit up on the couch and spot a note on the coffee table. I reach over and snatch it up and begin to read it. My heart sinks when I realize it's not from Lake.

Will,

I was going to warn you not to drive after you take

the medicine . . . but I see you already took it. So, never mind.

—Sherry

P.S. I had a talk with Layken today. You really should apologize, you know. That was kind of a dick move on your part. If you need any more medicine, you know where I live.

I toss the letter back on the table. Was the smiley face really necessary? I wince as the cramps in my stomach intensify. When was the last time I ate? I honestly can't remember. I open the refrigerator and see the basagna. Unfortunately, it's the perfect night for basagna. I cut a piece and throw it on a plate and toss it in the microwave. As I'm filling a glass with soda, the front door swings open.

She's walking across the room, heading for the bookshelf. I dart into the living room just as she reaches it. She's ignoring me. Rather than reaching in for a single star this time, she grabs the vase off the bookshelf.

She is *not* taking this vase with her. If she takes it, she won't have a reason to come back. I grab the vase out of her hands, but she won't let go. We tug back and forth, but I'm not letting go. I'm not letting her take it. She finally releases her grasp and glares at me.

"Give it to me, Will. My mother made it, and I want to take it home with me."

I walk back to the kitchen with the vase. She follows me. I set it on the corner of the counter against the wall and turn around to face her, then place my arms on either side of it so she can't reach it. "Your mother made it for both of us. I know you, Lake. If you take this home, you'll open every single one of them tonight. You'll be opening stars all night just like you carve pumpkins."

She throws her hands up in the air and groans. "Stop saying that! Please! I don't carve pumpkins anymore!"

I can't believe she thinks she doesn't carve pumpkins anymore. "You don't? Really? You're carving them right now, Lake. It's been twenty-four hours, and you still won't let me talk to you about it."

She wads her hands into fists and stomps her feet in frustration. "Ugh!" she yells. She looks like she wants to hit something. Or some*one.* God, she's so beautiful.

"Stop looking at me like that!" she snaps.

"Like what?"

"You've got that look in your eyes again. Just stop!"

I have absolutely no idea what look she's talking about, but I divert my attention away from her. I don't want to do anything to piss her off even more.

"Have you eaten anything today?" I ask. I take my plate out of the microwave, but she doesn't answer me. She just stands in the kitchen with her arms folded over her chest. I pull the pan of basagna out of the refrigerator and fold back the tinfoil.

"You're eating basagna? How appropriate," she says.

It's not the conversation I was hoping we would have, but it's conversation nonetheless. I cut another square and put it in the microwave. Neither of us says anything while it cooks. She just stands there, staring at the floor. I just stand here, staring at the microwave. When it's finished, I put our plates on the bar and pour another glass of soda. We sit down and eat in silence. Very uncomfortable silence.

When we're finished, I clear off the bar and sit across from her so I can see her. I wait for her to speak first. She has her elbows resting on the bar while she stares down at her nails, picking at them, attempting to look uninterested.

"So, talk," she says evenly, without looking up at me.

I reach my hands across the bar to touch hers, but she pulls away and leans back in her chair. I don't like the barrier of the bar between us, so I get up and walk to the living room. "Come sit," I say to her. She comes to the living room and sits on the same couch, but at the opposite end. I rub my face with my hands, trying to sort out just how I'm going to make her forgive me. I pull my leg up on the couch and turn to face her. "Lake, I love you. The last thing in the world I want to do is hurt you. You know that."

"Well, congratulations," she says. "You just succeeded with accomplishing the last thing in the world you wanted to do."

I lean my head back into the couch. This is going to be harder than I thought. She's tough to crack. "I'm sorry I didn't tell you she was in my class. I didn't want you to worry."

"Worry about what, Will? Is her being in class with you something I should worry about? Because if it's nothing like you say it is, why would I need to worry?"

Jesus! Am I picking the worst ways in the world to apologize, or is she just that good? If she ever stops being mad at me, I'll tell her she's finally figured out her major: prelaw.

"Lake, I don't feel that way about Vaughn anymore. I was planning to tell you about her being in my class next week; I just didn't want to bring it up before our getaway."

"Oh. So you wanted to make sure you got laid *before* you pissed me off. Good plan," she says sarcastically.

I slap my forehead with my hand and close my eyes. There isn't a fight this girl couldn't win.

"Think about it, Will. Put yourself in my shoes. Let's say I had sex with a guy before I met you. Then right when you and I were about to have sex, you walk into my bedroom, and I'm hugging this guy. Then you see me kiss him on the *neck:* your *favorite* place to be kissed by me. Then you find out I've been seeing this guy every other day for weeks and I've kept it a secret. What would you do? Huh?"

She's not picking at her nails anymore. She's glaring right at me, waiting for my response.

"Well," I say. "I would allow you the chance to explain without interrupting you every five seconds."

She flips me off and jerks off the couch and starts

toward the front door. I grab her arm and pull her back down on the couch. When she falls into the spot next to me, I wrap my arms around her and press her head into my chest. I try not to let her go. I don't want her to go. "Lake, please. Just give me a chance, I'll tell you everything. Don't leave again."

She doesn't struggle to pull away. She doesn't fight me, either. She relaxes into my chest and lets me hold her while I talk.

"I didn't know if you even knew about Vaughn. I know how much you hate talking about past relationships, so I thought it would be worse if I brought it up than if I didn't. Seeing her again meant nothing to me. I didn't want it to mean anything to you, either."

I run my fingers through her hair and she sighs, then starts crying into my shirt.

"I want to believe you, Will. I want to believe you so bad. But why was she here last night? If she doesn't still mean something to you, why were you holding her?"

I kiss her on top of the head. "Lake, I was asking her to leave. She was crying, so I hugged her."

She pulls her face away from my chest and looks up at

me, frightened. "She was crying? Why was she crying? Will, does she still *love* you?"

How do I answer that without coming off like a jerk again? Nothing I'm saying right now is helping my cause. Nothing at all.

She sits up and scoots away from me so she can turn toward me as she speaks. "Will, you're the one who wanted to talk. I want you to tell me everything. I want to know why she was here, what you were doing in your bedroom with her, why you were hugging her, why she was crying—*everything*." I reach over and take her hand, but she pulls it back. "Tell me," she says.

I try to think of where to begin. I inhale a deep breath and exhale slowly, preparing to be interrupted a million more times.

"She wrote me a note in class the other day and asked if we could talk. She showed up last night out of the blue. I didn't let her in, Lake. I was in my bedroom when she got here. I never would have let her in." I look her in the eyes when I say that because it's the truth. "My grandmother wanted her to eat with us, and I told her no and said I needed to talk to her. I just wanted her to leave. She started crying and told me she hated how she ended things with me. She said she knew about you and our whole situation with our parents and us raising our brothers. She said I 'owed it to you' to find out where my heart really lies, and that maybe I was with you because I felt sorry for you. She wanted me to give her another chance, to see if I was with you for the right reasons. I told her no. I told her I loved *you*, Lake. I asked her to leave, and she started crying again, so I hugged her. I felt like I was being a jerk; that's the only reason I hugged her."

I watch for some sort of reaction, but Lake looks down at her lap so I'm unable to see her face. "Why did you kiss her on the forehead?" she asks softly.

I sigh and stroke her cheek with the back of my hand, pulling her focus back to me. "Lake, I don't know. You've got to understand that I dated her for over two years. There are some things that, no matter how long it's been, they're just habit. It didn't mean anything. I was just consoling her."

Lake lies back on the arm of the couch and stares up at the ceiling. All I can do is let her think. I've told her everything. I watch her as she lies there, not saying a word. I want so badly to lie down beside her and hold her. It's killing me that I can't.

"Do you think there's a chance that she's right?" she asks, still staring at the ceiling.

"Right about what? That she loves me? Maybe, I don't know. I don't care. It doesn't change anything."

"I don't mean about that. It's obvious she wants to be with you, she said it herself. I mean do you think there's a chance she could be right about the other thing? About the possibility of you being with me because of our situation? Because you feel sorry for me?"

I spring forward on the couch and climb on top of her and grasp her jaw, pulling her face to mine. "Don't, Lake. Don't you dare think that for a second!"

She squeezes her eyes shut, and tears slide down over her temples, into her hair. I kiss them. I kiss her face and her tears and her eyes and her cheeks and her lips. I need her to know that it's not true. I need her to know how much I love her.

"Will, stop," she says weakly. I can hear her tears being suppressed in her throat; I can see it in her face. She doubts me.

"Baby, no. Don't believe that. *Please* don't believe that." I press my head into the crevice between her shoulder and her neck. "I love you because of *you*."

I've never needed anyone to believe anything more in my entire life. When she starts to resist and push against me, I slip my arm underneath her neck and pull her closer. "Lake, stop this. Please don't go," I beg. I realize as I'm speaking that my voice is shaking. I've never been so scared of losing something in my entire life. I completely lose control. I start to cry.

"Will, don't you see it?" she says. "How do you *know*? How do you *really* know? You couldn't leave me now if you wanted to. Your heart is too good for that, you would never do that to me. So how do I know that you would really be here if our circumstances were different? If our parents were alive and we didn't have Kel and Caulder, how do you know you would even love me?"

I clasp my hand over her mouth. "No! Stop saying that, Lake. *Please.*" She closes her eyes, and her tears flow even faster. I kiss them again. I kiss her cheek and I kiss her forehead and I kiss her lips. I grasp the back of her head and I kiss her with more desperation than I've ever kissed her. She puts her hands on my neck and kisses me back.

She's kissing me back.

We're both crying, frantically trying to hold on to the last bit of sanity between us. She pushes against me. She's still kissing me, but she wants me to sit up, so I do. I lean back into the couch, and she slides onto my lap and strokes my face with her hands. We stop kissing briefly and look at each other. I wipe tears away from her face and she does the same for me. I can see the heartache in her eyes, but she squeezes them shut and brings her lips back to mine. I pull her in to me so close that it's hard to breathe. We're gasping for air as we try to find a constant rhythm amid our frantic struggle. I have never needed her with more intensity. She pulls at my shirt, so I lean forward, allowing her to slip it off over my head. When her lips separate from mine, she crosses her arms and grasps the hem of her shirt and pulls it over her head. I help her. When her shirt is on top of mine on the floor, I wrap my arms around her, placing my hands on the bare skin of her back, and I pull her in to me.

"I love you, Lake. I'm so sorry. I'm so, so sorry. I love you so much."

She pulls back and looks me in the eyes. "I want you to make love to me, Will."

I wrap my arms tightly around her back and stand up as she clings to my neck. She wraps her legs around my waist and I carry her to my bedroom and we collapse onto the bed. Her hands find the button of my jeans, and she unbuttons them as my mouth slowly moves from her lips to her chin and down her neck. I can't believe this is actually happening. I don't allow myself time to second-guess my own actions. I slide my fingers under the straps of her bra and pull them off her shoulders. She slides her arms out of the straps and I move my lips along the edge of her bra while she begins to struggle with the button on her own jeans. I lift up to assist her, then I guide her hands as we slide them off and toss them behind me onto the floor. She scoots farther up on the bed until her head meets the pillows. I pull the covers out from beneath her and slide on top of her, then pull the covers back on top of us. When our eyes meet, I see the heartache behind her expression and the tears still streaming down her face. She grasps at the waist of my jeans and begins to slide them down, but I pull her hands away. She's hurting so much. I can't let her do this. She still doesn't trust me.

"Lake, I can't." I roll off of her and try to catch my

breath. "Not like this. You're upset. It shouldn't be like this."

She doesn't say anything, just continues to cry. We lie next to each other for several minutes without saying a single word. I reach over to put my hand on top of hers, but she pulls it away and slides off the bed. She picks her jeans up off the floor and walks back into the living room. I follow her and watch while she puts her shirt and pants back on. She sucks in a couple of breaths in an attempt to hold back her tears.

"Are you leaving?" I ask hesitantly. "I don't want you to go. Stay with me."

She doesn't respond. She goes to the door and slips her shoes on, then her jacket. I walk over to her and wrap my arms around her. "You can't be mad at me for this. You aren't thinking clearly, Lake. If we do this while you're angry, you'll regret it tomorrow. Then you'll be mad at yourself, too. You understand that, don't you?"

She wipes tears from her eyes and steps away from me. "You've had sex with her, Will. How do I get past that? How do I get past the fact that you've made love to Vaughn, but you won't make love to me? You don't know how it feels to be rejected. It feels like shit. You just made me feel like shit."

"Lake, that's absurd! I'm not about to have sex with you for the first time while you're crying. If we do this now, we'll *both* feel like shit."

She rubs her hands across her eyes again and looks at the floor, attempting not to cry. We stand in the living room, neither of us sure what happens next. I've said all I can say, and I just need her to believe me, so I give her time to think.

"Will?" She slowly brings her gaze back up to meet mine. It seems like it hurts her to even look at me. "I'm not sure I can do this," she says.

The look in her eyes makes my heart feel like it's come to a literal stop. I've seen this look in a girl before. She's about to break up with me.

"I mean . . . I'm not sure I can do *us*," she says. "I'm trying so hard, but I don't know how to get past this. How do I know this life is what you want? How do *you* know this is what you want? You need time, Will. We need time to think about it. We have to question everything."

I don't respond. I can't. Everything I say comes out wrong.

She's not crying anymore. "I'm going home now. I need you to let me go. Just let me go, okay?"

It's the clearheadedness behind her voice and the calm, reasonable expression in her eyes that rips my heart right out of my chest. She turns to leave, and all I can do is let her go. I just let her go.

AFTER AN HOUR of punching everything I can find to punch, cleaning everything I can find to clean, and screaming every cuss word I can think to scream, I knock on Sherry's door. When she opens it, she looks at me and doesn't say a word. She turns and comes back a moment later and holds out her fist. I open my palm, and she drops the pills in my hand and looks at me with pity. I hate pity.

When I'm back inside my house, I swallow the pills and lie on the couch, wishing it all away.

"WILL."

I try to open my eyes, to make sense of the voice I'm hearing. I try to move, but my entire body feels like concrete.

"Dude, wake up."

I'm discombobulated. I sit up on the couch and rub my eyes, attempting to open them, scared of the sunlight. When I finally do open them, it's not bright at all; it's dark. I look around the room and see Gavin sitting on the couch across from me.

"What time is it? What *day* is it?" I ask him.

"It's still today. Saturday. It's after ten, I think. How long have you been out?"

I think about that question. It was after seven when Lake and I had basagna. After eight when I let her go. When I just let her go. I lie back on the couch and don't answer Gavin as the scene from two hours before replays in my head.

"You want to talk about it?" Gavin asks.

I shake my head. I really don't want to talk about it.

"Eddie's over at Layken's house. She seemed pretty upset. It was a little awkward, so I thought I'd come hide out here. You want me to leave?"

I shake my head again. "There's basagna in the fridge if you're hungry."

"I am, actually," he says. He stands up and walks to the kitchen. "You need something to drink?"

I do. I do need a drink. I go into the kitchen, pressing my hand against my forehead. My head is pounding. I reach above the refrigerator and move the boxes of cereal out of the way to get to the cabinet. I pull out the bottle of tequila and grab a shot glass and pour myself a drink.

"I was thinking more along the lines of a soda," Gavin says as he sits down at the bar and watches me down a shot.

"Good idea." I open the refrigerator and pull out a soda. I grab an even bigger glass and mix the soda with the tequila. Not the best mix, but it goes down smoother.

"Will? I've never seen you like this. You sure you're okay?"

I tilt my head back and finish the entire drink, then put the glass in the sink. I choose not to answer him. If I say yes, he'll know I'm lying. If I say no, he'll ask me why. So I sit down next to him while he eats, and I don't say a thing.

"Eddie and I wanted to talk to you and Layken together. I guess right now that's not going to happen, so . . ." Gavin's voice trails off, and he takes another bite.

"Talk to us about what?"

He wipes his mouth with a napkin and sighs. He brings his right arm down, gripping his fork with his hand so tightly that his knuckles turn white. "Eddie's pregnant."

I don't trust my own ears at this point. My head is still pounding, and the alcohol mixed with Sherry's homemade concoction is causing me to see two of Gavin.

"Pregnant? How pregnant?" I ask.

"Pretty damn pregnant," he says.

"Shit." I stand up and grab the tequila off the counter and refill the shot glass. I normally don't promote underage drinking, but there are occasionally times when even I push my boundaries. I place the shot in front of him, and he downs it.

"What's the plan?" I ask.

He walks to the living room and sits down on the third couch. When did I get a third couch? I swipe the bottle of tequila off the counter and rub my eyes as I make my way into the living room. When I open them, there are two couches again. I hurry up and sit down before I fall.

"We don't have a plan. The same plan, anyway. Eddie wants to keep it. That scares the shit out of me, Will. We're nineteen. We're not prepared for this at all."

Unfortunately, I know *exactly* how it feels to unexpectedly become a parent at nineteen.

"Do *you* want to keep it?" I ask.

8.

SUNDAY, JANUARY 21

. . . I think. It might still be Saturday night. Whatever. WTF ever.

Lake . . . Lake, Lake, Lake, Lake. I'd take a mountain and then I need another drink. But I love you so much. Yeah I think I need more tequila . . . and more cow bell. I love you I'm so sorry. I'm not thirsty. But I'm not hungry, just thirsty. But I'm never drinking another cheeseburger again I love you so much.

EDDIE'S PREGNANT. GAVIN'S SCARED. I LET LAKE GO. That's all I remember about last night.

The sun is brighter than it's ever been. I throw the covers off and head to the bathroom. When I make it across the hall, I try to open the door, but it's locked. Why the hell is my bathroom door locked? I knock, which feels extremely odd—knocking on my own bathroom door when I should be the only person in my house.

"Just a sec!" I hear someone yell. It's a guy. It's not Gavin. What the hell is going on? I walk to the living room and see a blanket and pillow on the couch. There are shoes by the front door, next to a suitcase. I'm scratching my head when the bathroom door opens, so I turn around.

"Reece?"

"Mornin'," he says.

"What are you doing here?" I ask him.

He shoots me a confused look as he sits on the couch. "Are you kidding?" he asks.

Why would I be kidding? What would I be kidding about? I haven't seen him in over a year.

"No. What are you doing here? When did you get here?"

He shakes his head with the same bewildered

expression. "Will, do you not remember anything from last night?"

I sit down and try to remember. Eddie's pregnant. Gavin's scared. I let Lake go. That's all I remember. He can see from my struggle that I need a refresher.

"I got back last Friday. My mom kicked me out? I needed a place to stay last night, and you told me I could stay here. You really don't remember?"

I shake my head. "I'm sorry, Reece. I don't."

He laughs. "Dude, how much did you have to drink last night?"

I think back on the tequila, then remember the medicine Sherry gave me. "I don't think it was just the alcohol."

He stands up and looks awkwardly around the room. "Well, if you want me to leave . . ."

"No. No, I don't mind you staying here, you know that. I just don't remember. I've never blacked out before."

"You weren't making much sense when I got here, that's for sure. You kept saying something about a star . . . and a lake. I thought you were cracked out. You're not cracked out . . . are you?"

I laugh. "No, I'm not cracked out. I'm just having a really shitty weekend. The worst. And no, I don't feel like talking about it."

"Well, since you don't remember anything about last night . . . you kind of told me I could live here? For a month or two? Does that ring a bell?" Reece raises his eyebrows and waits for my reaction.

Now I know why I never drink. I always end up agreeing to things that I normally wouldn't agree to when I'm sober. I can't think of a reason not to let him stay here. We do have an extra bedroom. He practically lived here when we were growing up. Although I haven't seen him since his last break from deployment, I still consider him my best friend.

"Stay as long as you need to," I say. "Just don't expect me to be much fun. I'm not having a very good week."

"Obviously." He grabs his bags and shoes and takes them down the hallway to the spare bedroom. I walk to the window and look across the street at Lake's house. Her car is gone. Where would she be? She doesn't go anywhere on Sundays. They're her movies-and-junk-food days. I'm still looking out the window when Reece comes back.

"You don't have shit to eat," he says. "I'm hungry. You want me to grab you anything at the store?"

I shake my head. "I don't feel like eating," I say. "Just get whatever. I'll probably go later this afternoon, anyway. I need a few things before Caulder gets back tomorrow."

"Oh yeah, where is that little twerp?"

"Detroit."

Reece slides his shoes and his jacket on and slips out the front door. I walk to the kitchen to make coffee, but there's already a full pot. Nice.

AS SOON AS I step out of the shower, I hear the front door open. I don't know if it's Reece or Lake, so I rush to pull my pants on. When I emerge from the hallway, she's holding the vase in her hands, heading to the front door. When she sees me, she speeds up.

"Dammit, Lake!" I cut her off in the living room and don't let her by. "You aren't taking it. Don't make me hide it from you."

She tries to shove her way past me, but I block her again. "You have no right to keep them at your house, Will! It's just your excuse to make me keep coming over here!"

She's right. She's absolutely right, but I don't care. "No, I want them over here because I don't trust that you won't open them all."

She shoots me a dirty look. "While we're on the subject of trust, are you sabotaging these? Are you putting fake ones in here, trying to get me to forgive you?"

I laugh. She must be getting some great advice from her mom if she thinks I'm sabotaging the stars. "Maybe you should listen to your mother's advice, Lake."

She tries to brush past me again, so I grab the vase from her hands. She jerks it away harder than I expect, and the vase slips and lands on the floor, spilling out dozens of tiny stars onto the carpet. She bends down and starts scooping them up. Her hands are full, and I can see from her face that she doesn't know where to put them, since her pants don't have pockets. She pulls the collar of her shirt out and starts shoving them inside by the handful. She's determined.

I grab her hands and pull them away from her shirt. "Lake, stop it! You're acting like a ten-year-old!" I set the vase upright and start throwing the rest of them inside as fast as she's stuffing them inside her shirt. I do the only thing I can: I reach down her shirt and start grabbing them back. She slaps at my hands and tries to crawl backward, but I grab her shirt to stop her. She continues to back away as I continue holding her shirt until it slips over her head and is resting in my hands. She gathers more stars and stands and heads toward the front door with her hands clasped to her bra, trying to hold on to the stars.

"Lake, you aren't going outside without a shirt on," I say. She's relentless.

"Watch me!" she says. I jump up and wrap my arms around her waist and pick her up. Just as I'm about to release her onto the couch, the front door swings open. I look over my shoulder, and Reece walks in with groceries. He pauses and stares at us wide-eyed.

Lake is struggling to free herself from my grasp, ignoring the fact that someone she doesn't even know has a front-row seat to her tantrum. The only thing I can think of is that she's in her bra in front of another guy. I pick her up higher and toss her over the back of the couch. Just as fast as she's on the couch, she's back up, trying to make her way past me. She finally notices Reece standing in the doorway. "Who the *hell* are you?" she yells as she slaps at my arm.

He responds cautiously. "Reece? I live here?"

Lake stops struggling and folds her arms over her chest with an embarrassed look on her face. I take the opportunity to grab most of the stars out of her hands and toss them back toward the vase. I reach down and pick her shirt up and shove it at her. "Put your shirt on!"

"Ugh!" She throws the rest of the stars on the floor and turns her shirt right side out. "You're such a jerk, Will! You have no right to keep these here!" She pulls her shirt over her head and turns to Reece. "And when the *hell* did you get a roommate?"

Reece just stares at her. He clearly has no idea what to make of the scene. Lake goes back to the center of the room and grabs a small handful of stars, then rushes toward the front door. Reece steps aside as she goes outside. We watch as she crosses the street, stopping twice to pick up stars she drops in the snow. When she shuts her door behind her, Reece turns to me.

"Man, she's feisty. And *cute*," he says.

"And *mine*," I reply.

WHILE REECE IS cooking us lunch, I crawl around the living room and pick up all the stars that scattered, then

I hide the vase in a kitchen cabinet. If she can't find it, she'll have to speak to me to ask me where it is.

"What are those, anyway?" Reece asks.

"They're from her mother," I say. "Long story."

Lake might find them too easily if I hide them in such an obvious spot. I move the cereal again and place the vase right behind the tequila.

"So is this chick your girlfriend?"

I'm not sure how to answer his question. I don't know how to label what's going on between us. "Yep," I say.

He cocks his head at me. "Doesn't seem like she likes you very much."

"She loves me. She just doesn't like me right now."

He laughs. "What's her name?"

"Layken. I call her Lake," I say as I pour myself a drink. A nonalcoholic drink this time.

He laughs. "That explains your incoherent rambling last night." He spoons some pasta into our bowls, and we sit at the table to eat. "So, what'd you do to piss her off so bad?"

I rest my elbows on the table and drop my fork into my bowl. I guess now is as good a time as any to fill him in on the last year. He's been my best friend since we were ten, minus the last couple of years or so, after he left for the army. I tell him everything. The entire story. From the day we met, to Lake's first day at school, to our fight about Vaughn, all the way up to last night. When I finish, he's on his second bowl of pasta, and I haven't even touched mine.

"So," he says, stirring his pasta around. "You think you're really over Vaughn?"

Out of all the things I just told him, *that's* what he focuses on? I laugh. "I'm absolutely over Vaughn."

He shifts in his chair and looks at me. "Just tell me if this isn't cool with you, but . . . would you care if I asked her out? If you say no, I won't, man. I swear."

He hasn't changed a bit. Of course this is the *one* thing he would pick up on. The *single* girl.

"Reece? I could honestly care less what you do with Vaughn. Honestly. Just don't bring her here. That's one rule you can't break. She's not allowed in this house."

He smiles. "I can live with that."

I SPEND THE next few hours finishing homework and studying the notes Vaughn left for me. I rewrite them and throw away her original notes. I hate looking at her handwriting.

I've cut down my spying to about once an hour. I don't want Reece to think I'm crazy, so I look out the window only when he leaves the room. I'm at the table studying, and he's watching TV, when Kiersten walks in—without knocking, of course.

"Who the hell are you?" she says to Reece as she walks across the living room.

"Are you even old enough to talk like that?" he asks.

She rolls her eyes and walks to the kitchen and takes a seat across from me. She puts her elbows on the table and rests her chin in her hands, watching me study.

"You see Lake today?" I ask without looking up from my notes.

"Yep."

"And?"

"Watching movies. And eating a lot of junk food."

"Did she say anything about me?"

Kiersten folds her arms on the table and leans in closer. "You know, Will, if I'm going to be working for you, I think it's a good time to negotiate fair compensation."

I look at her. "Are you agreeing to help me?"

"Are you agreeing to pay me?"

"I think we could work out a deal," I say. "Not with currency. But maybe I could help you build your port folio."

She leans back in her seat and eyes me curiously. "Keep talking."

"I've got a lot of performance experience, you know. I could give you some of my poetry . . . help you prepare for a slam."

I can see her thoughts churning behind her expression. "Take me to the slam. Every Thursday for at least a month. There's a talent show coming up at the school in a few weeks that I want to enter, so I need all the exposure I can get."

"An entire month? No way. This reconciliation between Lake and me better happen before four weeks! I can't go through this for a whole month."

"You really are an idiot, aren't you?" She stands up and pushes her chair in. "Without my help, you'll be lucky if she forgives you this *year.*" She turns to walk away.

"Fine! I'll do it. I'll take you," I say.

She turns back and smiles at me. "Good choice," she says. "Now . . . is there anything you want me to plant in her head while I go to work?"

I stew on this for a moment. What's the best way to win Lake back? What in the world can I possibly say to get her to see how much I really love her? What can I have Kier sten do? I jump up when it hits me. "Yes! Kiersten, you need to ask her to take you to the slams. Tell her I refused to take you and that I said I'm never going back. Beg her to take you if you have to. If there's one way I can get her to believe me, it's while I'm on that stage."

She gives me an evil grin. "Devious. I love it!" she says on her way out.

"Who *is* she?" Reece says.

"*She* is my new best friend."

OTHER THAN THE fight we had over the stars today, I've given Lake all the alone time I possibly can. Kiersten reported back that Lake agreed to take her on Thursday, after an intense bout of begging on Kiersten's part. I rewarded her with one of my old poems.

It's after ten now. I know I shouldn't, but I can't seem to go to bed without trying to talk to Lake at least one more time. I can't decide whether leaving her alone or hounding her is the better choice. I figure it's time for another star. I hate that we're opening them so fast, but I consider this an emergency.

When I get to the kitchen, I'm shocked to see Lake peering in one of the cabinets. She's getting sneakier. When I pass by her, she jumps. I don't say anything as I reach into the cabinet and pull out the vase. I set it on the counter and take out one of the stars. She looks at me as though waiting for me to yell at her again. I hold the vase out to her, and she grabs her own star. We lean against opposite ends of the counter while we open them and read them silently to ourselves.

Adopt the pace of nature: her secret is patience.

—RALPH WALDO EMERSON

I do just that . . . I practice patience. I don't speak as Lake reads hers. As much as I want to run up to her and kiss her and make it all better, I decide to be patient instead. She scowls as she reads the paper in her hand.

She wads it up and throws it on the counter, then walks away. Again I let her go.

When I know she's gone, I grab her slip of paper and unfold it.

So if you could find it in your heart
To give a man a second start
I promise things won't end the same.

—THE AVETT BROTHERS

I couldn't have said it better if I'd written it myself. "Thank you, Julia," I whisper.

9.

MONDAY, JANUARY 23

I'm not giving up
You're not giving in
This battle will turn into a war
Before I let it come to an end.

I KNOW LAKE DOESN'T LIKE ME RIGHT NOW, BUT I know she doesn't hate me, either. I can't help but wonder if I should give her the space she's asking for. Part of me wants to respect where she's coming from, but part of me is scared that if I do back off, she may decide she likes the space. I'm terrified of that. So maybe I won't give her space. I wish I knew where to draw the line between desperation and suffocation.

Reece is in the kitchen drinking coffee. The fact that he actually makes coffee is a good enough reason alone to let him stay.

"What are your plans today?" he says.

"I have to go to Detroit to get the boys at some point. You want to go with me?"

He shakes his head. "Can't. I have plans with . . . I have plans today." He looks away nervously as he rinses out his coffee cup.

I laugh and take my own cup out of the cabinet. "You don't have to hide it. I already told you I was cool with it."

He places his cup upside down in the dish drainer and turns to face me. "It's still a little weird, though. I mean, I don't want you to think I was trying to get with her while you two were together. It wasn't like that."

"Stop worrying about it, Reece. Really. It's not weird for me at all. What is a little weird is that just a few days ago she was professing her love for me, and now she's about to spend the day with you. Does that not bother you just a little bit?"

He grins at me as he grabs his wallet and keys off the counter. "Believe me, Will, I've got skills. When Vaughn's with me, you'll be the last thing on her mind."

Reece has never been much for modesty. He puts on his jacket and heads out. As soon as the front door shuts, my phone vibrates. I pull it out of my pocket and smile. It's a text from Lake.

What time will Kel be home today? I have to go pick up a textbook on back order, and I won't be home for a while.

The text seems too impersonal. I read it a few times, trying to gain hints from any hidden meanings. Unfortunately, I'm pretty positive that it states exactly what she intended to say. I text her back, hoping to somehow talk her into going with me to pick the boys up.

Where are you going to pick up textbooks? Detroit?

I know which bookstore she's going to. It's a long shot, but I'm hoping I can trap her into riding with me instead of taking her own car. She replies almost immediately.

Yes. What time will Kel be home?

She's so hard to crack. I hate her short responses.

I'm going to Detroit to pick the boys up later. Why don't you just ride with me? I can take you to get your book.

Having the long drive to talk things over might give me a chance to convince her that things need to go back to the way they were.

I don't think that's a good idea. I'm sorry.

Or not. Why does she have to be so damn difficult? I throw my phone on the couch and don't bother texting her back. I walk to the window and pathetically stare at her house. I hate that her need for space is stronger than her need for me. I really need her to go to Detroit with me today.

I CAN'T BELIEVE I'm doing this. As I'm crossing the street, I double-check to make sure Lake isn't peeking out the window. She'll be so pissed if she catches me. I quickly open her car door and push the lever to pop the hood. I have to work fast. I decide the best way to disable her Jeep is to disconnect the battery. It's probably the most obvious, but she would never notice, considering her lack of mechanical knowledge. As soon as I succeed with my goal, I glance toward her window again, then make a mad dash back home. When I shut the door behind me, I almost regret what I just did. Almost.

I WAIT FOR her to come out that afternoon before I leave. I watch as she attempts to crank her vehicle. It doesn't start. She hits the steering wheel and swings open the car door. This is my opportunity. I grab my things and head out the front door to my car, pretending not to notice her. When I back up and pull onto the street, she has her hood up. I stop in front of her driveway and roll down my window. "What's wrong? Car won't start?"

She peers around the front of the hood and shakes her head. I pull my car over and get out to take a look. She steps aside and allows me by without speaking. I fidget with a few wires here and there and pretend to crank her car a couple of times. The whole time, she's just silently standing back.

"Looks like your battery is shot," I lie. "If you want, I can pick a new one up for you while I'm in Detroit. Or . . . you could ride with me, and I'll take you to get your book." I smile at her, hoping she'll cave.

She looks back at her house, then at me. She looks

torn. "No, I'll just ask Eddie. I don't think she has plans today."

That isn't what I need her to say. It isn't going how I planned. *Play it cool, Will.*

"I'm only offering you a ride. We both need to go to Detroit anyway. It's ridiculous to get Eddie involved just because you don't want to talk to me right now." I use the authoritative tone I've perfected on her. It usually works.

She hesitates.

"Lake, you can carve pumpkins the whole trip. Whatever you need. Just get in the car," I say.

She scowls at me, then turns and grabs her purse out of the Jeep. "Fine. But don't think this means anything." She walks down the driveway and toward my car.

I'm glad she's in front of me, because I can't hide my excitement as I punch at the air with my fists. An entire day together is exactly what we need.

AS SOON AS we pull away, she turns the Avett Brothers on, her way of letting me know she's carving pumpkins. The first few miles to Detroit are awkward. I keep wanting to bring everything up, but I don't know how. Kel and Caulder will be with us on the way home, so I know if I want to lay it all out, I need to do it now.

I reach over and turn the volume down. She's got her foot propped up on the dash, and she's staring out the window in an obvious attempt to avoid confrontation, like she always does. When she notices I've turned down the volume, she glances at me and sees me staring at her, then returns her attention to the window. "Don't, Will. I told you . . . we need time. I don't want to talk about it."

She is so damn *frustrating*. I sigh and shake my head, feeling another round of defeat coming on. "Could you at least give me an estimate of how long you'll be carving pumpkins? It'd be nice to know how long I have to suffer." I don't try to mask my aggravation.

I can tell by her scowl that I said the absolute wrong thing again.

"I knew this was a bad idea," she mumbles.

I grip the steering wheel even tighter. You would think after a year I would have found a way to get through to her or to manipulate her in some way. She's almost impenetrable. I have to remind myself that her indomitable will is one of the reasons I fell in love with her in the first place.

Neither of us says another word during the remainder of the drive. It doesn't help that neither of us turns the radio back up. The entire trip is incredibly awkward as I try my best to search for the right thing to say and she tries her best to pretend I don't exist. As soon as we arrive at the bookstore in Detroit and I pull into a parking spot, she swings open the car door and runs inside. I'd like to think she's running from the cold, but I know she's running from me. From confrontation.

While she's inside, I get a text from my grandfather informing me that my grandmother is cooking us dinner. His text ended with the word "roast," preceded by a hash tag.

"Great," I mutter to myself. I know Lake has no intention of spending the evening with my grandparents. As soon as I text my grandfather letting him know we're almost there, Lake returns to the car.

"They're cooking dinner for us. We won't stay long," I say.

She sighs. "How convenient. Well, take me to get a new battery first so we can get it over with."

I don't respond as I head toward my grandparents' house. She's been to their house a couple of times, so she knows when we get closer that I have no intention of stopping at the store.

"You've passed like three stores that sell batteries," she says. "We need to get one now, in case it's too late on the way back."

"You don't need a battery. Your battery is fine," I say. I avoid looking at her, but out of the corner of my eye, I can see her watching me, waiting for explanation. I don't immediately respond. I flick the blinker on and turn onto my grandparents' street. When I pull into their driveway, I turn off the car and tell her the truth. What harm could it do at this point?

"I unhooked your battery cable before you tried to leave today." I don't wait for her reaction as I get out of the car and slam the door. I'm not sure why. I'm not mad at her, I'm just frustrated. Frustrated that she doubts me after all this time.

"You *what*?" she yells. When she gets out of the car, she slams her door, too.

I keep walking, shielding the wind and snow with my jacket until I reach the front door. She rushes after me.

I almost walk inside without knocking but remember how it feels, so I knock.

"I said I unhooked your battery cable. How else was I going to convince you to ride with me?"

"That's real mature, Will." She huddles closer to the front door, farther away from the wind. I hear footsteps nearing the entryway when she turns to face me, opening her mouth as if to say something else. Then she rolls her eyes and turns away. The front door swings open, and my grandmother steps aside to let us in.

"Hi, Sara," Lake says with a fake smile as she hugs my grandmother. My grandmother returns her hug, and I walk in behind them.

"You two got here just in time. Kel and Caulder are setting the table," Grandma says. "Will, take your jackets and put them in the dryer so they won't be so wet when you leave."

My grandmother goes back to the kitchen, and I remove my jacket and head to the laundry room without offering to take Lake's. I smile when I hear her stomping angrily after me. Being the nice guy has not helped my case at all, so I guess I'll start being the jerk. I throw my jacket into the dryer and step aside so she can do the same. After she shoves her jacket inside, she slams the dryer door shut and turns it on. She spins around to exit the laundry room, but I'm blocking her way. She shoots me a dirty look and tries to ease past me, but I don't budge. She steps back and looks away. She's going to stand there until I move out of her way. I'm going to stand here until she talks to me. I guess we'll be here all night.

She tightens her ponytail and leans against the dryer, crossing one foot over the other. I lean against the laundry room door in the same position as I stare her down, waiting for something. I'm not sure what I'm trying to get out of her right now; I just want her to talk to me.

She wipes snow off the shoulder of her shirt. She's wearing the Avett shirt I bought her at the concert we went to a month ago. We had the best time that night; I never would have imagined then that we would be in this predicament.

I give in and speak first. "You know, you sure are quick to accuse me of being immature for someone giving me the silent treatment like a five-year-old."

She cocks her eyebrows at me and laughs. "Seriously?

You have me trapped in a laundry room, Will! Who's being immature?"

She tries to move past me again, but I continue to block her way. She's flush against me, pathetically trying to shove against my chest. I have to fight the urge to wrap my arms around her. We're practically face-to-face when she finally stops pushing me. She's inches from me, staring at the floor. She may have doubts about my feelings for her, but there is no way she can doubt the sexual tension between us. I take her chin in my hand and gently pull her face toward mine.

"Lake," I whisper. "I'm not sorry about what I did to your car. I'm desperate. I'd do anything at this point just to be with you. I miss you."

She looks away, so I bring my other hand to her face and force her to look me in the eyes. She tries to pull my hands away, but I refuse to let go. The tension between us increases as we hold the stare. I can tell she wants to hate me so bad right now, but she loves me too much. There's a struggle of emotion in her eyes. She can't decide whether she wants to punch me or kiss me.

I take advantage of her moment of weakness and slowly lean in and touch my lips to hers. She presses her hands against my chest and halfheartedly tries to push me away, but she doesn't pull her mouth away from mine. Rather than honor her request for space, I lean in to her even farther and part her lips with mine. Her pressure against my chest weakens as her stubbornness finally dissolves and she lets me kiss her.

I place my hand on the back of her head and slowly move my lips in rhythm with hers. Our kiss is different this time. Rather than pushing it to the point of retreat, like we've been doing, we continue to slowly kiss, pausing every few seconds to look at each other. It's almost as if neither of us believes this is happening. I feel like this kiss is my last chance to remove any doubt from her mind, so I pour into it every single emotion I have. Now that I have her in my arms, I'm afraid to let her go. I take a step forward, and she takes a step back, until we end up against the dryer. The situation reminds me of the last time we were alone together in a laundry room, over a year ago.

It was the day after her kiss with Javi at Club N9NE. The moment I walked around his truck and saw his mouth on hers, I immediately felt jealousy coupled with intense hurt like nothing I'd ever experienced. I had never been in a physical fight. The fact that he was my student and I was his teacher was lost on me as soon as I began to pull him away from her. I don't know what would have happened if Gavin hadn't shown up when he did.

The day after the fight, when I heard Lake tell her version of events, I felt like such an idiot that I believed she'd kissed him back. I knew her better than that, and I hated myself for assuming the worst. As difficult as it was to allow her to believe I had chosen my career over her, I knew it was the right thing to do at the time. That night in my laundry room, though, I allowed my emotions to control my conscience, and I almost messed up the best thing that ever happened to me.

I push the fear of losing her again out of my mind. She moves her hands to my neck, sending chills down my entire body. Slow and steady loses out as we simultaneously pick up the pace. When she runs her hands through my hair, it sends me over the edge. I grab her by the waist and lift her up until she's seated on the dryer. Out of every single kiss we've ever shared, this is by far the best. I place my hands on the outside of her thighs and pull her to the edge of the dryer, and she wraps her legs around me. Just as my lips meet the spot directly below her ear, she gasps and shoves against my chest.

"Eh-hem," my grandmother says, rudely interrupting one of the best moments of my life.

Lake immediately jumps off the dryer, and I step back. My grandmother is standing in the doorway with her arms crossed, glaring at us. Lake straightens her shirt and looks down at her feet, embarrassed.

"Well, it's nice to see you two made up," my grandmother says, eyeing me disapprovingly. "Dinner is ready when you can find time to join us at the table." She turns and walks away.

As soon as she's gone, I turn back to Lake and wrap my arms around her again. "Babe, I've missed you so bad."

"Stop," she says, pulling away from me. "Just stop."

Her sudden hostility is unexpected and confusing. "What do you mean, *stop*? You were just kissing me back, Lake."

She looks up at me, agitated. She seems disappointed in herself. "I guess I had a *weak moment*," she says in a mocking tone.

I recognize the phrase, and more than likely, I deserve

her reaction. "Lake, quit doing this to yourself. I know you love me."

She lets out a sigh as though she's unsuccessfully trying to get through to a child. "Will, I'm not struggling with whether or not I love *you.* It's whether or not you really love *me.*" She heads into the dining room, leaving me behind in yet another laundry room.

I punch the wall, frustrated. I thought for a second I'd gotten through to her. I don't know how much longer I can take this. She's starting to piss me off.

"THIS ROAST IS delicious, Sara," Lake says to my grandmother. "You'll have to give me the recipe."

I snatch the bowl of potatoes off the table and silently seethe at the way Lake is so casually exchanging pleasantries with my grandmother. I have no appetite, but I'm piling on the food anyway. I know my grandmother: If I don't eat, she'll be offended. I scoop potatoes onto my plate, then take an exaggerated spoonful and drop them on Lake's plate, right on top of her roast. She's seated next to me, doing her best to pretend nothing is amiss as she eyes the massive mound of potatoes. I don't know whether she's putting on this fake display of happiness for my grandparents' sake or for Kel and Caulder's sake. Maybe for all of them.

"Layken, did you know Grandpaul used to be in a band?" Kel says.

"No, I didn't. And did you just call him Grandpaul?" Lake says.

"Yeah. That's my new name for him."

"I like it," my grandfather says. "Can I call you Grandkel?"

Kel smiles and nods at him.

"Will you call me Grandcaulder?" Caulder asks.

"Sure thing, Grandcaulder," he says.

"What was the name of your band, Grandpaul?" Lake asks.

It's almost scary how good she is at putting up a front. I make a mental note to retain this little detail about her for future reference.

"Well, I was in several, actually," he replies. "It was a hobby when I was younger. I played the guitar."

"That's neat," Lake says. She takes a bite and talks around the mouthful. "You know, Kel has always wanted to learn how to play the guitar. I've been thinking about putting him in lessons." She wipes her mouth and takes a sip of water.

"Why? You should just get Will to teach him," Grandpaul says.

Lake turns and looks at me. "I wasn't aware that Will knew how to play the guitar," she says in a somewhat accusatory tone.

I guess I've never shared that with her. It's not like I was trying to keep it from her; I just haven't played in a couple of years. I'm sure she thinks it's one more secret I've been keeping from her.

"You've never played for her?" my grandfather says to me.

I shrug. "I don't own a guitar."

Lake is still glaring at me. "This is really interesting, Will," she says sarcastically. "There sure is a lot about you that I don't know."

I look at her straight-faced. "Actually, sweetie . . . there isn't. You know pretty much everything about me."

She shakes her head and places her elbows on the table and squints at me, putting on that fake smile I'm growing to hate. "No, *sweetie.* I don't think I do know everything about you." She says this in a tone that only

I could recognize as false enthusiasm. "I didn't know you played the guitar. I also didn't know you were getting a roommate. In fact, this Reece seems to have been a pretty big part of your life, and you've never even mentioned him—along with a few other 'old friends' who have popped up recently."

I set my fork down and wipe my mouth with the napkin. Everyone at the table is staring at me, waiting for me to speak. I smile at my grandmother, who seems oblivious to what's going on between Lake and me. She smiles back at me, interested in my response. I decide to raise the stakes, so I wrap my arm around Lake and pull her closer to me and kiss her on the forehead.

"You're right, *Layken.*" I say her name with the same feigned enthusiasm. I know how much it pisses her off. "I did fail to mention a few old friends from my past. I guess this means we'll just have to spend a lot more time together, getting to know every single aspect of each other's lives." I pinch her chin with my thumb and finger and smile as she narrows her eyes at me.

"Reece is back? He's living with us?" Caulder asks.

I nod. "He needed a place to crash for a month or so."

"Why isn't he staying with his mother?" my grandmother asks.

"She got remarried while he was overseas. He doesn't get along with his new stepdad, so he's looking for his own place," I say.

Lake leans forward in an attempt to inconspicuously remove my arm from her shoulder. I squeeze her tighter and pull my chair closer to hers. "Lake sure made a good first impression on Reece," I say, referring to her shirtless tantrum in my living room. "Right, sweetie?"

She presses the heel of her boot into the top of my foot and smiles back at me. "Right," she says. She scoots her chair back and stands up. "Excuse me. I need to go to the restroom." She slaps her napkin down on the table and gives me the evil eye as she walks away.

Everyone else at the table is oblivious to her anger. "You two seem to have moved past your hump from last week," my grandfather says after she's disappeared down the hallway.

"Yep. Getting along great," I say. I shove a spoonful of potatoes in my mouth.

Lake remains in the bathroom for quite a while. When she returns, she doesn't speak much. Kel, Caulder, and

Grandpaul talk video games while Lake and I finish eating in silence.

"Will, can you help me in the kitchen?" my grandmother says.

My grandmother is the last person who would ask for help in the kitchen. I'm about to either change a lightbulb or receive a lecture. I get up from the table and grab Lake's and my plates and follow her through the kitchen door.

"What's that all about?" she says as I scrape food off the plates and into the disposal.

"What's what all about?" I reply.

She wipes her hands on the dish towel and leans against the counter. "She's not very happy with you, Will. I may be old, but I know a woman's scorn when I see it. Do you want to talk about it?"

She's more observant than I give her credit for. "I guess it can't hurt at this point," I say, leaning against the kitchen counter next to her. "She's pissed at me. The whole thing with Vaughn last week left her doubting me. Now she thinks I'm with her just because I feel sorry for her and Kel."

"Why *are* you with her?" my grandmother asks.

"Because I'm in love with her," I say.

"I suggest you show her," she says. She takes the rag and begins wiping down the counter.

"I have. I can't tell you how many times I've told her. I can't get it through her head. Now she wants me to leave her alone so she can think. I'm getting so frustrated; I don't know what else I can do."

My grandmother rolls her eyes at my perceived ignorance. "A man can *tell* a woman he's in love with her until he's blue in the face. Words don't mean anything to her when her head is full of doubt. You have to *show* her."

"How? I disabled her car so she'd have to ride here with me today. Short of stalking her, I don't know what else I can do to show her."

My pathetic confession prompts a disapproving look. "That's a good way to get yourself put in jail, not win back the heart of the girl you're in love with," she says.

"I know. It was stupid. I was desperate. I'm out of ideas."

She walks to the refrigerator and pulls out a pie. She sets it on the counter next to me and starts cutting slices. "I think the first step is for you to take some time to question just why you're in love with her, then figure out a way to relay that to her. In the meantime, you need to give her the space she needs. I'm surprised your little spectacle at dinner didn't get you punched."

"The night is still young."

My grandmother laughs and places a slice of pie on a plate, then turns around and hands it to me. "I like her, Will. You better not screw this up. She's good for Caulder."

My grandmother's comment surprises me. "Really? I didn't think you liked her very much."

She continues slicing the pie. "I know you think that, but I do like her. What I don't like is the way you're always all over her when you're around her. Some things are better left in private. And I'm referring to the bedroom, not the laundry room." She frowns at me.

I didn't realize how publicly I displayed my affection for Lake. Now that my grandmother and Lake have both brought it up, it's kind of embarrassing. I guess the laundry room incident from earlier didn't help to dispel what Lake believes my grandmother thinks of her.

"Grandma?" I ask. She never gave me a fork, so I tear off a piece of pie crust and pop it in my mouth.

"Hum?" She reaches into the drawer, pulls out a fork, and drops it on my plate.

"She's still a virgin, you know."

My grandmother's eyes grow wide, and she turns back to cut another slice. "Will, that's none of my business."

"I know," I say. "I just want you to know that. I don't want you thinking the opposite of her."

She hands me two more plates of dessert, then grabs two of her own and nods at the kitchen door. "You have a good heart, Will. She'll come around. You just need to give her time."

LAKE SITS IN the backseat with Kel on the way home, and Caulder rides in front with me. The three of them talk the entire way. Kel and Caulder are droning on to Lake about everything they did with Grandpaul. I don't say a word. I tune them out and drive in silence.

After I pull into my driveway and we all get out of the car, I follow Lake and Kel across the street. She heads inside without saying a word. I pop the hood on her Jeep and reconnect the battery, then head back to my house.

It's not even ten o'clock at night. I'm not tired at all.

Caulder's in bed, and Reece is more than likely out with Vaughn. I'm sitting down on the couch to turn the TV on when someone knocks at the door.

Who would be coming over this late? Who would knock? I open the door, and my stomach flips when I see Lake shivering on the patio. She doesn't look angry, which is a good sign. She's pulling her jacket tightly around her neck and wearing her snow boots over her pajama bottoms. She looks ridiculous . . . and beautiful.

"Hey," I say a little too eagerly. "Here for another star?" I step aside and she walks in. "Why'd you knock?" I ask, shutting the door behind her. I hate that she knocked. She never knocks. That small gesture reveals some sort of change in our entire relationship that I can't pinpoint, but I know I don't like it.

She just shrugs. "Can I talk to you?"

"I wish you *would* talk to me," I say. We head to the couch. Normally, she would curl up next to me and sit on her feet. This time she makes sure there's plenty of space between us as she drops down on the opposite end of the couch. If I've learned anything at all this week, it's the fact that I hate space. Space sucks.

She looks at me and musters a smile, but it doesn't

come off right. It looks more like she's trying not to pity me.

"Promise me you'll hear me out without arguing first," she says. "I'd like to have a mature conversation with you."

"Lake, you can't sit there and say I don't hear you out. It's impossible to hear you out when you're carving pumpkins all the damn time!"

"See? Right there. Don't do that," she says.

I grab the throw pillow next to me and cover my face with it to muffle a groan. She's impossible. I bring the pillow back down and rest my elbow on it as I prepare for her lecture. "I'm listening," I say.

"I don't think you understand where I'm coming from at all. You have no clue why I'm having doubts, do you?"

She's right. "Enlighten me," I say.

She takes her jacket off and throws it over the back of the couch and gets comfortable. I was wrong, she's not here to lecture; I can tell by the way she's speaking. She's here to have a serious conversation, so I decide to respectfully hear her out.

"I know you love me, Will. I was wrong to say that earlier. I know you do. And I love you, too."

It's obvious this confession is merely a preface to something else. Something I *don't* want to hear.

"But after I heard the things Vaughn said to you, it made me look at our relationship in a different way." She sits Indian-style, facing me. "Think about it. I started thinking back on that night at the slam last year, when I finally told you how I felt. What if I wouldn't have shown up that night? What if I hadn't come to you and told you how much I loved you? You never would have read me your slam. You would have taken the job at the junior high, and we probably wouldn't even be together. So you can see where my doubt comes into play, right? It seems like you wanted to sit back and let the chips fall where they may. You didn't fight for me. You were just going to let me go. You *did* let me go."

I did let her go, but not for the reasons she's telling herself. She knows that. Why does she doubt it now? I do my best to be patient when I respond, but my emotions are all jumbled up. I'm frustrated, I'm pissed, I'm happy she's here. It's exhausting. I hate fighting.

"You *know* why I had to let you go, Lake. There were bigger things going on last year than just us. Your mother needed you. She didn't know how much time she had. The way we felt about each other would have interfered with your time left with her, and you would have hated yourself for it later. That's the only reason why I gave up, and you *know* that."

She shakes her head in disagreement. "It's more than that, Will. We've both experienced more grief in the past couple of years than most people experience in a lifetime. Think about the effect that had on us. When we finally found each other, our grief was how we related. Then when we found out we couldn't be together, that made it even worse. Especially since Kel and Caulder were best friends by then. We had to interact constantly, which made it harder to shut off our feelings. Top it all off, my mom ended up having cancer, and I was about to become a guardian, just like you. That was how we related. There were all these external influences at play. Almost like life was forcing us together."

I let her continue without interrupting, as she requested, but I want to scream out of sheer frustration. I'm not sure what point she's getting at, but it seems to me she's been thinking way too hard.

"Remove all the external factors for a second," she

says. "Imagine if things were like this: Your parents are alive. My mom is alive. Kel and Caulder aren't best friends. We aren't both guardians with huge responsibilities. We have no sense of obligation to help each other out. You were never my teacher, so we never had to experience those months of emotional torture. We're just a young couple with absolutely no responsibilities or life experiences tying us together. Now, tell me, if all that was our current reality, what is it about *me* that you love? Why would you want to be with me?"

"This is ridiculous," I mutter. "That's *not* our reality, Lake. Maybe some of those things are why we're in love. What's wrong with that? Why does it matter? Love is love."

She scoots closer to me on the couch and takes my hands in hers, looking me straight in the eyes. "It matters, Will. It matters because five or ten years from now, those external factors aren't going to be at play in our relationship. It'll just be you and me. My biggest fear is that you'll wake up one day and realize all the reasons you're in love with me are gone. Kel and Caulder won't be here to depend on us. Our parents will be a memory. We'll both have careers that could support us individually. If these are the reasons you love me, there won't be anything left to hold you to me other than your conscience. And knowing you, you would live with it internally because you're too good a person to break my heart. I don't want to be the reason you end up with regrets."

She stands up and puts her jacket back on. I start to protest, but as soon as I open my mouth, she interrupts me. "Don't," she says with a serious expression. "I want you to think before you object. I don't care if it takes you days or weeks or months. I don't want to hear from you again until you can be completely real with me and leave my feelings for you out of your decision. You owe it to me, Will. You owe it to me to make sure we aren't about to live a life together that someday you'll regret."

She walks out the door and calmly closes it behind her.

Months? Did she just say she didn't care if it takes *months*?

She did. She said months.

My God, everything she said makes sense. She's completely wrong, but it makes sense. I get it. I can see why she's questioning everything. I can see why she doubts me now.

Half an hour goes by before I so much as move a muscle. I'm completely lost in thought. When I finally break free from the trance, I come to one conclusion. My grandmother is right. Lake needs me to show her why I love her.

I decide to grab inspiration out of the jar. I unfold the star and read it.

Life's hard. It's even harder when you're stupid.

—JOHN WAYNE

I sigh. I miss Julia's sense of humor.

10.

TUESDAY, JANUARY 24

The heart of a man
is no heart at all
If his heart isn't loved by a woman.
The heart of a woman
is no heart at all
If her heart isn't loving a man.
But the heart of a man and a woman in love
Can be worse than not having a heart
Because at least if you have no heart at all
It can't die when it breaks apart.

IT'S TUESDAY, AND SO FAR I'VE SPENT THE MAJORITY of the day studying. I've spent only a portion of it being paranoid. Paranoid that someone's going to see me sneaking into Lake's house. Once I'm inside, I search around for everything I need and quickly head back out before everyone gets home from school. I throw my satchel over my shoulder and bend down to hide Lake's key under the pot.

"What are you doing?"

I jump back and nearly trip over the concrete patio rise. I control my balance on the support beam and look up. Sherry is standing in Lake's driveway with her hands on her hips.

"I . . . I was just . . ."

"I'm kidding." Sherry laughs, walking toward me.

I shoot her a dirty look for almost giving me a heart attack and turn back to push the pot into its original position. "I needed some things out of her house," I say without going into detail. "What's up?"

"Not much," she says. She has a shovel in her hands, and I glance behind her to see part of Lake's sidewalk cleared. "I'm just wasting time . . . waiting on my husband to get home. We've got errands to run."

I cock my head at her. "You have a husband?" I don't mean to sound surprised, but I am. I've never seen him.

She laughs at my response. "No, Will. My children are the result of immaculate conception."

I laugh. Her sense of humor reminds me of my mother's. *And* Julia's. *And* Lake's. How was I so lucky to be surrounded by such amazing women?

"Sorry," I say. "It's just that I've never seen him before."

"He works a lot. Mostly out of state . . . business trips and the like. He's home for two weeks. I'd really like you to meet him."

I don't like that we're standing in front of Lake's house. She'll be home soon. I start walking away from the house as I respond. "Well, if Kel and Kiersten get married someday, we'll technically be in-laws, so I guess I should meet him."

"That's assuming you and Kel have a different type of relationship by then," she says. "Are you planning on popping the question?" She begins walking with me toward her house. I think she can sense I want to be off of Lake's property before they return home.

"I'd planned on it," I say. "I'm just not so sure now what Lake's answer would be."

Sherry tilts her head, then sighs. She's looking at me with pity again. "Come inside for a sec. I want to show you something."

I follow her into her house. "Sit down on the couch," she says. "Do you have a few minutes?"

"I've got more than a few."

She returns a moment later with a DVD. After she inserts it in the DVD player, she sits down on the couch beside me and turns the television on with the remote.

"What is it?" I ask.

"A close-up of me giving birth to Kiersten."

I jump up in protest, and she rolls her eyes and laughs. "Sit down, Will. I'm kidding."

I reluctantly sit back down. "That's not funny."

She presses play on the remote, and the screen shows a shot of a much younger Sherry. She looks about nineteen or twenty. She's sitting on a porch swing laughing, hiding her face with her hands. The person holding the camera is laughing, too. I assume it's her now-husband. When he walks up the porch steps, he angles the camera around and sits beside her, focusing the lens on both of them. Sherry uncovers her face and leans her head against his and smiles.

"Why are you filming us, Jim?" Sherry says to the camera.

"Because. I want you to remember this moment forever," he says.

The camera shuffles again and comes to a rest on what is probably a table. It's positioned on both of them as he kneels in front of her. It's obvious he's about to propose, but you can see Sherry attempting to suppress her excitement, in case that's not his intention. When he pulls a small box out of his pocket, she gasps and starts to cry. He brings a hand up to her face and wipes away her tears, then briefly leans forward and kisses her.

When he settles back onto his knees, he wipes a tear away from his own eyes. "Sherry, until I met you, I didn't know what life was. I had no clue that I wasn't even alive. It's like you came along and woke up my soul." He's looking straight at her as he talks. He doesn't sound nervous at all, as if he's determined to prove to her how serious he is. He takes a deep breath and then continues. "I'll never be able to give you everything you deserve, but I'll definitely spend the rest of my life trying." He pulls the ring out of the box and slides it on her finger. "I'm not asking you to marry me, Sherry. I'm *telling* you to marry me, because I can't live without you."

Sherry wraps her arms around his neck, and they hold on to each other and cry. "Okay," she says. When they begin to kiss, he reaches over and turns off the camera.

The television screen goes black.

Sherry presses the power button on the remote, and she's silent for a moment. I can tell the video brought back a lot of emotions for her. "What you saw in that video?" she says. "The connection Jim and I had? That's true love, Will. I've seen you and Layken together, and she loves you like that. She really does."

The front door to Sherry's house opens wide and a man enters, shaking the snow out of his hair. Sherry looks nervous as she hops up and hits eject on the DVD player and puts it back inside the case.

"Hey, sweetie," she says to him. She motions for me to stand up, so I do. "This is Will," she says. "He's Caulder's older brother from across the street."

The man walks across the living room, and I reach my hand out to him. As soon as we're eye to eye, Sherry's agitation is explained. This isn't Jim. This is a completely different man than whoever it was I just saw propose to Sherry on that DVD.

"I'm David. Nice to meet you. Heard a lot about you."

"Likewise," I say. I'm lying.

"I've been giving Will relationship advice," Sherry says.

"Oh yeah?" he says. He smiles at me. "Hopefully you take it with a grain of salt, Will. Sherry thinks she's a real guru." He leans in and kisses her on the cheek.

"Well, she is pretty smart," I say.

"That she is," he says as he takes a seat on the couch. "But take it from me . . . never accept any of her medicinal concoctions. You'll regret it."

Too late for that.

"I better get going," I say. "Nice meeting you, David."

"I'll walk you out," Sherry says.

Her smile fades after she shuts the door behind her. "Will, you need to know that I love my husband. But there are very few people in this world lucky enough to experience love on the same level that I've had in the past . . . on the same level that you and Layken have. I'm not getting into the details of why mine didn't work out, but take it from someone who's had it before . . . you don't want to let it slip away. Fight for her."

She steps back inside her house and shuts the door.

"That's what I'm trying to do," I whisper.

"CAN WE HAVE pizza tonight?" Caulder says as soon as he walks through the front door. "It's Tuesday. Gavin can get us the Tuesday special that comes with the dessert pizza."

"Whatever. I don't feel like cooking, anyway." I text Gavin and offer to buy pizza if he'll bring it over when he gets off work.

By the time eight o'clock comes around, I've got a houseful. Kiersten and Kel showed up at some point. Gavin and Eddie walk in with the pizza, and we all sit down at the table to eat. The only one missing is Lake.

"Should you invite Lake?" I ask Eddie as I toss a pile of paper plates onto the table.

Eddie looks at me and shakes her head. "I just texted her. She said she's not hungry."

I sit down and grab one of the paper plates and toss a

slice on it. I take a bite and drop the pizza back on the plate. I'm suddenly not hungry, either.

"Thanks for bringing a cheese pizza, Gavin," Kiersten says. "At least someone around here respects the fact that I don't eat meat."

I don't have anything to throw at her, or I would. I shoot her a dirty look instead.

"What's the plan of attack for Thursday?" Kiersten asks me.

I glance at Eddie, who's looking right at me. "What's Thursday?" she says.

"Nothing," I reply. I don't want Eddie ruining this. I'm afraid she'll go warn Lake.

"Will, if you think I'll tell her whatever it is you're planning to do, you're wrong. No one wants you two to work things out more than I do, believe me." She takes a bite of her pizza. She seems genuinely serious, although I'm not sure why.

"He's doing a slam for her," Kiersten blurts out.

Eddie looks back up at me. "Seriously? How? You aren't gonna be able to talk her into going."

"He didn't have to," Kiersten says. "I talked her into going."

Eddie grins at her. "You're a sly little thing. And just how are you planning to keep her there?" She looks back at me. "As soon as she sees you on that stage, she'll get pissed and leave."

"Not if I steal her purse and keys," Kel says.

"Good idea, Kel!" I say. As soon as I say it, the reality of the moment hits me. I'm sitting here praising eleven-year-olds for stealing and lying to my girlfriend. What kind of role model am I?

"And we can sit in the same booth we sat in last time," Caulder says. "We'll make sure Lake gets in first; that way we can trap her in. Once you start doing your slam, she won't be able to get up. She'll have to watch you."

"Great idea," I say. I may not be a role model, but at least I'm raising smart children.

"I want to go," Eddie says. She turns to Gavin. "Can we go? Aren't you off Thursday? I want to watch Will and Layken make up."

"Yeah, we can go. But how are we all getting there if she doesn't know you're going, Will? We can't all fit in Layken's car, and I don't need to be driving all the way to Detroit in mine after all the deliveries I've been making."

"You can ride with me," I say. "Eddie can tell Lake you're working or something. Everyone else can ride with Lake."

We all seem to agree on the plans. The fact that everyone seems determined to help me win her back gives me a sense of hope. If everyone in this room can see how much we need to be together, surely Lake will see it, too.

I throw three slices of pizza on another plate, then take it to the kitchen. I glance over my shoulder to make sure no one is paying attention. I reach into the cabinet and pull out a star and set it under one of the slices of pizza before wrapping the plate.

"Eddie, will you take this to Lake? Make sure she eats something?"

Eddie grabs the plate, smiles at me, and goes.

"Kids, clean the table. Put the pizza in the fridge," I say.

Gavin and I go into the living room. He lies on the couch, pinches his forehead, and closes his eyes.

"Headache?" I say.

He shakes his head. "Stress."

"You guys decide on anything?"

He's quiet. He inhales a slow, deep breath, then exhales even slower. "I told her I was nervous about going through with it. Told her I think we need to weigh our options. She got really upset," he says. He sits up and puts his elbows on his knees. "She accused me of thinking she would make a bad mom. That's not what I think at all, Will. I think she would make a great mom. I just think she would make an even better mom if we wait until we're ready. Now she's pissed at me. We haven't talked about it since. We're both pretending like it's not happening. It's weird."

"So you're both carving pumpkins?" I say.

Gavin looks at me. "I still don't get that analogy."

I guess he wouldn't. I wish I had better advice for him.

Kiersten comes into the living room and sits down next to Gavin. "Know what I think?" she says.

Gavin looks at her, agitated. "You don't even know what we're talking about, Kiersten. Go play with your toys."

She glares at him. "I'm going to let that insult slide because I know you're in a bad mood. But for future reference, I don't *play*." She stares at him to make sure he doesn't have a response, then continues talking.

"Anyway, I think you should quit feeling sorry for yourself. You're acting like a little bitch. You aren't even the one pregnant, Gavin. How do you think Eddie feels? I'm sorry, but as much as the guy likes to think he's got an equal part in these situations, he's wrong. You screwed up when you knocked her up. Now you need to shut your mouth and be there for her. For whatever she decides to do." She stands up and walks to the front door. "And Gavin? Sometimes things happen in life that you didn't plan for. All you can do now is suck it up and start mapping out a new plan."

She shuts the door behind her, leaving Gavin and me speechless.

"Did you tell her Eddie was pregnant?" I finally ask.

He shakes his head. "No." He continues to stare at the door, in deep thought. Then, "Dammit!" he yells. "I'm such an idiot! I'm a selfish idiot!" He jumps up from the couch and puts on his jacket. "I'll call you Thursday, Will. I've got to go figure out how to make this right."

"Good luck," I say. As soon as Gavin opens the front door, Reece walks in.

"Hi-Reece-bye-Reece," Gavin says.

Reece turns and watches Gavin run across the street. "You've got strange friends," he says.

I don't argue. "There's pizza in the fridge if you want some."

"Nah. I'm just here to grab some clothes. I already ate," he says as he heads down the hallway.

It's Tuesday. I'm pretty sure he and Vaughn went out for the first time yesterday. Not that it bothers me in the least, but things seem to be progressing a little fast. Reece comes back through the living room toward the front door. "You work things out with Layken yet?" He's shoving an extra pair of pants into his bag.

"Almost," I say, eyeing his overnight bag. "You and Vaughn seem to be hitting it off pretty well."

He grins and walks backward out the door. "Like I said, I've got skills."

I sit there on the couch and ponder my situation. I've got an old best friend who's dating the girl I spent two years of my life with. My new best friend is freaking out about becoming a dad. My girlfriend isn't speaking to me. I've got class in the morning with the very reason my girlfriend isn't speaking to me. My eleven-year-old neighbor gives better advice than I do. I'm feeling a tad bit defeated right now. I lie down on the couch and try to think of something going *right* in my life. Anything.

Kel and Caulder come in and sit on the other couch. "You with wrong what's?" Kel says backward.

"Wrong *not* what's?" I sigh.

"I'm too tired to talk backward," Caulder says. "I'm just gonna talk frontward. Will . . . can you come to school next Thursday and sit with me at lunch? It's supposed to be Dad Day, but Dad's dead, so that leaves you."

I close my eyes. I hate that he's so casual about not having a dad. Or maybe I'm glad he's so casual about it. Either way, I hate it for him. "Sure. Just let me know what time I need to be there."

"Eleven," he says as he stands up. "I'm going to bed now. See ya later, Kel."

Caulder goes toward his bedroom. Kel looks just as defeated as I feel as he heads toward the front door. When the door closes behind him, I slap myself in the forehead. You're such an idiot, Will!

I jump off the couch and follow Kel outside. "Kel!" I yell when I open the front door. He walks back toward me. We meet in my front yard.

"What about you?" I say. "Can I have lunch with you, too?"

Kel tries to suppress a smile, just like his sister. He shrugs. "If you want to," he says.

I ruffle his hair. "I'd be honored."

"Thanks, Will." He turns and walks back to his house. As I watch him close the front door behind him, it occurs to me that if things don't work out between Lake and me, it's not just *her* I'm afraid of losing.

I'M NOT SURE how today is going to go. When I get to my first class, all I can do is wait. I'm hoping she doesn't sit by me. Surely she knows that much. Most of the students arrive, and the professor walks in and hands out the tests. It's ten minutes after the start of class, and Vaughn still hasn't shown up. I've let out a sigh of relief and begun to focus on the test when she bursts through the door. She never has been much for subtlety. After she grabs her test, she comes straight up the stairs and sits right next to me. Of course she does.

"Hey," she whispers. She's smiling. She looks happy. I'm hoping it has everything to do with Reece and nothing to do with me. She rolls her eyes. "Don't worry. This is the last day I'm sitting by you," she says. I guess she could see the disappointment written across my face when she walked up. "I just wanted to say I was sorry about last week. I also wanted to say thanks for being so cool about Reece and me dating again." She picks her bag up from the table and starts sifting through it for a pen.

"Again?" I whisper.

"Yeah. I mean, I thought you'd be pissed that we started dating right after you and I broke up. Before he left for the military? Actually, it kind of upset me that it didn't piss you off," she says with a strange look in her eyes. "Anyway, we decided to give it another shot. But that's all I wanted to say." She turns her attention to the test in front of her.

Again? I want to ask her to repeat everything she just said, but that would mean I was inviting conversation, so I don't. But *again*? And I could swear she just said they dated before he left for the military. Reece left for the military two months after my parents died. If he and Vaughn dated before that . . . that means one thing . . . he was dating her right after she broke my heart. He was *dating* her? The entire time I was venting to him about her, he was *dating* her? What a *jackass*. Hopefully, he and Vaughn have gotten to know each other pretty well the whole three days they've been "back" together—because he's about to need a new place to live.

I EXPECT TO confront Reece about it when I get home, but he isn't here. The entire night is relatively quiet. Kel and Caulder are spending most of the evening at Lake's house. Kiersten is, too, I guess. It's just me and my thoughts. I use the rest of the evening to perfect what I want to say tomorrow night.

IT'S THURSDAY MORNING, the day Lake will forgive me. I hope. Caulder and Kel have already left with Lake. I hear Reece in the kitchen making coffee and decide that now would be a good time to have a talk with him. To thank him for being such a great friend all these years. Jackass.

When I walk into the kitchen, ready to confront him, it's not Reece making coffee. It's not Lake, either.

Vaughn is standing in my kitchen with her back turned to me. In her *bra.* Making coffee in *my* kitchen. Using *my* coffeepot. In *my* house. In her *bra.*

Why the hell is this my life?

"What the hell are you doing here, Vaughn?"

She jumps and turns around. "I . . . I didn't know you were here," she stutters. "Reece said you weren't here last night."

"Ugh!" I yell, frustrated. I turn my back to her and rub my face, trying to sort out how the hell to fix this "roommate" situation. Just as I'm about to kick Vaughn out, Reece walks into the kitchen. "What the hell, Reece? I told you not to bring her here!"

"Chill out, Will. What's it matter? You were asleep. You didn't even know she was here."

He casually walks to the cabinet and grabs a coffee cup. He's wearing boxer shorts. She's in her bra. I can't imagine what Lake would think if she walked in and saw Vaughn in my kitchen in her bra. I'm *this close* to getting Lake to forgive me. This would derail my entire plan.

"Get out! Both of you, get out!" I yell.

Neither of them moves. Vaughn looks at Reece, waiting for him to say something or do something. Reece looks at me and rolls his eyes. "Let me give you a piece of advice, Will. Any girl who can make you as miserable as you've been this week isn't worth it. You're being an ass. You need to drop that chick. Move on."

This little piece of advice, coming from a man who could care less about anyone but himself, pushes me over the edge. I don't know what comes over me. I don't know if it's the comment about Lake not being worth it, or the fact that I'm now aware he lied to me for months. Either way, I lunge forward and punch the shit out of him. As soon as my fist meets his face, it's agony. Vaughn is screaming at me as I back away from him, holding my fist with my other hand.

Jesus! In the movies, it always looks like the one being hit is the only one hurt. They never show the damage it does to the hand *doing* the hitting.

"What the hell?" Reece yells, holding his jaw. I expect him to try to punch me back, but he doesn't. Maybe deep down, he knows he deserves it.

"Don't tell me she isn't worth it," I say, turning toward the refrigerator. I reach in and grab two ice packs. I throw one to Reece and put the other one on my fist. "And thanks, Reece. . . . for being such a *great* friend.

After my parents died and she broke up with me . . ." I point to Vaughn. "You were the only one willing to stick around and help me through it. Too bad I didn't know you were helping *her* out, too."

Reece looks at Vaughn. "You told him?" he says.

Vaughn looks confused. "I thought he knew," she says defensively.

Reece becomes flustered. "Will, I'm sorry. I didn't mean for it to happen. It just did."

I shake my head. "Things like that don't just happen, Reece. We've been best friends since we were *ten*! My whole damn world collapsed around me. For an entire month, you acted like you were trying to help me get her back, but instead, you were *screwing* her!" Neither of them can look me in the eyes. "I know I said I'd let you stay here, but things are different now." I throw the ice pack on the counter and walk toward the hallway. "I want you both gone. Now."

I shut my bedroom door and collapse onto the bed. I can probably count the friends I have left on one hand. Actually, I can count them on one finger. I lie there for a while longer, wondering how I could have been so blind to his selfishness. I hear Reece go into the spare bedroom, then the bathroom, packing up his things. When I hear his car pull away, I go out to the kitchen and pour myself a cup of coffee. I guess I'll have to start making my own again.

This isn't a very good start to the day. I reach into the cabinet and grab a star out of the vase and unfold it.

I want to have friends that I can trust, who love me for the man I've become . . . not the man that I was.

—THE AVETT BROTHERS

As soon as I read it, I look over my shoulder, half expecting Julia to be there, smiling. It's eerie sometimes how fitting these quotes have been to the situation. Almost like she's writing them as life is happening.

11.

THURSDAY, JANUARY 26

I can only hope that the next entry I write in this journal, after my performance tonight, will read something like this:

Now that I have you back, I'm never letting you go. That's a promise. I'm not letting you go again.

GAVIN WALKS THROUGH THE FRONT DOOR RIGHT around seven o'clock. It's the first time he's walked in without knocking. It must be contagious.

He can tell I'm a nervous wreck as soon as he sees me. "They just left. We should let them get a head start," he says.

"Good idea," I say. I make another walk-through of the house, trying to find something to add to my satchel. I'm pretty sure I have it all. We give Lake and Eddie a good fifteen-minute head start before we leave. I warn Gavin that I'm not going to be much for conversation on the ride there. Luckily, he understands. He always understands. That's what best friends do, I guess.

During the drive, I recite everything I need to say over and over in my head. I've got the poem down. I already talked to the guys at Club N9NE, so everything is in place there. Unfortunately, I get only one shot with her. I've got to make it count.

When we arrive, Gavin goes inside first. He texts me a minute later to ensure that the plan is in place. I walk inside with my satchel across my shoulder and wait for my cue from the entryway. I don't want her to see me. If she sees me before it's time, she'll get angry and leave.

The seconds turn into minutes, and the minutes turn into eternity. I hate this. I've never been so nervous about performing. Normally, when I perform, there's nothing on the line. This performance could very well determine my path in life. I take a deep breath and focus on my nerves. Then the emcee takes the microphone. "We've got something special planned for open mike tonight. So without further ado . . ." He walks off the stage.

This is it. Now or never.

Everyone in the audience has their eyes glued to the stage, so I go unnoticed as I walk along the wall on the right of the room toward the front. Right before I walk onstage, I glance at the booth where they're all sitting. Lake is right in the middle with nowhere to go. She's looking down at her phone. She has no clue what's about to hit her. I've already prepared myself for her reaction . . . she's going to be pissed. I just need her to hear me out long enough to get through to her. She's hard-headed, but she's also reasonable.

The spotlight dims and focuses on a stool on the stage, just as I asked of the lighting tech. I don't like the bright lights hindering my view of the audience, so I made sure they would all be turned off. I want to see Lake's face the entire time. I need to be able to look her in the eyes, so she'll know just how serious I am.

Before I take the stairs, I stretch my neck and arms out to ease the apprehension building up inside of me. I exhale a few times, then take the stage.

I take a seat on the stool as I place my satchel on the

floor. I remove the microphone from the stand and look straight at Lake, who looks up from her phone. As soon as she sees me, she frowns and shakes her head. She's pissed. She says something to Caulder, who's seated at the edge of the booth, and she points to the door. He shakes his head and doesn't move. I watch as she fidgets her hands around beside her, looking for her purse. She can't find it. She points to Kiersten, seated at the other end of the booth, and Kiersten shakes her head, too. Lake looks at Gavin and Eddie, then at Kiersten again, then she realizes they're all in on it. After accepting that they won't let her out of the booth, she folds her arms over her chest and returns her focus to the stage. To me.

"Are you finished trying to run away yet?" I say into the microphone. "Because I have a few things I'd like to say to you."

The audience members turn, searching for the person I'm speaking to. When Lake notices everyone staring at her, she buries her face in her hands.

I bring the audience's attention back to me. "I'm breaking the rules tonight," I say. "I know that slams can't involve props, but I've got a few I need to use. It's an *emergency*."

I bend down and pick up the satchel, then stand and place it on the stool. I put the microphone back in the stand and position it at the right height.

"Lake? I know you told me you wanted me to think about everything you said the other night. I know it's only been two days, but honestly, I didn't even need two seconds. So instead of spending the last two days thinking about something I already know the answer to, I decided to do this. It's not a traditional slam, but I have a feeling you aren't that particular. My piece tonight is called 'Because of You.' "

I exhale and smile at her before I begin.

"There are moments in every relationship that define when two people start to fall in love.

"A first ***glance***
A first ***smile***
A first ***kiss***
A first ***fall*** "

I remove the Darth Vader house shoes from my satchel and look down at them.

"You were wearing these during one
of those moments.
One of the moments I first started to
fall in love with you.
The way you made me feel that morning
had absolutely ***nothing*** to do with ***anyone*** else,
and ***everything*** to do with ***you.***
I was falling in love with you that morning
because of you."

I take the next item out of the satchel. When I pull it out and look up, she brings her hands to her mouth in shock.

"This ugly little ***gnome***
with his smug little ***grin,***
He's the reason I had an excuse to invite
you into my house.
Into my life.
You took a lot of aggression out on him
over those next few months.
I would watch from my window as you kicked
him over every time you walked by him.

Poor little guy.
You were so ***tenacious.***
That ***feisty, aggressive, strong-willed***
side of you . . .
the side of you that ***refused*** to take crap
from this concrete gnome?
The side of you that refused to take crap
from me?
I fell in love with that side of you
because of you."

I set the gnome down on the stage and grab the CD.

"This is your favorite CD.
'Layken's Shit.'
Although now I know you intended for
'shit' to be ***possessive,***
rather than ***descriptive.***
The banjo started playing through the
speakers of your car
and I immediately recognized my favorite band.
Then when I realized it was ***your***
favorite band, ***too***?

The fact that these ***same lyrics*** inspired
both of us?
I fell in love with that about you.
That had absolutely ***nothing*** to do
with ***anyone*** else.
I fell in love with that about you
because of you."

I take a slip of paper out of the satchel and hold it up. When I look over, I notice Eddie sliding Lake a napkin. I can't see from up here, but that can only mean she's crying.

"This is a receipt I kept.
Only because the item I purchased that night
was on the verge of ***ridiculous.***
Chocolate milk on the rocks? ***Who orders that?***
You were ***different,*** and you didn't ***care.***
You were being ***you.***
A piece of me fell in love with you
at that moment,
because of you."

"This?" I hold up another sheet of paper.

"*This* I didn't really like so much.
It's the poem you wrote about me.
The one you titled 'Mean'?
I don't think I ever told you . . .
but you made a ***zero.***
And then I ***kept*** it
to remind myself of all the things I ***never***
want to be to you."

I pull her shirt from my bag. When I hold it up to the light, I sigh into the microphone.

"This is that ugly shirt you wear.
It doesn't really have anything to do with
why I fell in love with you.
I just saw it at your house and thought
I'd steal it."

I pull the second-to-last item out of my bag. Her purple hair clip. She told me once how much it meant to her and why she always kept it.

"This purple hair clip?
It really ***is*** magic . . . just like your dad told
you it was.
It's magic because, no matter how many times it
lets you down, you keep having ***hope*** in it.
You keep ***trusting*** it.
No matter how many times it ***fails*** you,
You never fail ***it.***
Just like you never fail ***me.***
I love that about you,
because of you."

I set it down and pull out a strip of paper and unfold it.

"Your mother."

I sigh.

"Your mother was an amazing woman, Lake.
I'm blessed that I got to know her,
And that she was a part of my life, too.
I came to love her as my ***own*** mom . . . just as she
came to love Caulder and me as ***her*** own.

I didn't love her because of ***you,*** Lake.
I loved her because of ***her.***
So, thank you for sharing her with us.
She had more advice about
life and ***love*** and ***happiness*** and ***heartache*** than
anyone I've ever known.
But the ***best*** advice she ever gave me?
The best advice she ever gave ***us***?"

I read the quote in my hands. " 'Sometimes two people have to fall apart to realize how much they need to fall back together.' "

She's definitely crying now. I place the slip back in the satchel and take a step closer to the edge of the stage as I hold her gaze.

"The last item I have wouldn't fit, because
you're actually sitting in it.
That booth.
You're sitting in the exact same spot where you
sat when you watched your first performance
on this stage.

The way you watched this stage with passion in
your eyes . . . I'll ***never*** forget that moment.
It's the moment I knew it was too late.
I was too far gone by then.
I was in ***love*** with you.
I was in love with you because of ***you.***"

I back up and sit down on the stool, still holding her gaze.

"I could go on all night, Lake.
I could go ***on and on and on*** about all the reasons
I'm in love with you.
And you know what? Some of them ***are*** the
things that life has thrown our way.
I ***do*** love you because you're the only other
person I know who understands my situation.
I ***do*** love you because both of us know what it's
like to lose your mom ***and*** your dad.
I ***do*** love you because you're raising your little
brother, just like I am.
I love you because of what you went through with
your ***mother.***

I love you because of what *we* went through
with your mother.
I love the way you love *Kel.*
I love the way you love *Caulder.*
And I love the way *I* love Kel.
So I'm not about to apologize for loving all these
things about you, *no matter* the reasons or the
circumstances behind them.
And no, I don't need *days,* or *weeks,* or *months*
to think about *why* I love you.
It's an easy answer for me.
I love you because of *you.*
Because of
every
single
thing
about *you.*"

I take a step back from the microphone when I'm finished. I keep my eyes locked on hers, and I'm not sure because she's pretty far away, but I think she mouths "I love you." The stage lights come back up, and I'm blinded. I can't see her anymore.

I gather the items and the satchel and jump off the stage. I immediately head to the back of the room. When I get there, she's gone. Kel and Caulder are both standing up. They let her get out. They let her leave! Eddie sees the confusion on my face, so she holds up Lake's purse and shakes it. "No worries, Will. I've still got her keys. She just walked outside, said she needed air."

I head to the exit and shove the door open. She's in the parking lot, next to my car with her back to me, staring up at the sky. She's letting the snow fall on her face as she stands there. I watch her for a minute, wondering what she's thinking. My biggest fear is that I misread her reaction from the stage and that everything I said meant nothing to her. I slide my hands in my jacket pockets and walk toward her. When she hears the snow crunch beneath my feet, she turns around. The look in her eyes tells me everything I need to know. Before I take another step, she rushes to me and throws her arms around my neck, almost knocking me backward.

"I'm so sorry, Will. I'm so, so sorry." She kisses me on the cheek, the neck, the lips, the nose, the chin. She keeps saying she's sorry, over and over between each kiss. I wrap my arms around her and pick her up, giving her the biggest hug I've ever given her. When I plant her feet back on the ground, she takes my face in her hands and looks into my eyes. I don't see it anymore . . . the heartache. She's not heartbroken anymore. I feel like the weight of the world has been lifted off my shoulders and I can finally breathe again.

"I can't believe you kept that damn gnome," she whispers.

"I can't believe you threw him away," I say.

We continue to stare at each other, neither of us fully trusting that the moment is real. Or that it will last.

"Lake?" I stroke her hair, then the side of her face. "I'm sorry it took me so long to get it. It's my fault you had doubts. I promise there won't be a day that goes by that I won't show you how much you mean to me."

A tear rolls down her cheek. "Me, too," she says.

My heart pounds against my chest. Not because I'm nervous. Not even because I want her worse than I've ever wanted her. It's pounding against my chest because I realize I've never been more sure about the rest of my life than I am in this moment. This girl is the rest of my life. I lean in and kiss her. Neither of us closes our eyes; I don't think we want to miss a single second of the moment.

We're two feet from my car, so I walk her backward until she's up against it. "I love you," I somehow mutter while my lips are meshed with hers. "I love you so much," I say again. "God, I love you."

She pulls away from me and smiles. Her thumbs move to my cheeks, and she wipes at the tears that I didn't even realize were streaming down my face. "I love *you*," she says. "Now that we have that out of the way, will you just shut up and kiss me?"

And so I do.

After several minutes of making up for all the kisses we missed out on over the last week, the temperature begins to affect us. Lake's bottom lip starts shivering. "You're cold," I say. "Do you want to get in my car and make out with me, or should we go inside?" I'm hoping she chooses the car.

She smiles. "The car."

I've taken a step toward the car door when I realize I set my satchel on the booth where everyone's sitting.

"Crap," I say as I step back to Lake and wrap my arms around her. "My keys are inside." Her whole body is trembling against me from the cold.

"Then break your butterflying window and unlock the door," she says.

"A broken window would defeat the purpose of trying to keep you warm," I say. I do my best to warm her by pressing my face against her neck.

"I guess you'll have to try and keep me warm in other ways."

Her suggestion tempts me to break the damn window. Instead, I take her hand in mine and pull her toward the entrance. As soon as we walk inside but before we pass through the entryway, I turn around to kiss her one more time before we head to our booth. I was just going in for a quick peck, but she pulls me in to her, and the kiss lingers.

"Thank you," she says when she pulls away. "For what you did up there tonight. And for trapping me in the booth so I couldn't leave. You know me too well."

"Thank you for listening."

We head back to the booth hand in hand. When Kiersten sees us walking in together, she starts clapping.

"It worked!" she squeals. They all scoot toward the center so Lake and I can slide in. "Will, that means you owe me more poems," Kiersten says.

Lake looks at me and then at Kiersten. "Wait. You mean you two were conspiring this whole time?" she says. "Kiersten, did he put you up to begging me to bring you here tonight?"

Kiersten shoots me a look, and we both laugh.

"And last weekend!" Lake says. "Did you knock on my door just so he could get in my house?"

Kiersten doesn't answer as she looks back at me. "You owe me an early return fee," she says. "I think twenty bucks should do it." She holds out her palm.

"We didn't agree to monetary compensation, if I remember correctly," I say, pulling twenty dollars from my wallet. "But I would have paid triple that."

She takes the money and puts it in her pocket with a satisfied expression. "I would have done it for free."

"I feel used," Lake says.

I put my arm around Lake and kiss her on top of the head. "Yeah, sorry about that. You're really hard to manipulate. I had to rally the forces."

She looks up at me, and I take the opportunity to give

her a quick kiss on the mouth. I can't help it. Every time her lips come within a certain proximity to mine, it's impossible not to kiss them.

"I liked it better when you two weren't speaking," Caulder says.

"Same here," Kel says. "I forgot how gross it was."

"I think I'm gonna be sick," Eddie says.

I laugh because I think Eddie's making a joke about our public display of affection. She's not. She covers her mouth with her hand, and her eyes get big. Lake shoves against me, and I hop out of the booth, followed by Lake and Kiersten. Eddie scoots out of the booth with her hand still over her mouth and makes a mad dash for the bathroom. Lake runs after her.

"What's wrong with her?" Kiersten asks. "Is she having nausea?"

"Yep," Gavin says flatly. "Constantly."

"Well, you don't look very worried about her," Kiersten says.

Gavin rolls his eyes and doesn't respond. We're sitting quietly through another performance when I notice Gavin watching the hallway with concern. "Will, hop up. I need to go check on her," he says. Kiersten and I get back out of the booth, and Gavin exits. I grab Lake's purse and my satchel, and we all follow.

"Kiersten, go inside and see if she needs me," Gavin says.

Kiersten opens the door to the women's restroom. A minute later, she returns. "She said she'll be fine. Layken said for all you boys to go on and head home and us three will follow you in a few minutes. Layken needs her purse, though."

I hand Kiersten the purse. I'm a little bummed that Lake isn't riding with me, but I guess she did bring her own car. I'm anxious to get back to Ypsilanti. Back to our houses. I'm definitely sneaking into her room tonight.

We head outside to my car. I crank it and wipe the snow from the windows, then walk over to Lake's car and wipe the snow off her windows as well. When I get back to my car, the three of them are coming outside.

"You okay?" I ask Eddie. She just nods.

I walk over to Lake and give her a quick peck on the cheek as she unlocks her door. "I'll follow you guys in case she gets sick again and you have to pull over."

"Thanks, babe," she says, unlocking the doors for

everyone else. She turns around and gives me a hug before climbing into her car.

"The boys are staying at my house tonight," I whisper in her ear. "After they fall asleep, I'm coming over. Wear your ugly shirt, okay?"

She smiles. "I can't. You stole it, remember?"

"Oh yeah," I whisper. "In that case . . . I guess you just shouldn't wear one at all." I wink at her and walk back to my car.

"She okay?" Gavin asks when I get in the car.

"I guess so," I say. "You want to go ride with them?"

Gavin shakes his head and sighs. "She doesn't want me to. She's still mad at me."

I feel bad. I hate that Lake and I just made up right in front of them. "She'll come around," I say as I pull out of the parking lot.

"Why do you two even bother with girls?" Kel asks. "Both of you have been miserable for days. It's pathetic."

"Someday you'll see, Kel," Gavin says. "You'll see."

He's right. Making up with Lake later tonight will make this entire week of hell worth every second. Deep down I know it'll happen tonight. We're both way beyond the point of retreat. I suddenly become nervous at the thought.

"Kel, you want to stay at my house tonight?" I try to act casual with my plan to corral the boys at my place. I feel like Kel can see right through me, even though I know he can't.

"Sure," he says. "But it's a school night, and Lake takes us to school on Fridays. Why doesn't Caulder just stay with me?"

I didn't think about that. I guess Lake could sneak over to my house after they fall asleep at her house. "Whichever," I say. "Doesn't really matter where."

Gavin laughs. "I see what you're up to," he whispers.

I just smile.

WE'RE ABOUT HALFWAY home when the snow begins to fall pretty heavily. Luckily, Lake is a pretty cautious driver. I'm following behind her even though I would normally drive about ten miles an hour faster. It's a good thing Eddie isn't driving; we'd all be in trouble.

"Gavin, you awake?" He's staring out the window and

hasn't said much since we left Detroit. I can't tell whether he's lost in thought or passed out.

He grumbles a response, informing me that he's still awake.

"Have you and Eddie talked since you left my house the other night?"

He stretches in his seat and yawns, then puts his hands behind his head and leans back. "Not yet. I worked a double shift yesterday. We were both in school all day today and didn't even see each other until tonight. I pulled her aside and told her I wanted to talk to her later. I have a feeling she thinks it's bad. She hasn't said much to me since then."

"Well, she'll be—"

"Will!" Gavin yells. My first instinct is to slam on the brakes, but I'm not sure why I'm slamming on the brakes. I glance at Gavin, and his eyes are glued to the oncoming traffic in the lanes to the left of us. I turn my head and see it just as the truck crosses the median and hits the car in front of us.

Lake's car.

part two

12.

THURSDAY, JANUARY 26

I OPEN MY EYES BUT DON'T HEAR ANYTHING RIGHT away. It's cold, though. I feel wind. And glass. Glass is on my shirt. Then I hear Caulder.

"Will!" he's screaming.

I turn around. Caulder and Kel both look fine, but they're panicking and trying to get out of their seat belts. Kel looks terrified. He's crying and yanking on the car door.

"Kel, don't get out of the car. Stay in the backseat." My hand goes up to my eye. I pull my fingers back, and there's blood on them.

I'm not sure what just happened. We must have been

hit. Or we ran off the road. The back window is busted out, and there's glass all over the car. The boys don't look cut anywhere. Gavin is swinging his door open. He tries to jump out of the car, but he's stuck in his seat belt. He's frantic, trying to unlatch it. I reach over and push the button, releasing him. He trips as he lunges out of the car but catches himself with his hands and pushes himself back up and runs. What is he running from? My gaze follows as he runs around the car next to us. He's gone. I can't see him. I lean my head back into the headrest and close my eyes. *What the hell just happened?*

And then it hits me. "Lake!" I yell. I swing open the car door and get hung up in the seat belt just like Gavin did. After I free myself, I run. I don't know where I'm running. It's dark, it's snowing, and there are cars everywhere. Headlights everywhere.

"Sir, are you okay? You need to sit down, you're hurt." A man grabs my arm and tries to pull me aside, but I yank my arm away from him and keep running. There are pieces of glass and metal all over the highway. My eyes dart from one side of the road to the other, but I can't make anything out. I glance back to my car and to the space in front of us where Lake's car should be. My eyes follow the broken glass to the median on the right of the highway. I see it. Her car.

Gavin is on the passenger side. He's pulling Eddie out of the car, so I run around to help him. Her eyes are closed, but she winces when I pull on her arm. She's okay. I glance inside the car, but Lake's not there. Her door is wide open. A sense of relief washes over me when I realize she must be okay if she's able to walk away. My eyes dart to the backseat, and I see Kiersten. As soon as Eddie is safely on the ground, I climb into the backseat and shake Kiersten.

"Kiersten," I say. She doesn't respond. There's blood on her, but I'm not sure where it's coming from. "Kiersten!" I yell. She still doesn't respond. I take her wrist and hold it between my fingers. Gavin climbs into the backseat with me and sees me checking her pulse. He looks at me with terror in his eyes.

"She's got a pulse," I say. "Help me get her out." He unbuckles her seat belt as I put my hands underneath her arms and pull her over the front seat. Gavin climbs out and grabs her legs and helps me pull her out of the car. We lay her next to Eddie. Next to a growing crowd of concerned bystanders. I glance at all of them but don't see Lake.

"Where the hell did she go?" I stand up and look around. "Stay with them," I tell Gavin. "I need to find Lake. She's probably looking for Kel." Gavin nods.

I walk around several vehicles and pass the truck that hit them. What's left of the truck, anyway. There are several people surrounding it, talking to the driver inside, telling him to wait for help before he gets out. I'm in the middle of the highway, calling Lake's name. Where did she go? I run back to my car. Kel and Caulder are still inside.

"Is she okay?" Kel asks. "Is Layken okay?" He's crying.

"Yeah, I think so. She walked away . . . I can't find her. You guys stay here, I'll be right back."

I finally hear sirens as I'm making my way back to Lake's car. When the emergency vehicles come closer, their flashing lights illuminate all the chaos, almost emphasizing it. I look at Gavin. He's hovering over Kiersten, checking her pulse again. The sirens fade as I watch everyone around me move in slow motion.

All I can hear is the sound of my own breath.

An ambulance pulls up beside me, and the lights

slowly make their way in a circle, as if their job as lights is to display the perimeter of the damage. I follow along with my eyes as one of the red lights slowly illuminates my car, then the car next to mine, then over the top of Lake's car, then on top of the truck that hit them, then across Lake lying in the snow. *Lake!* As soon as the red light circles farther, it's dark, and I don't see her anymore. I run.

I try to scream her name, but nothing comes out. Though there are people in my way, I shove past them. I keep running and running, but it feels like the distance between us keeps growing.

"Will!" I hear Gavin yell. He's and running after me.

When I finally reach her, she's lying there in the snow with her eyes closed. There's blood on her head. So much blood. I tear off my jacket and throw it in the snow and remove my shirt. I begin wiping the blood off her face with it, trying desperately to find her injuries.

"Lake! No, no, no. Lake, no." I touch her face, trying to get some sort of reaction. It's cold. She's so cold. As soon as I put my hands under her shoulders to pull her into my lap, someone pulls me back. Paramedics swarm her. I can't see her anymore. I can't see her.

"Will!" Gavin yells. He's in my face. He's shaking me. "Will! We need to get to the hospital. They'll take her there. We need to go."

He's trying to push me away from her. I can't speak, so I shake my head and push him out of my way. I start to run back to them. Back to her. He pulls me back again. "Will, don't! Let them help her."

I turn around and shove him, then run back to her. They're moving her onto a gurney when I skid to a stop in the snow next to her. "Lake!"

One of the paramedics pushes me back as the others carry her to the ambulance. "I need in there!" I yell. "Let me in there!" The paramedic won't let me by as they shut the doors and tap on the glass. The ambulance pulls away. As soon as its lights fade into the distance, I fall to my knees.

I can't breathe.

I can't breathe.

I still can't breathe.

13.

THURSDAY, JANUARY 26, 2012

WHEN I OPEN MY EYES, I IMMEDIATELY HAVE TO close them again. It's so bright. I'm shaking. My whole body is shaking. Actually, it's not my body that's shaking at all. It's whatever I'm lying on that's shaking.

"Will? Are you okay?"

I hear Caulder's voice. I open my eyes and see him sitting next to me. We're in an ambulance. He's crying. I try to sit up to hug him, but someone pushes me back down.

"Be still, sir. You've got a pretty bad gash I'm working on here."

I look at the person talking to me. It's the paramedic who was holding me back. "Is she okay?" I feel myself succumb to the panic again. "Where is she? Is she okay?"

He puts his hand on my shoulder to hold me still and places gauze over my eye. "I wish I knew something, but I don't. I'm sorry. I just know I need to get this injury of yours closed. We'll find out more when we get there."

I look around the ambulance, but I don't see Kel. "Where's Kel?"

"They put him and Gavin in the other ambulance to check on them. They said we would see them at the hospital," Caulder says.

I lay my head back, close my eyes, and pray.

AS SOON AS the ambulance doors open and they pull me out, I unfasten the straps and jump off the gurney.

"Sir, get back here! You need stitches!"

I keep running. I glance back to make sure Caulder is following me. He is, so I keep running. When I get inside, Gavin and Kel are standing at the nurses' station. "Kel!" I yell. Kel runs up to me and hugs me. I pick him up, and he wraps his arms around my neck. "Where are they?" I say to Gavin. "Where'd they take them?"

"I can't find anyone," Gavin says. He looks as panicked as I do. He sees a nurse round the corner, and he runs up to her. "We're looking for three girls who were just brought here?"

She glances at all four of us, then walks around the desk to her computer. "Are you family?"

Gavin looks at me, then back at her. "Yes," he lies.

She eyes Gavin and picks up the phone. "The family is here . . . yes, sir." She hangs up the phone. "Follow me." She leads us around the corner and into a room. "The doctor will be with you as soon as possible."

I set Kel down in a chair next to Caulder. Gavin takes off his jacket and hands it to me. I look down and realize for the first time since I took it off that I'm not wearing a shirt. Gavin and I pace the room. Several minutes pass with no word. I can't take it anymore. "I've got to find her," I say.

I start to walk out of the room, but Gavin pulls me back. "Just give it a minute, Will. If they need to find you, you won't be here. Just give it a minute."

I begin to pace again; it's all I can do. Kel is still crying, so I bend down and hug him again. He hasn't said anything. Not a single word.

She has to be okay. She *has* to.

I glance across the hall and see a restroom. I go inside, and as soon as I shut the door behind me, I get sick. I lean over the toilet and vomit. When I think I'm finished, I wash my hands in the sink and rinse my mouth. I grip the edges of the sink and take a deep breath, trying to calm down. I need to calm down for Kel. He doesn't need to see me like this.

When I look in the mirror, I don't even recognize myself. There's dried blood all over the side of my face. The bandage the paramedic placed above my eye is already saturated. I grab a napkin and try to wipe off some of the blood. As I'm wiping, I find myself wishing I had some of Sherry's medicine.

Sherry. "Sherry!" I yell. I throw open the bathroom door. "Gavin! We have to call Sherry! Where's your phone?"

Gavin pats his pockets. "I think it's in my jacket," he says. "I need to call Joel."

I reach into his jacket and pull out his phone. "Shit! I don't know her number, it's in my phone."

"Hand it to me, I'll dial," Kel says. He wipes his eyes and reaches for the phone, so I hand it to him. After he punches in the numbers and hands me the phone, I suddenly feel sick again.

Sherry picks up on the second ring. "Hello?"

I can't speak. What am I supposed to say?

"Hello?" she says again.

"Sherry," I say. My voice cracks.

"Will?" she says. "Will? What's wrong?"

"Sherry," I say again. "We're at the hospital . . . they . . ."

"Will! Is she okay? Is Kiersten okay?"

I can't respond. Gavin takes the phone from my hand, and I run back to the bathroom.

THERE'S A KNOCK on the bathroom door a few minutes later. I'm sitting on the floor against the wall with my eyes closed. I don't respond. When the door opens, I look up. It's the paramedic.

"We've still got to get you stitched up," he says. "You've got a pretty bad cut." He offers his hand. I take it and he pulls me up. I follow him down the hall and into an exam room, where he instructs me to lie back on the table. "Your friend said you've had some nausea. You more than likely have a concussion. Stay here, the nurse will be by in a minute."

AFTER I'VE BEEN stitched up and given instructions on how to care for the apparent concussion, I'm told to go to the nurses' station to fill out paperwork. When I get there, the nurse grabs a clipboard and hands it to me. "Which patient is your wife?" she asks.

I just stare at her. "My wife?" Then it dawns on me that Gavin told her we were related. I guess it's better if they think that. I'll get more information that way. "Layken Cohen . . . Cooper. Layken Cohen Cooper."

"Fill out these forms and bring them back to me. And if you don't mind, take this clipboard to the other gentleman with you. What about the little girl? Is she related to you?"

I shake my head. "She's my neighbor. Her mother's on

the way." I grab the paperwork and head back to the waiting room. "Any news?" I ask, handing Gavin his clipboard. He just shakes his head.

"We've been here almost an hour! Where is everybody?" I throw my clipboard in the chair and sit down. Just as I land, a man in a white lab coat rounds the corner toward us, followed by a frantic Sherry. I jump back up.

"Will!" she yells. She's crying. "Where is she? Where's Kiersten? Is she hurt?"

I put my arms around her, then look to the doctor for answers, since I don't have any.

"You're looking for the little girl?" the doctor asks. Sherry nods. "She'll be okay. She's got a broken arm and got hit on the head pretty hard. We're still waiting on a few test results, but you're welcome to go see her. I've just put her in room 212. If you'll head to the nurses' station, they can direct you."

"Oh, thank God," I say. Sherry lets go of me and darts around the corner.

"Which one of you is with the other young lady?" he asks.

Gavin and I look at each other. The doctor's singular

reference makes my heart stop. "There are two!" I'm frantic. "There are two of them!"

He looks puzzled as to why I'm yelling at him. "I'm sorry," he says. "I was only brought the girl and a young lady. Sometimes, depending on the injuries, they don't come to me first. I only have news on a young lady with blond hair."

"Eddie! Is she okay?" Gavin asks.

"She's stable. They're running tests, so you can't go back yet."

"What about the baby? Is the baby okay?"

"That's why they're running tests, sir. I'll be back as soon as I know more." He starts to walk away, so I cut him off in the hallway.

"Wait!" I say. "What about Lake? I haven't heard anything. Is she okay? Is she in surgery?"

He looks at me with pity. It makes me want to punch him.

"I'm sorry, sir. I only treated the other two. I'll do my best to find some answers and get back with you as soon as I can." He hurries away.

They're not telling me anything! They aren't telling me a damn thing! I lean against the wall and slide down to the floor. I pull up my knees and rest my elbows on them and bury my face in my hands.

"Will?"

I look up. Kel is looking down at me.

"Why won't they just tell us if she's okay or not?"

I grab his hand and pull him to the floor with me. I put my arm around him, and he hugs me back. I stroke his hair and kiss him on top of the head, because I know that's what Lake would do. "I don't know, Kel. I don't know." I hold him while he cries. As much as I want to scream, as much as I want to cry, as much as my world is crashing down around me, I have to hold it all in for this little boy. I can't even begin to imagine what he's feeling. How scared he must be. Lake is the only person he has in this world. I hold him and kiss his head until he cries himself to sleep.

"WILL?"

I look up and see Sherry standing over me. I start to get up, but she shakes her head and points at Kel, who has fallen asleep in my lap. She sits down on the floor next to me.

"How's Kiersten?" I ask.

"She'll be okay. She's asleep. They may not even keep her overnight." She reaches over and strokes Kel's hair. "Gavin said you guys haven't heard anything about Layken yet?"

I shake my head. "It's been well over an hour, Sherry. Why aren't they telling me anything? They won't even tell me if she's . . ." I can't finish the sentence. I take a deep breath, trying to maintain my composure.

"Will . . . if that were the case, they would have told you by now. That means they're doing everything they can."

I know she's trying to help, but her statement hits me hard. I pick Kel up and carry him back to the waiting room and lay him in the chair next to Gavin. He wakes up and looks at me. "I'll be back," I say. I run down the hallway to the nurses' station, but there isn't anyone there. The doors leading to the emergency rooms are locked. I look around for someone. There are a few people staring at me in the general waiting area, but no one offers to assist me. I walk behind the nurses' station and look around until I find the button that opens the emergency doors. I press the button, then jump over the desk and run through the doors just as they open.

"Can I help you?" a nurse asks when I pass her in the hallway. I round a corner and see a sign that says patient rooms are to the right and surgery is to the left. I turn left. As soon as I see the double doors to the operating rooms, I hit the button on the wall to open them. Before they're even open far enough, I try to squeeze myself through them, but a man pushes me back. "You can't be in here," he says.

"No! I need to be in there!" I try to shove past him.

He's a lot stronger than I am. He pushes me against the wall and lifts his leg, kicking the button with his foot. The doors close behind him. "You aren't allowed in there," he says calmly. "Now, who are you looking for?" He releases his grip on my arms and stands back.

"My girlfriend," I say. I'm out of breath. I lean forward and put my hands on my knees. "I need to know if she's okay."

"I've got a young woman who sustained injuries in a vehicle accident. Is that the person you're referring to?"

I nod. "Is she okay?"

He leans against the wall next to me. He slides his hands into the pockets of his white coat and pulls one of his knees up, settling his foot against the wall behind him. "She's hurt. She has an epidural hematoma that's going to require surgery."

"What is that? What does that mean? Will she be okay?"

"She experienced severe head trauma that has caused bleeding in her brain. It's too early to give you any more information at this point. Until we get her into surgery, we won't know the extent of her injuries. I was just coming to speak to the family. Do you need me to relay this information to her parents?"

I shake my head. "She doesn't have any. She doesn't have anyone. I'm all she's got."

He straightens up and walks back to the doors and presses the button. He turns just as they open. "What's your name?" he asks.

"Will."

He looks me in the eyes. "I'm Dr. Bradshaw," he says. "I'll do everything I can for her, Will. In the meantime, go back to the waiting room. I'll find you as soon as I know something." The doors close behind him.

I slide down to the floor in an attempt to regain my bearings.

She's alive.

WHEN I MAKE it back to the waiting room, Kel and Caulder are the only ones there.

"Where's Gavin?" I ask.

"Joel called. Gavin went outside to meet him," Caulder says.

"Did you hear anything?" Kel asks.

I nod. "She's in surgery."

"So she's alive? She's alive?" He jumps up and wraps his arms around me. I return his hug.

"She's alive," I whisper. I sit down and gently guide him back into his chair. "Kel, she's hurt pretty bad. It's too soon to know anything, but they'll keep us updated, okay?" I grab a tissue from one of the many boxes scattered around the room and hand it to him. He wipes his nose.

We all sit there in silence. I close my eyes and think back to the conversation I just had with the doctor. Were there any hints in his expression? In his voice? I know he knows more than he's telling me, which scares the hell out of me. What if something happens to her? I can't think about it. I don't think about. She'll be okay. She has to be.

"Anything?" Gavin asks as he and Joel walk into the waiting room. "I had Joel grab you a shirt," he says, handing it to me.

"Thanks." I give Gavin his jacket and pull the shirt on. "Lake's in surgery. She's got a head injury. They don't know anything yet. That's all I know. What about Eddie?" I ask. "Have you heard anything else? Is the baby okay?"

Gavin looks at me, wide-eyed.

Joel jumps up. "Baby?" he yells. "What the hell is he talking about, Gavin?"

Gavin stands up. "We were going to tell you, Joel. It's still so early . . . we . . . we haven't had a chance."

Joel storms out, and Gavin follows him. I'm such an idiot.

"Can we go see Kiersten?" Kel asks.

I nod. "Don't stay too long. She needs her rest."

Kel and Caulder leave.

I'm alone. I close my eyes and lean my head against

the wall. I take several deep breaths, but the pressure in my chest keeps building and building and building. I try to keep holding it all in. I try to hold it in like Lake does. I can't. I bring my hands to my face and break down. I don't just cry; I *sob.* I *wail.* I *scream.*

14.

THURSDAY OR FRIDAY, JANUARY 26 OR 27,
SOMEWHERE AROUND MIDNIGHT . . .

Now that I have you back, I'm never letting you go. That's a promise. I'm not letting you go again.

I'M IN THE BATHROOM SPLASHING WATER ON MY face when I hear someone talking outside the door. I swing it open to see if it's the doctor, but it's Gavin and Joel. I've started to shut the door when Gavin reaches in and stops me.

"Will, your grandparents are here. They're looking for you."

"My grandparents? Who called them?"

"I did," he says. "I thought maybe they could take Kel and Caulder for you."

I step out of the bathroom. "Where are they?"

"Around the corner," he says.

I see my grandparents standing in the hallway. My grandfather has his coat folded over his hands. He's saying something to my grandmother when he catches a glimpse of me. "Will!" They both run toward me.

"Are you okay?" my grandmother says, brushing her fingers against the bandages on my forehead.

I pull away from her. "I'm fine," I say.

She hugs me. "Have you heard anything?"

I shake my head. I'm getting really tired of this question.

"Where are the boys?"

"They're up in Kiersten's room," I say.

"Kiersten? She was involved, too?"

I nod.

"Will, the nurse is asking about paperwork. They need it. Have you finished filling it out yet?" my grandfather says.

"I haven't started it yet. I don't feel like doing paperwork right now." I begin walking back to the waiting room. I need to sit down.

Gavin and Joel are seated in the waiting room. Gavin looks awful. I didn't notice before, but his arm is in a sling.

"You okay?" I ask, nodding in the direction of the sling.

"Yeah."

I sit down and prop my legs up on the table in front of me and tilt my head against the back of the chair. My grandparents take seats opposite me. Everyone's staring at me. I feel like they're all waiting on me. I don't know why. Waiting for me to cry, maybe? To yell? To hit something?

"*What!*" I yell at all of them. My grandmother flinches. I immediately feel guilty, but I don't apologize. I close my eyes and inhale, trying to figure out the order of events. I remember talking to Gavin about Eddie, and I remember Gavin yelling. I even remember slamming on the brakes, but I can't remember why. I can't remember anything after that . . . up to opening my eyes in the car.

I bring my legs off the table and turn to Gavin. "What happened, Gavin? I don't remember."

He makes a face as if he's tired of explaining. He does it anyway, though. "A truck crossed the median and hit their car. You slammed on your brakes, so we weren't involved in that wreck. But when you slammed on your brakes, we were hit from behind. It knocked us into the ditch. As soon as I got out of the car, I ran to Layken's car. I saw her get out, so I thought she was okay . . . that's when I went to check on Eddie."

"So you saw her? She got out on her own? She wasn't thrown from the car?"

He shakes his head. "No, I think she was confused. She must have passed out. But I saw her walking."

I don't know if the fact that she got out on her own makes a difference, but it somehow eases my mind a little.

My grandfather leans forward in his chair and looks at me. "Will. I know you don't want to deal with it right now, but they need as much information as you can give them. They don't even know her name. They need to know if she's allergic to anything. Does she have insurance? If you give them her social security number, they may be able to figure a lot of this out."

I sigh. "I don't know. I don't know if she has

insurance. I don't know her social. I don't know if she's allergic to anything. She hasn't got anyone but me, and I don't know a damn thing!" I lay my head in my hands, ashamed that Lake and I have never discussed any of this before. Didn't we learn anything? From my parents' deaths? From Julia's death? Here I am, possibly facing my past head-on again . . . *unprepared* and *overwhelmed.*

My grandfather walks over to me and wraps his arms around me. "I'm sorry, Will. We'll figure it out."

ANOTHER HOUR PASSES with no word. Not even about Eddie. Joel goes with my grandparents and Kel and Caulder to the cafeteria for food. Gavin stays with me.

I guess he gets tired of sitting in the chairs because he gets up and lies down on the floor. It looks like a good idea, so I do the same thing. I put my hands under my head and raise my feet up in a chair.

"I'm trying not to think about it, Will. But if the baby isn't okay . . . Eddie . . ."

I hear the fear in his voice. "Gavin . . . stop. Stop thinking about it. Let's just think about something else for a while. We'll drive ourselves insane if we don't."

"Yeah . . ." he says.

We're silent, so I know we're both still thinking about it. I try to think about anything else.

"I kicked Reece out this morning," I say, doing my best to tear our minds away from reality.

"Why? I thought you guys were best friends," he says. He sounds relieved to be talking about something else.

"We used to be. Things change. People change. People get new best friends," I say.

"That they do."

We're quiet again for a while. My mind starts drifting back to Lake, so I reel myself back in. "I punched him," I say. "Right in the jaw. It was beautiful. I wish you could've seen it."

Gavin laughs. "Good. I never have liked him."

"I'm not so sure I did, either," I say. "It's just one of those things where you feel obligated to the friendship, I guess."

"Those are the worst kind," he says.

Every now and then, one of us will lift our head when we hear someone walk by. We eventually become too tired even to do that. I've begun to drift off to sleep when I'm sucked back into reality. "Sir?" someone says from the doorway. Gavin and I jump up.

"She's in a room now," the nurse says to Gavin. "You can go see her. Room 207."

"She's okay? Is the baby okay?"

The nurse nods at him and smiles.

And Gavin is gone. Just like that.

The nurse turns to me. "Dr. Bradshaw wanted me to let you know they're still in surgery. He doesn't have any updates yet, but we'll let you know as soon as we find something out."

"Thank you," I say.

MY GRANDPARENTS EVENTUALLY come back with Kel and Caulder. My grandfather and Kel are trying to fill out the paperwork for Lake. There aren't any questions I could answer that Kel doesn't already know the answers to. They leave most of the questions blank. My grandfather walks the forms to the nurses' station and returns with a box. "These are some of the personal items found in the vehicles," he says to me.

I lean forward and look inside the box. My satchel is on top, so I pull it out. Lake's purse is there. So are my cell phone and my jacket. I don't see her phone.

Knowing Lake, she probably lost it *before* the wreck. I open her purse and pull out her wallet and hand it to my grandfather. "Look in there. She might have an insurance card or something."

He takes the wallet out of my hands and opens it. They must have already given Eddie's things to Gavin, because there's nothing left in the box.

"It's late," my grandmother says. "We'll take the boys home with us so they can get some rest. Do you need anything before we go?"

"I don't want to go," Kel says.

"Kel, sweetie. You need some rest. There isn't anywhere you can sleep here," she says.

Kel looks at me and silently pleads.

"He can stay with me," I say.

My grandmother picks up her purse and coat. I follow them out and walk down the hall with them. When we get to the end of the hallway, I stop and give Caulder a hug. "I'll call you as soon as I find out anything," I say to him. My grandparents hug me goodbye, and they leave. My entire family leaves.

*

I'M ALMOST ASLEEP when I feel someone shaking my shoulder. I jerk up and look around, hoping someone's here with some news. It's just Kel.

"I'm thirsty," he says.

I look down at my watch. It's after one in the morning. Why haven't they told me anything? I reach into my pocket and take out my wallet. "Here," I say, handing him some cash. "Bring me a coffee." Kel takes the money and leaves just as Gavin walks back into the room. He looks at me for answers, but I shake my head. He sits down in the seat next to me.

"So Eddie's okay?" I ask.

"Yeah. She's bruised up but okay," he says.

I'm too tired to make small talk. Gavin fills the silent void.

"She's further along than we thought she was," he says. "She's about sixteen weeks. They let us see the baby on a monitor. They're pretty sure it's a girl."

"Oh yeah?" I say. I'm not sure how Gavin feels about the whole thing, so I refrain from congratulating him. Doesn't feel like a good situation for congratulations, anyway.

"I saw her heart beating," he says.

"Whose? Eddie's?"

He shakes his head and smiles at me. "No. *My* baby girl's." His eyes tear up and he looks away.

Now is the right time. I smile. "Congratulations."

Kel walks in with two coffees. He hands me one and plops down in the chair and takes a sip of the other.

"Are you drinking coffee?" I ask him.

He nods. "Don't try to take it from me, either. I'll run."

I laugh. "Okay, then." I bring the coffee up to my mouth, but before I take a sip, Dr. Bradshaw walks in. I jump up, and the coffee splashes on my shirt. Or Joel's shirt. Or Gavin's. Whoever the hell's shirt I have on, it's got coffee all over it now.

"Will? Walk with me?" Dr. Bradshaw tilts his head toward the hallway.

"Wait here, Kel, I'll be right back." I set the coffee down on the table.

We've gotten to the end of the hallway before he starts to speak. When he does, I have to brace myself against the wall. I feel like I'm about to collapse.

"She made it through surgery, but we aren't close to being in the clear. She had a lot of bleeding. Some swelling. I did what I could without removing a portion of her parietal bone. Now all we can do is watch and wait."

My heart is pounding against my chest. It's hard to pay attention when I have a million questions on the tip of my tongue. "What is it we're waiting for? If she made it this far, what are the dangers?"

He leans against the wall next to me. We're staring at our feet, as if he's trying to avoid looking me in the eyes. He has to hate this part of his job. I hate this part of his job *for* him. That's why I don't look at him—I feel like maybe it takes the pressure off.

"The brain is the most delicate organ in the human body. Unfortunately, we aren't able to tell just by looking at scans what exactly a person's injuries are. It's more like a waiting game, so for right now we're keeping her under anesthesia. Hopefully, by morning we'll have more of an idea what we're dealing with."

"Can I see her?"

He sighs. "Not yet. She's in recovery throughout the night. I'll let you know as soon as they take her to ICU." He straightens up and puts his hands in the pockets of his lab coat. "Do you have any more questions, Will?"

Now I look him in the eyes. "A million," I reply.

He takes my response as it was rhetorically intended and he walks away.

WHEN I RETURN to the waiting room, Gavin is still sitting with Kel, who jumps up and rushes to me. "Is she okay?"

"She's out of surgery," I say. "But they won't know anything until tomorrow."

"Know anything about what?" Kel asks.

I sit and motion for him to sit down next to me. I pause so I can find the right words. I want to explain in a way that he'll understand. "When she hit her head, she hurt her brain, Kel. We won't know how badly she's hurt, when she'll wake up, or even if there's any damage until they take her off the anesthesia."

Gavin says, "I'll go tell Eddie. She's been hysterical," and he leaves the room.

I was hoping a weight would be lifted off my shoulders after finally speaking with the doctor, but it doesn't feel that way at all. It feels worse. I feel so much worse. I just want to see her.

"Will?" Kel says.

"Yeah?" I reply. I'm too tired to look at him. I can't even keep my eyes open.

"What'll happen to me? If . . . she can't take care of me? Where will I go?"

I manage to open my eyes and look at him. As soon as we make eye contact, he starts crying. I wrap my arms around him and pull his head against my chest. "You aren't going anywhere, Kel. We're in this together. You and me." I pull back and look him in the eyes. "I mean it. No matter what happens."

15.

FRIDAY, JANUARY 27

Kel,

I don't know what's about to happen in our lives. I wish I did. God, I wish I did.

I was lucky enough to be nineteen when I lost my parents; you were only nine. That's a lot of growing up left to do for a little boy without a dad.

But whatever happens . . . whichever road we have to take when we leave this hospital . . . we're taking it together.

I'll do my best to help you finish growing up with the closest thing to a dad you can have. I'll do my absolute best.

I don't know what's about to happen in our lives. I wish I did. God, I wish I did.

But whatever happens, I'll love you. I can promise you that.

"WILL."

I try to crack my eyes, but only one of them opens. I'm lying on the floor again. I close my eye before my entire head explodes.

"Will, wake up."

I sit up and run my hands along the chairs next to me, pulling myself into one by the arm. I still can't open my other eye. I shield my vision from the fluorescent lights and turn toward the voice.

"Will, I need you to listen to me."

I finally recognize the voice as Sherry's. "I'm listening," I whisper. It feels like if I spoke any louder, it would be too painful. My whole head hurts. I bring my hand to the bandage, then to my eye. It's swollen. No wonder I can't open it.

"I'm having the nurse bring you some medicine. You need to eat something. They aren't keeping Kiersten, so we're going home soon. I'll be back to wake up Kel after I get Kiersten into the car. I'll bring him back up here during the day; I just think he needs some rest. Is there anything you need from your house? Besides a change of clothes?"

I shake my head, which hurts less than speaking.

"Okay. Call me if you think of anything."

"Sherry," I say before she exits. Then I realize nothing audible came out of my mouth. "Sherry!" I say louder, and wince. Why does my head hurt so bad?

She comes back.

"There's a vase in my cabinet. Above the fridge. I need it."

She acknowledges that with a nod and leaves the room.

"Kel," I say, shaking him awake. "I'm going to get something to drink. Do you want anything?"

He nods. "Coffee."

He must not be a morning person: just like his sister. When I pass the nurses' station, one of the nurses calls my name. I back-step and she holds out her hand. "These will help your head," she says. "Your mother said you needed them."

I laugh. My mother. I pop the pills into my mouth and swallow them and head to find coffee. The double doors in the lobby open as I pass them, sending a swarm of cold air around me. I stop and look outside, then decide some fresh air might do me some good. I take a seat on a bench under the awning. Everything's so white. The snow is still falling. I wonder how deep our driveways will be by the time Lake and I get home.

I don't know how it happens, how the thought even creeps its way into my head, but for a second I wonder what would happen to everything in Lake's house if she died. She doesn't have family to finalize anything. To deal with her bank accounts, her bills, her insurance, her possessions. She and I aren't related, and Kel's only eleven. Would they even let me do those things? Am I even legally allowed to keep Kel? As soon as the thoughts register, I force them back. It's pointless thinking like this, because that isn't going to happen. I get pissed at myself for letting my mind get carried away, so I head back inside to get the coffee.

WHEN I RETURN to the waiting room, Dr. Bradshaw is sitting with Kel. They don't notice me right away. He's telling a story, and Kel's laughing, so I don't interrupt. It's nice to hear Kel laugh. I stand outside the door and listen.

"Then when my mother told me to go get the box to bury the cat, I told her there was no need. I'd already brought him back to life," Dr. Bradshaw says. "It was that moment, after I resuscitated that kitten, I knew I wanted to be a doctor when I grew up."

"So you saved the kitten?" Kel asks him.

Dr. Bradshaw laughs. "No. He died again a few minutes later. But I had already made up my mind by then," he says.

Kel laughs, too. "At least you didn't want to be a veterinarian."

"No, clearly, I'm not cut out for animals."

"Any news?" I walk into the room and hand Kel his coffee.

Dr. Bradshaw stands up. "We've still got her under anesthesia. We were able to run some tests. I'm waiting on the results, but you can see her for a few minutes."

"Now? We can see her? Right now?" I'm gathering up my things as I reply.

"Will . . . I can't let anyone else in," he says. He looks down at Kel, then back at me. "She hasn't been moved from recovery yet . . . I'm not even supposed to let you in. But I'm doing some rounds and thought I'd let you walk with me."

I want to beg Dr. Bradshaw to let me take Kel with

us, but I know he's already doing me a huge favor. "Kel, if I'm not back before you leave with Sherry, I'll call you."

He nods. I expect him to argue, but I think he understands. The fact that he's being so reasonable fills me with a sense of pride. I bend over and hug him and kiss him on top of the head. "I'll call you. As soon as I hear anything, I'll call you." He nods once more. I reach over and grab her clip from my satchel, then turn back toward the door.

I follow Dr. Bradshaw past the nurses' station, through the doors, and down the hall to the double doors leading to surgery. Before we go any farther, he takes me into a room where we both wash our hands. When we get to the door, I can barely catch my breath. I'm so nervous. My heart is about to explode through my chest.

"Will, you need to know a few things first. She's on a ventilator to help her breathe, but only because we've got her in a medically induced coma. There's no chance of her waking up right now with the amount of medicine we're giving her. Most of her head is bandaged. She looks worse than she feels; we're keeping her comfortable. I'll allow you a few minutes with her, but that's all I can give you right now. Understand?"

I nod.

He pushes open the door and lets me in.

As soon as I see her, I struggle to breathe. The reality of the moment knocks the air from my lungs. The ventilator sucks in a rush of air and releases it. With each repetitive sound of the machine, it's as if hope is being pushed out of me.

I go to the bed and take her hand. It's cold. I kiss her forehead. I kiss it a million times. I just want to lie down with her, hug her. There are too many wires and tubes and cords running everywhere. I pull a chair up next to the bed and interlock her fingers with mine. It's getting hard to see her through my tears, so I have to wipe my eyes on my shirt. She looks so peaceful, like she's just taking a nap.

"I love you, Lake," I whisper. I kiss her hand. "I love you," I whisper again. "I love you."

The covers are pulled tightly around her, and she's got a hospital gown on. Her head is wrapped in a bandage, but most of her hair is hanging down around her neck. I'm relieved they didn't cut all of her hair. She'd be pissed. The ventilator tube is taped over her mouth, so I kiss her forehead again and her cheek. I know she can't hear me, but I talk to her anyway.

"Lake, you have to pull through this. You *have* to." I stroke her hand. "I can't live without you." I turn her hand over and kiss her palm, then press it against my cheek. The feel of her skin against mine is surreal. I wasn't sure if I'd ever feel it again. I close my eyes and kiss her palm again and again. I sit there and cry and kiss the only parts of her I can.

"Will," Dr. Bradshaw says. "We need to go now."

I stand up and kiss her on the forehead. I take a step back, then take a step forward and kiss her hand. I take two steps back, then walk two steps toward her and kiss her cheek.

Dr. Bradshaw takes my arm. "Will, we need to go."

I take a few steps toward the door. "Wait," I say. I put my hand in my pocket and pull out her purple hair clip. I open her hand and place it in her palm and close her fingers over it, then kiss her on the forehead again before we leave.

*

THE REST OF the morning drags by. Kel left with Sherry. Eddie was discharged. She wanted to stay with me, but Gavin and Joel wouldn't let her. All I can do now is wait. Wait and think. Think and wait. That's all I can do. That's all I do.

I wander the halls for a while. I can't keep sitting in that waiting room. I've spent way too much of my life in there, and in this hospital. I was here for six solid days after my parents died, when I stayed with Caulder. I don't remember much from those days. Caulder and I were both in a daze, not really believing what was happening. Caulder had hit his head in the wreck and broken his arm. I'm not sure his injuries were near extensive enough to warrant six days in the hospital, but the staff didn't seem to feel comfortable just letting us go. Two orphans, into the wild.

Caulder was seven at the time, so the hardest part was all the questions he had. I couldn't get through to him that we weren't going to see our parents again. I think that six-day hospital stay is why I hate pity so much. Every single person who spoke to me felt sorry for me, and I could see it in their eyes. I could hear it in their voices.

I was here with Lake for two months off and on when Julia was sick. When Kel and Caulder would stay at my grandparents' house, Lake and I would stay here with Julia. Lake stayed most nights, in fact. When Kel wasn't with me, he was here with them. By the end of Julia's first week here, Lake and I ended up bringing an air mattress. Hospital furniture is the worst. They asked us a few times to remove the mattress from the room. Instead, we would just deflate it every morning and then blow it up again every night. We noticed they weren't so quick to ask us to remove it when we were asleep on it.

Out of all the nights I've spent here, this time feels different. It feels worse. Maybe it's the absence of finality, the lack of knowledge. At least after my parents had died and Caulder was here, I didn't question anything. I knew they were dead. I knew Caulder was going to be okay. Even with Julia, we knew her death was inevitable. We weren't left with questions while we waited; we knew what was happening. But this time . . . this time is much harder. It's so hard not knowing.

*

AS SOON AS I begin to doze off, Dr. Bradshaw walks in. I sit up in my chair, and he takes a seat next to me.

"We've moved her to a room in ICU. You'll be able to see her in an hour, during visiting hours. The scans look good. We'll try easing her off the anesthesia over time and see what happens. It's still touch and go, Will. Anything can happen. Getting her to respond to us is our priority now."

The relief washes over me, but a new sense of worry creeps in just as fast. "Does . . ." It feels like my throat is squeezed shut when I try to speak. I grab my bottle of water off the table in front of me and take a drink, then try again to speak. "Does she have a chance? At full recovery?"

He sighs. "I can't answer that. Right now the scans show normal activity, but that may not mean anything when it comes to trying to wake her up. Then again, it could mean she'll be perfectly fine. Until that moment, we won't know." He stands up. "She's in room five in ICU. Wait until one o'clock before you head down there."

I nod. "Thank you."

As soon as I hear him round the corner, I grab my

things and run as fast as I can in the opposite direction to ICU. The nurse doesn't ask any questions when I walk in. I act like I know exactly what I'm doing and head straight to room five.

There aren't as many wires, though she's still hooked up to the ventilator, and she has an IV in her left wrist. I walk around to the right side of the bed and pull the rail down. I climb into bed with her and wrap my arm around her and lay my leg over her legs. I take her hand in mine and I close my eyes . . .

"WILL," SHERRY SAYS. I jerk my eyes open, and she's standing on the other side of Lake's bed.

I stretch my arms out above my head. "Hey," I whisper.

"I brought you some clothes. And your vase. Kel was still asleep, so I just let him stay. I hope that's okay. I'll bring him back when he wakes up."

"Yeah, that's fine. What time is it?"

She looks at her watch. "Almost five," she says. "The nurse said you've been asleep for a couple of hours."

I push my elbow into the bed and lift myself up. My

arm is asleep. I slide off the bed and stand up and stretch again.

"You do realize visitors are only allowed fifteen minutes," she says. "They must like you."

I laugh. "I'd like to see them try to kick me out," I say. I walk over to the chair and sit. The worst thing about hospitals is the furniture. The beds are too small for two people. The chairs are too hard for any people. And there's never a recliner. If they would just have a recliner, I might not detest them so much.

"Have you eaten anything today?" she asks.

I shake my head.

"Come downstairs with me. I'll buy you something to eat."

"I can't. I don't want to leave her," I say. "They've been reducing her meds. She could wake up."

"Well, you need to eat. I'll grab you something and bring it back up."

"Thanks," I say.

"You should at least take a shower. You've got dried blood all over you. It's gross." She smiles at me and starts to head out the door.

"Sherry. Don't bring me a hamburger, okay?"

She laughs.

After she's gone, I get up, take out a star, and then crawl back in the bed with Lake. "This one's for you, babe." I unfold the star and read it.

Never, under any circumstances, take a sleeping pill and a laxative on the same night.

I roll my eyes. "Jesus, Julia! Now's not the time to be funny!" I reach over and grab another star, then lie back down. "Let's try this again, babe."

Strength does not come from physical capacity. It comes from an indomitable will.

—MAHATMA GANDHI

I lean over and whisper in her ear. "You hear that, Lake? Indomitable will. That's one of the things I love about you."

I MUST HAVE fallen asleep again. The nurse shakes me awake. "Sir, can you step outside for a moment?"

Dr. Bradshaw walks into the room. "Is she okay?" I ask him.

"We're removing the ventilator now. The anesthesia is wearing off, so she's not getting anything other than the pain medicine through her IV." He raises the bed rail. "Just step outside for a few minutes. I promise we'll let you back in." He smiles.

He's smiling. *This is good.* They're taking her off the ventilator. *This is good.* He's looking me in the eyes. *This is good.* I step outside and impatiently wait.

I pace the hallway for fifteen minutes before he emerges from the room. "Her vitals look fine. She's breathing on her own. Now we wait," he says. He pats me on the shoulder and turns to leave.

I go back in the room and crawl in the bed with her. I put my ear to her mouth and listen to her breathe. It's the most beautiful sound in the world. I kiss her. Of course I kiss her. I kiss her a million times.

SHERRY MADE ME take a shower when she got back with our food. Gavin and Eddie showed up around six o'clock and stayed for an hour. Eddie cried the whole time, so

Gavin got worried and made her leave again. Sherry came back with Kel before visiting hours were over. He didn't cry, but I think he was upset seeing her like this, so they didn't stay long. I've been giving my grandmother hourly calls, although nothing has changed.

Now it's somewhere around midnight, and I'm just sitting here. Waiting. Thinking. Waiting and thinking. I keep imagining I see her toe move. Or her finger. It's driving me crazy, so I stop watching. I start thinking about everything that happened Thursday night. Our cars. Where *are* our cars? I should probably be calling the insurance company. What about school? I missed school today. Or was it yesterday? I don't know if it's Saturday yet. I probably won't be in school next week, either. I should figure out who Lake's professors are and let them know she won't be there. I should probably let my professors know, too. And the elementary school. What do I tell them? I don't know when the boys will go back. If Lake is still in the hospital next week, I know Kel won't want to go to school. But he just missed an entire week. He can't miss many more days. And what about Caulder? Where are Kel and Caulder going to stay while Lake and I are here? I'm not leaving the hospital without Lake. I may not even leave *with* Lake if I don't figure out what to do about a car. My car. Where *is* my car?

"Will."

I glance to the door. No one's there. Now I'm hearing things. Too many thoughts are jumbled up in my head right now. I wonder if Sherry left me any of her medicine. I bet she did. She probably sneaked it in my bag.

"Will."

I jerk up in my seat and look at Lake. Her eyes are closed. She isn't moving. I know I heard my name. I know I did! I rush to her and touch her face. "Lake?"

She flinches. She flinches! "Lake!"

Her lips part and she says it again. "Will?"

She squints. She's trying to open her eyes. I flick the light switch off, then pull the string to the overhead light until it clicks off. I know how much these fluorescent lights hurt.

"Lake," I whisper. I pull the rail down and climb into the bed with her. I kiss her on the lips, the cheek, the forehead. "Don't try to talk if it hurts. You're okay. I'm right here. You're okay." She moves her hand, so I take it in mine. "Can you feel my hand?"

She nods. It's not much of a nod, but it's a nod.

"You're okay," I say. I keep saying it over and over until I'm crying. "You're okay."

The door to her room opens, and a nurse walks in.

"She said my name!"

She looks up at me, then rushes out of the room and comes back with Dr. Bradshaw. "Get up, Will," he says. "Let us examine her. We'll let you back in soon."

"She said my name," I say as I slide off the bed. "She said my name!"

He smiles at me. "Go outside."

And so I do. For over half an hour. No one has left the room and no one has entered and it's been half a freakin' hour. I knock on the door, and the nurse cracks it. I try to peek past her, but she doesn't open the door far enough. "Just a few more minutes," she says.

I contemplate calling everyone, but I don't. I just need to make sure I wasn't hearing things, though I know she heard me. She spoke to me. She moved.

Dr. Bradshaw opens the door and steps outside. The nurses follow him out.

"I heard her, right? She's okay? She said my name!"

"Calm down, Will. You need to calm down. They

won't let you stay in here if you keep freaking out like this."

Calm down? He has no idea how calm I'm being!

"She's responding," he says. "Her physical responses were all good. She doesn't remember what happened. She may not remember a lot of stuff right away. She needs rest, Will. I'll let you back inside, but you'll need to let her rest."

"Okay, I will. I promise. I swear."

"I know. Now go," he says.

When I open the door, she's facing me. She smiles a really pathetic, pained smile.

"Hey," I whisper.

"Hey," she whispers back.

"Hey." I walk to her bed and stroke her cheek.

"Hey," she says again.

"Hey."

"Stop it," she says. She tries to laugh, but it hurts her. She closes her eyes.

I take her hand in mine, and I bury my face in the crevice between her shoulder and her neck, and I cry.

*

FOR THE NEXT few hours, she goes in and out of consciousness, just like Dr. Bradshaw said she would. Every time she wakes up, she says my name. Every time she says my name, I tell her to close her eyes and get some rest. Every time I tell her to close her eyes and get some rest, she does.

Dr. Bradshaw comes in a few times to check on her. They lower the dose in the IV one more time so she can stay awake for longer periods. I decide again not to call anyone. It's still too early, and I don't want everyone bombarding her. I just want her to rest.

It's almost seven in the morning and I'm walking out of the bathroom when she finally says something besides my name. "What happened?" she asks.

I pull a chair up beside her bed. She's rolled over onto her left side, so I rest my chin on the bed rail and stroke her arm. "We were in a wreck."

She looks confused, then terror washes over her face. "The kids—"

"Everyone's fine," I reassure her. "Everyone's okay."

She breathes a sigh of relief. "When? What day was it? What day *is* it?"

"It's Saturday. It happened Thursday night. What's the last thing you remember?"

She closes her eyes. I reach up and pull the string to the light above her bed, and it flicks off. I don't know why they keep turning it on. What hospital patient wants a fluorescent light three feet from her head?

"I remember going to the slam," she says. "I remember your poem . . . but that's all. That's all I can remember." She opens her eyes again and looks at me. "Did I forgive you?"

I laugh. "Yes, you forgave me. And you love me. A bunch."

She smiles. "Good."

"You were hurt. They had to take you into surgery."

"I know. The doctor told me that much."

I stroke her cheek with the back of my hand. "I'll tell you everything that happened later, okay? Right now you need to rest. I'm going outside to call everyone. Kel's worried sick. Eddie, too. I'll be back, okay?"

She nods and closes her eyes again. I lean forward and kiss her on the forehead. "I love you, Lake." I grab my phone off the table and stand up.

"Again," she whispers.

"I love you."

VISITING HOURS ARE strictly enforced once everyone starts to arrive. They make me wait in the waiting room just like everyone else. Only one person is allowed in at a time. Eddie and Gavin got here first. Kel shows up with Sherry about the same time my grandparents show up with Caulder.

"Can I go see her?" Kel asks.

"Absolutely. She keeps asking for you. Eddie's with her right now. It's ICU, so Lake can only have visitors for fifteen minutes, but you're next."

"So she's talking? She's okay? She remembers me?"

"Yeah. She's perfect," I say.

Grandpaul walks over to Kel and puts a hand on his shoulder. "Come on, Grandkel, we'll get you some breakfast before you go see her."

My grandparents take Kel and Caulder to the cafeteria. I ask them to bring me something back. I finally have an appetite.

"Do you need me and Eddie to stay with the boys for a few days?" Gavin asks.

"No. Not now, anyway. My grandparents are keeping them for a couple of days. I don't want them to miss a lot of school, though."

"I'm sending Kiersten back to school on Wednesday," Sherry says. "If your grandparents have them home on Tuesday, they can stay with me until Layken is discharged."

"Thanks, guys," I say to both of them.

Eddie walks around the corner. She's wiping her eyes and sniffing. I sit up in my chair, and Gavin takes Eddie's arm and guides her to a seat. She rolls her eyes at him. "Gavin, I'm pregnant. Quit treating me like I'm an invalid."

Gavin sits next to her. "I'm sorry, babe. I just worry about you." He leans forward and kisses her stomach. "Both of you."

Eddie smiles and kisses him on the cheek.

It's good to see that he's accepted his upcoming role as a dad. I know they've got a lot of hurdles ahead of them, but I have faith that they'll make it. I guess Lake and I could start recycling our stars for them, just in case they need them. "How's Lake feeling?" I ask.

Eddie shrugs. "Like shit," she says. "But she did just have her head cut open, so that's understandable. I told her all about the wreck. She felt kind of bad once she found out she was the one driving. I told her it wasn't her fault, but she still said she wishes you were driving. That way she could blame her injuries on you."

I laugh. "She can blame them on me anyway, if it makes her feel better."

"We're coming back this afternoon," Eddie says. "She really needs some TLC in the makeup department. Is two o'clock okay? Does anyone have that time slot yet?"

I shake my head. "See you guys at two."

Before they leave, Eddie walks over and gives me a hug. An unusually long hug.

After she and Gavin walk out, I look down at my watch. Kel will see her next, then Sherry. My grandmother may want to see her. I guess I'll have to wait until after lunch before they'll let me back in.

"You've got great friends," Sherry says.

I raise my eyebrows at her. "You don't think they're weird? Most people think my friends are weird."

"Yeah, I do. That's why they're great," she says.

I smile and scoot down in my seat until my head is resting against the back of the chair. I close my eyes. "You're pretty weird yourself, Sherry."

She laughs. "You, too."

I can't get comfortable in the chair, so I resort to lying on the floor again. I stretch my arms out above my head and sigh. The floor actually feels comfortable. Now that I know Lake will be okay, I'm starting not to despise the hospital as much.

"Will?" Sherry says.

I open my eyes. She's not looking at me. She's got her legs crossed in the chair, and she's picking at the seam of her jeans.

"What's up?" I reply.

She looks at me and smiles. "You did a great job," she says quietly. "I know it was hard, calling me about Kiersten. And taking care of the boys during all of this. How you've handled everything with Layken. You're too young to have so much responsibility, but you're doing a good job. I hope you know that. Your mom and dad would be proud."

I close my eyes and inhale. I didn't know how much I needed to hear that until this very second. Sometimes it feels good to have your biggest fears discounted with a simple compliment. "Thank you."

She gets out of the chair and lies down next to me on the floor. Her eyes are closed, but I can tell from the set of her face that she's trying not to cry. I look away. Sometimes women just need to cry.

We're quiet for a little while. She blows out a deep breath. "He was killed a year later. A year after he proposed. In a car accident," she says.

I realize she's telling me the story about Jim. I roll over and face her, resting my head on my elbow. I don't really know what to say, so I don't say anything.

"I'm okay," she says. She smiles at me. This time it seems like she's trying not to pity herself. "It's been a long time. I love my family and wouldn't trade them for the world. But sometimes it's still hard. Times like these . . ." She pulls herself up and sits Indian-style on the floor. She begins to pick at the seam of her pants again. "I was so scared for you, Will. I was scared she wouldn't make it. Seeing you go through that brought back a lot of memories. That's why I haven't been up here very much."

I understand the expression in her eyes and the

heartache in her voice. I understand it, and I hate it for her. "It's okay," I say. "I didn't expect you to stay. You had Kiersten to worry about."

"I know you didn't expect me to stay. I wouldn't have been any help. But I worry about you. I worry about all of you. Kel, Caulder, you, Layken. Now I even like your damn weird friends, and I'm gonna have to worry about them, too." She laughs.

I smile at her. "It's nice to be worried about, Sherry. Thank you."

16.

SUNDAY, JANUARY 29

I've learned something about my heart.

It can break.

It can be ripped apart.

It can harden and freeze.

It can stop. Completely.

It can shatter into a million pieces.

It can explode.

It can die.

The only thing that made it start beating again?

The moment you opened your eyes.

ALL THE VISITS WEAR LAKE OUT, AND SHE SLEEPS the majority of the afternoon. She slept through Eddie's second visit, which was probably good, for Lake's sake. I highly doubt she would feel like being pampered. The nurse brought her soup at dinnertime, and she sipped most of it. It was the first thing she's eaten since Thursday.

She asked more questions about the night of the wreck. She wanted to know all about her forgiving me and our making up. I told her everything that happened after I performed. For the most part, I was honest, but I may have thrown in a more climactic make-out scene for emphasis.

IT'S SUNDAY, AND the fact that she's in the hospital doesn't deter her from her routine. I walk into her hospital room and set the bags of movies and junk food down in the chair. Lake is sitting up on the side of the bed, and the nurse is working with the IV.

"Oh, good. You're right on time," the nurse says. "She doesn't want a sponge bath, she wants a standard bath. I was about to assist her in the bathroom, but if you'd rather do it, you can." She unhooks the IV and clamps it, then tapes the end of it to Lake's hand.

Lake and I look at each other. It's not like I've never seen her naked—just not for prolonged periods. And with the lights *on*.

"I . . . I don't know," I mutter. "Do you want me to help you?"

Lake shrugs. "It wouldn't be the first time you've put me in a shower. Although I hope you help me take my clothes *off* this time." She laughs at her own joke. She regrets the laugh, though. Her hand goes up to her head, and she winces.

The nurse can sense the slight awkwardness between us. "I'm sorry. I thought you guys were married. It said on her chart that you were her husband."

"Yeah . . . about that," I say. "Not quite yet."

"It's fine," the nurse says. "If you'll just go back to the waiting room, I'll let you know when we're finished."

"No," Lake says. "He'll help me." She looks up at me. "You'll help me." I nod at the nurse, who takes a few items off the tray next to Lake's bed and leaves the room.

"Have you walked any more today?" I take Lake's arm and help lift her off the bed.

She nods. "Yeah. They had me walk down the hall between visits. I feel better than yesterday, just dizzy."

The nurse comes back with a towel. "Just don't let her get her head wet. There's a handheld shower, or she can use the bathtub. The tub may be better for her, so she can lie down." The nurse leaves the towel in the chair and exits again.

Lake slowly stands up, and I assist her into the bathroom. Once we're inside, I close the door behind us.

"This is so embarrassing," she says.

"Lake, you asked me to stay. If you want, I'll go back and get the nurse."

"No. I just mean because I need to pee."

"Oh. Here." I walk around her and grab her other arm as she backs up.

She grabs hold of the metal bar attached to the wall and pauses. "Turn around," she says.

I face the opposite direction. "Babe, if you're already making me look away, it'll be kind of hard for me to help you in the shower. You aren't even naked yet."

"That's different. I just don't want you to watch me pee."

I laugh. And I wait. And I wait some more. Nothing happens.

"Maybe you need to leave for a minute," she says.

I shake my head and walk out of the bathroom. "Don't try to stand up without me." I leave the door open a few inches so I can hear her if she needs me. When she's finished, I go back in and help her stand up. "Shower or bath?" I ask.

"Bath. I don't think I can stand up long enough for a shower."

I make sure she's holding on to the bar before I let go of her arm. I adjust the tub faucet until the water turns warm. I grab the washcloth and get it wet, then set it on the side of the tub. It's a large tub, with two steps leading up to make it easier to walk down into. I take Lake's arm again and lead her to the bathtub. I stand behind her and brush her hair over her shoulder and untie the top of her gown. When it drapes open, I have to suppress a gasp. She's got bruises all over her back. There's one more tie on the gown, so I pull the string until it separates.

She slides the gown forward and down her arms. I run my fingers under the stream of water to check the temperature, then help her up the steps and into the bathtub. Once she's seated, she pulls her knees up to her chest and wraps her arms around them, then rests her head on them. "Thank you," she says. "For not trying to put the moves on me just now."

I smile at her. "Don't thank me yet. We just got started." I dip the washcloth in the water and kneel beside the bathtub. The steps come out pretty far, so it's hard to reach her without hovering.

She takes the washcloth out of my hand and begins washing her arm. "It's weird how much energy everything takes. I feels like my arms weigh a hundred pounds each."

I open the bar of soap and hand it to her, but it slips out of her grasp. She feels around in the water until she finds it, then she rubs it in the washcloth.

"Do you know how long before they let me go home?" she asks.

"Hopefully by Wednesday. The doctor said recovery can take anywhere from a few days to two weeks depending on how the injury heals. You seem to be doing pretty well."

She frowns. "I don't feel like I'm doing well."

"You're doing great," I say.

She smiles and sets the washcloth back on the side of the tub and wraps her arms around her knees again. "I have to rest," she says. "I'll get to the other arm in a minute." She closes her eyes. She looks so tired.

I reach over and turn off the water, then stand up and take off my shoes and my shirt but leave my pants on. "Scoot up," I say to her.

She does, and I step into the bathtub and slide down into the water behind her. I put my legs on either side of her and gently lay her back on my chest. I grab the washcloth and run it up the arm she was too tired to get to.

"You're crazy," she says quietly.

I kiss her on top of the head. "So are you."

We're silent as I wash her. She rests against my chest until I tell her to lean forward so I can get her back. I put more soap on the washcloth and gently touch it to her skin. She's bruised so badly, I'm afraid I'll hurt her.

"You really got banged up. Does your back hurt?"

"Everything hurts."

I wash her back as softly as I can. I don't want to make

it worse. When I've covered every inch, I lean forward and kiss her right on top of her bruise. I kiss her other bruise, and her other bruise, and her other bruise. I kiss every spot of her back that's hurt. When she leans back against my chest, I lift her arm and kiss the bruises on her arm, too. Then I do the same to the other arm. When I've kissed all the bruises I can find, I lay her arm back down in the water. "There. Good as new," I say. I wrap my arms around her and kiss her cheek. She closes her eyes, and we just sit there for a while.

"This isn't how I pictured our first bath together," she says.

I laugh. "Really? 'Cause this is exactly how I pictured it. Pants and all."

She takes a deep breath and exhales, then tilts her head back so she can look me in the eyes. "I love you, Will."

I kiss her on the forehead. "Say it again."

"I love you, Will."

"One more time."

"I love you."

*

LAKE IS DISCHARGED today after five days in the hospital. Luckily, since yesterday was a Monday, I was able to finalize reports with the insurance companies. Lake's Jeep was totaled. The damage to my car wasn't as bad, so I was given a rental until it's repaired.

Dr. Bradshaw is really pleased with Lake's progress. She has to go back to see him in two weeks. In the meantime, he's put her on bed rest. She's excited because that means she gets to sleep in my comfortable bed every night. I'm excited because that means I get to spend two solid weeks with her at my house.

I end up withdrawing her from all of her classes for the semester. She was upset, but she doesn't need the added stress of school right now. I told her she needs to focus on getting well. I'm taking the rest of the week off but plan on going back to school Monday, depending on how she's feeling. For now, we've got almost a whole week of nothing to do but watch movies and eat junk food.

KEL AND CAULDER bring their plates to the coffee table in the living room and set them down next to mine.

Lake's lying on the couch, so we're eating in the living room rather than at the table.

"Suck-and-sweet time," Caulder says. He crosses his legs and scoots around to the opposite side of the coffee table so we're seated in a semicircle that includes Lake. "My suck is that I have to go back to school tomorrow. My sweet is that Layken's finally home."

She smiles. "Awe, thanks Caulder. That *is* a sweet," she says.

"My turn," Kel says. "My suck is that I have to go back to school tomorrow. My sweet is that Layken's finally home."

She scrunches her nose up at Kel. "Copycat."

I laugh. "Well, my suck is that my girlfriend made me rent six different Johnny Depp movies. My sweet is right now." I lean over and kiss her on the forehead. Kel and Caulder have no objection to my sweet tonight. I guess they're getting used to it, or maybe they're just grateful that she's home.

"My suck is obvious. I've got staples in my head," Lake says. She looks at me and smiles, then her eyes drift to Kel and Caulder as she watches them eat.

"What's your sweet?" Caulder says with a mouthful of food.

Lake stares at him for a moment. "You guys," she says. "All three of you."

It's quiet, then Kel picks up a french fry and throws it at her. "Quit being cheesy," he says. Lake grabs the french fry and throws it back at him.

"Hey," Kiersten says as she walks through the door. "Sorry I'm late." She heads to the kitchen. I didn't know she was coming over. Looks like she'll have to eat bread again.

"You need some help?" I ask her. She's only got one good arm, but she seems to be adjusting pretty well.

"Nope. I got it." She brings her plate into the living room and sits down on the floor. We all stare at her when she takes a huge bite of a chicken strip. "Oh my God, it's so gooood," she says. She shoves the rest of it in her mouth.

"Kiersten, that's meat. You're eating meat," I say.

She nods. "I know. It's the weirdest thing. I've been dying to come over here since you guys got home so I could try some." She takes another bite. "It's *heaven*," she says around her mouthful. She hops up and walks to the kitchen. "Is it good in ketchup?" She brings the bottle back and squirts some on her plate.

"Why the sudden change of heart?" Lake asks her.

Kiersten swallows. "Right when we were about to be hit by that truck . . . all I could think was how I was about to die and I'd never tasted meat. That was my only regret in life."

We all laugh. She grabs the chicken off of my plate and throws it on her own.

"Will, are you still coming to Dad Day on Thursday?" Caulder asks.

Lake looks at me. "Dad Day?"

"I don't know, Caulder. I'm not sure I feel comfortable leaving Lake alone yet," I say.

"Dad Day? What's Dad Day?" Lake asks again.

"It's Father Appreciation Day at our school," Kiersten says. "They're having a luncheon. Kids get to eat lunch with their dads in the gymnasium. Mom Day isn't until next month."

"But what about the kids who don't have dads? What are they supposed to do? That's not very fair."

"The kids who don't have dads just go with Will," Kel says.

Lake looks at me again. She doesn't like being out of the loop.

"I asked Kel if I could eat with him, too," I say.

"Will you eat with me, too?" Kiersten asks. "My dad won't be back until Saturday."

I nod. "If I go. I don't know if I should."

"Go," Lake says. "I'll be fine. You need to quit babying me so much."

I lean forward and kiss her. "But you *are* my baby," I say.

I'm not sure which direction it comes from, maybe all three, but I'm hit in the head with french fries.

I HELP LAKE into the bed and pull the covers over her. "You want something to drink?"

"I'm fine," she says.

I turn off the light and walk around to the other side of the bed and crawl in. I scoot closer to her and put my head on her pillow and wrap my arm around her. Her bandages come off at her next doctor's visit. She's so worried about how much hair they had to cut. I keep telling her not to worry about it. I'm sure they didn't cut much, and the incision is on the back of her head, so it won't be that noticeable.

It hurts her if she's not lying on her side, so she's facing me. Her lips are in close proximity to mine, so I have to kiss them. I lay my head back down on her pillow and brush her hair behind her ear with my fingers.

This entire past week has been hell. Mentally *and* physically. But especially mentally. I came so close to losing her. *So close.* Sometimes when it's quiet, my mind wanders to the possibility of having lost her and what I would have done. I have to keep reeling myself back in, reminding myself that she's okay. That everyone's okay.

I didn't think it was possible, but everything Lake and I have been through this past month has somehow made me love her even more. I can't begin to imagine my life without her in it. I think back to the video Sherry showed me and what Jim said to her: "It's like you came along and woke up my soul."

That's exactly what Lake did to me. She woke up my soul.

I lean in and kiss her again, longer this time. But not too long. I feel like she's so fragile.

"This sucks," she says. "Do you realize how hard it'll

be sleeping in the same bed with you? Are you sure he specified an entire month? We have to retreat for a whole month?"

"Technically, he said four weeks," I say, stroking her arm. "I guess we could stick to four weeks, since it's a few days shy of a whole month."

"See? You should have taken me up on the offer when you had the chance. Now we have to wait four more weeks!" she says. "How many weeks is that, total?"

"It'll be sixty-five," I quickly respond. "Not that I'm counting. And four weeks from today is February twenty-eighth. Not that I'm counting that, either."

She laughs. "February twenty-eighth? But that'll be a Tuesday. Who wants to lose their virginity on a Tuesday? Let's make it the Friday before. February twenty-fourth. We'll get Kel and Caulder to stay with your grandparents again."

"Nope. Four weeks. Doctor's orders," I say. "We'll make a deal. I'll get my grandparents to watch the boys again if we can make it to March second. The Friday *after* it's been four weeks."

"March second is a Thursday."

"It's a leap year."

"Ugh! Fine. March second," she says. "But I want a suite this time. A big one."

"You got it."

"With chocolates. And flowers."

"You got it," I say. I lift my head off her pillow and kiss her, then roll over.

"And a fruit tray. With strawberries."

"You got it," I say again. I yawn and pull the covers up over my head.

"And I want those fluffy hotel robes. For both of us. That way we can wear them all weekend."

"Whatever you want, Lake. Now go to sleep. You need the rest."

She's done nothing but sleep for five days, so I'm not surprised she's wide awake. I, on the other hand, have had close to zero sleep for five days. I could barely keep my eyes open today. It feels so good to be back home, back in my bed. It especially feels good that Lake's right next to me.

"Will?" she whispers.

"Yeah?"

"I have to pee."

*

"ARE YOU SURE you'll be okay?" I ask Lake for the tenth time this morning.

"I'll be fine," she says. She holds the phone up to show me that she has it close by.

"Okay. Sherry's at home if you need her. I'll be back in an hour; the luncheon shouldn't last long."

"Babe, I'm fine. Promise."

I kiss her on the forehead. "I know."

And I do know she's fine. She's more than fine. She's been so focused and determined to get better that she's doing way too much on her own. Even things she shouldn't be doing on her own, which is why I worry. Her indomitable will that I fell in love with sometimes irritates the hell out of me, too.

WHEN I WALK into the gymnasium, I scan the area for the boys. Caulder is waving when I see him, so I head to his table.

"Where are Kel and Kiersten?" I say as I take a seat.

"Mrs. Brill wouldn't let them come," he says.

"Why?" I jerk my head around, looking for Mrs. Brill.

"She said they were just using this lunch as an excuse

to get out of study hall. She made them go to regular lunch at ten-forty-five. Kel told her you'd be mad."

"Well, Kel's right," I say. "I'll be right back."

I exit the gymnasium and turn left for the cafeteria. When I walk inside, the noise penetrates my eardrums. I forgot how loud kids were. I also forgot how much my head still hurt. I glance at all the tables, but there are so many kids, I can't spot either of them. I walk over to a lady who looks like she's monitoring the cafeteria.

"Can you tell me where Kel Cohen is?" I ask.

"Who?" she says. "It's too loud, I didn't hear you."

I say it louder. "Kel Cohen!"

She points to a table at the other end of the cafeteria. Before I reach the table, Kel spots me and waves. Kiersten is seated next to him, wiping her shirt with a wad of wet napkins. They both stand up when I reach the table.

"What happened to your shirt?" I ask Kiersten.

She looks at Kel and shakes her head. "Stupid boys," she says. She points to the table across from theirs. There are three boys who look a little older than Kiersten and Kel. They're all laughing.

"Did they do something to you?" I ask her.

She rolls her eyes. "When do they *not*? If it's not chocolate milk, it's applesauce. Or pudding. Or Jell-O."

"Yeah, it's usually Jell-O," Kel says.

"Don't worry about it, Will. I'm used to it now. I always keep an extra change of clothes in my backpack just in case."

"Don't worry about it?" I ask. "Why the hell isn't something being done about it? Have you talked to a teacher?"

She nods. "They never see it when it happens. It's gotten worse since the suspension. Now kids just make sure they only throw things at me when the monitors aren't looking. But it's fine, Will. Really. I have Abby and Kel and Caulder. They're all the friends I need."

I'm pissed. I can't believe she has to go through this every day! I look at Kel. "Who's the one Caulder was telling me about? The dickhead?" Kel points at the boy seated at the head of the table. "You guys wait here." I turn around and walk toward Dickhead's table. As I get closer, their laughter succumbs to confusion. I grab one of the empty chairs at their table and pull it around next to Dickhead and straddle the chair backward, facing him. "Hey," I say.

He just looks at me, then at his friends. "Can I help you?" he says sarcastically. His friends laugh.

"Yes. Actually, you can," I say. "What's your name?"

He laughs again. I can tell he's trying to play the part of the big, bad twelve-year-old that he is. He reminds me of Reece at that age. He can't hide the anxiety on his face, though.

"Mark," he says.

"Well, hi, Mark. I'm Will." I extend my hand, and he reluctantly shakes it. "Now that we've been formally introduced, I think it's safe to say that we can be frank with each other. Can we do that, Mark? Are you tough enough to take a little bit of honesty?"

He laughs nervously. "Yeah, I'm tough."

"Good. Because you see that girl over there?" I point back at Kiersten. Mark glances over my shoulder at her, then looks back at me and nods.

"Let me be candid with you. That girl is very important to me. *Very* important. When bad things happen to important people in my life, I don't take it very well. I guess you could say I have a bit of a temper." I scoot my chair closer to his and look him straight in the eyes. "Now, while we're being frank with each other, you should know that I used to be a teacher. You know why I'm not a teacher anymore, Mark?"

He's no longer smiling. He shakes his head.

"I don't teach anymore because one of my *dickhead* students decided to mess with one of my important people. It didn't end well."

All three of the boys are staring at me, wide-eyed.

"You can take that as a threat if you want to, Mark. But honestly, I have no intention of hurting you. After all, you're only twelve. When it comes to kicking someone's ass, I usually draw the line at fourteen-year-olds. But I will tell you this—the fact that you bully people? And *girls*, for that matter? Girls younger than you?" I shake my head in disgust. "It only goes to show what a pathetic human being you'll turn out to be. But that's not the worst of it." I look at his friends. "The worst of it is the people who follow you. Because anyone weak enough to let someone as pathetic as you be a leader is even *worse* than pathetic."

I look back at Mark and smile. "It was nice meeting you." I stand up and swing the chair under the table, then I place my hands on the table in front of him. "I'll be keeping in touch."

I look all three of them in the eyes as I back away from their table, then turn back to Kiersten and Kel. "Let's go. Caulder's waiting on us."

When the three of us get back to the gymnasium, we go to Caulder's table and take a seat. We haven't been seated for two minutes when Mrs. Brill marches up with a scowl. Right before she opens her mouth, I stand up and reach a hand out to her. "Mrs. Brill," I say with a smile. "It's so good of you to let Kiersten and the boys eat with me today. It really means a lot that you recognize there are families in this world in nontraditional situations. I love these kids as if they're my own. The fact that you respect our relationship even though I'm not a typical father says a lot about your character. So I just wanted to say thank you."

Mrs. Brill lets go of my hand and steps back. She eyes Kiersten and Kel, then me. "You're welcome," she says. "Hope you all enjoy the luncheon." She turns and walks away without another word.

"Well," Kel says, "that was definitely my *sweet*."

17.

THURSDAY, FEBRUARY 16

One more day . . .

"SO WHAT'S THE DAMAGE?" LAKE ASKS DR. BRADSHAW.

"To what? You?" He laughs as he slowly unwraps the bandage from her head.

"To my hair," she says. "How much did you chop off?"

"Well," he says, "we did have to cut through your skull, you know. We tried to save as much hair as we could, but we were faced with a pretty tough decision . . . it was either your hair or your life."

She laughs. "I guess I'll forgive you, then."

AS SOON AS we get home from the doctor, she heads straight for the shower to wash her hair. I'm pretty comfortable with leaving her home now, so I go to pick up the boys. When I get there, I remember that the school talent show is tomorrow night, and the students who signed up to perform get to stay and practice. Kiersten and Caulder both signed up, but neither of them is giving hints as to what they're doing. I've given Kiersten copies of all my poems. She says she needed them for research. I didn't argue. There's just something about Kiersten that you don't argue with.

When the boys and I finally get home, Lake is still in the bathroom. I know she's tired of me babying her, but I check on her anyway. The fact that she's been in there so long worries me. When I knock on the door, she tells me to go away. She doesn't sound happy, which means I'm not going away.

"Lake, open the door," I say. I jiggle the doorknob, but it's locked.

"Will, I need a minute." She sniffs.

She's crying.

"Lake. Open the door!" I'm really worried now. I know how stubborn she is, and if she hurt herself, she's probably trying to hide it. I beat on the door and shake the knob again. She doesn't respond. "Lake!" I yell.

The doorknob turns, and the door slowly opens. She's staring down at the floor, crying. "I'm okay," she says. She wipes at her eyes with a wad of toilet paper. "You really need to quit freaking out, Will."

I step into the bathroom and hug her. "Why are you crying?"

She pulls away from me and shakes her head, then sits down on the seat in front of the bathroom mirror. "It's stupid," she says.

"Are you in pain? Does your head hurt?"

She shakes her head and wipes her eyes again. She brings her arm up and pulls the rubber band out of her hair, and it falls down over her shoulder. "It's my hair."

Her hair. She's crying about her damn hair! I breathe a sigh of relief. "It'll grow back, Lake. It's okay." I walk around behind her and pull her hair away from her shoulders to her back. She's got an area on the back of her head that's been shaved. It can't be covered up, because it's smack dab in the middle of her hair. I run my fingers over it. "I think you would look cute with short hair. Wait till it grows out some more, and you can get it cut."

She shakes her head. "That'll take forever. I'm not going anywhere like this. I'm not leaving the house for another month," she says.

I know she doesn't mean it, but I hate that she's so upset. "I think it's beautiful," I say, running my fingers over her scar. "It's what saved your life." I reach around her and open the cabinet doors underneath the sink.

"What are you doing? You aren't cutting the rest of my hair off, Will."

I reach inside and pull out the black box that contains my hair trimmer. "I'm not cutting your hair." I plug in the cord and take off the guard and turn it on. I reach behind my head and press it against the back of my hair and make a quick swipe. When I bring it back around, I pull the pieces of my hair out and toss them in the trash can. "There. Now we match," I say.

She swings around in her seat. "Will! What the hell? Why did you do that?"

"It's just hair, babe." I smile at her.

She brings the wad of toilet paper back up to her eyes and looks at our reflection in the mirror. She shakes her head and laughs. "You look ridiculous," she says.

"So do you."

OTHER THAN HER doctor's appointment yesterday, tonight is Lake's first time out of the house. Sherry is watching the boys for a few hours after the talent show so we can have a date. Of course, Lake got upset when I told her about our date. "You never ask me, you always tell me," she whined. So I had to get down on my knee and ask her out. I'm keeping her in the dark again. She has no clue what I have planned for tonight. No clue.

Eddie and Gavin are already in the school auditorium with Sherry and David when we arrive. I let Lake sit next to Eddie, and I take the seat next to Sherry. Lake was able to pull her hair back into a ponytail and hide most of her scar. I'm not so lucky.

"Ummm . . . Will? Is this some sort of new trend I'm not aware of?" Sherry asks when she sees my hair.

Lake laughs. "See? You look ridiculous."

Sherry leans in to me and whispers, "Can you give me a hint as to what Kiersten's doing tonight?"

I shrug. "I don't know what she's doing. I'm assuming it's a poem. She didn't read it to you guys?"

Sherry and David both shake their heads. "She's been pretty secretive about it," David says.

"So has Caulder," I say. "I have no idea what he's up to. I don't even think he has a talent."

The curtain opens, and Principal Brill walks up to the microphone and gives her introductions to kick off the evening. For every child who performs, there's a different parent holding a video camera at the front of the audience. Why didn't I bring my camera? I'm an idiot. A real parent would have brought a camera. When Kiersten is called to the stage, Lake reaches inside her purse and pulls out a camera. Of course she does.

Principal Brill introduces Kiersten, who doesn't look nervous at all. She really is a miniature version of Eddie. There's a small sack draped over her wrist with the cast. She lifts her good arm to lower the microphone.

"I'm doing something tonight called a slam. It's a type of poetry that I was introduced to this year by a friend of mine. Thank you, Will."

I smile.

Kiersten takes a deep breath and says, "My poem tonight is called 'Butterfly You.' "

Lake and I look at each other. I know she's thinking the same thing I'm thinking, which is: Oh, no.

"Butterfly.
What a beautiful word
What a delicate creature.
Delicate like the cruel ***words*** that flow right
out of your ***mouths***
and the ***food*** that flies right out of your ***hands*** . . .
Does it make you feel ***better***?
Does it make you feel ***good***?
Does picking on a ***girl*** make you more of a ***man***?
I'm standing ***up*** for myself
Like I ***should*** have done ***before***
I'm not putting ***up*** with your
Butterfly anymore."

Kiersten slides the sack off her wrist and opens it, pulling out a fistful of handmade butterflies. She takes the microphone out of the stand and walks down the stairs as she continues speaking. "I'd like to extend to others what others have extended to me." She walks up to Mrs. Brill first and holds out a butterfly. "*Butterfly* you, Mrs. Brill."

Mrs. Brill smiles at her and takes the butterfly. Lake laughs out loud, and I have to nudge her to be quiet. Kier sten walks around the room, passing out butterflies to several of the students, including the three from the lunchroom.

"Butterfly ***you,*** Mark.
Butterfly ***you,*** Brendan.
Butterfly ***you,*** Colby."

When she's finished passing out the butterflies, she walks back on the stage and places the microphone in the stand.

"I have something to ***say*** to ***you***
I'm not referring to the ***bullies***

Or the ones they ***pursue.***
I'm referring to those of you who just ***stand by***
The ones who don't ***take up*** for those
of us who cry
Those of you who just . . . turn a blind eye.
After all, it's not ***you*** it's happening to
You aren't the one being ***bullied***
And ***you*** aren't the one being ***rude***
It isn't ***your*** hand that's throwing the ***food***
But . . . it is ***your mouth*** not ***speaking up***
It is ***your feet*** not taking ***a stand***
It is your ***arm*** not lending a ***hand***
It is your ***heart***
Not ***giving*** a damn.
So ***take up*** for yourself
Take up for your ***friends***
I challenge you to be someone
Who doesn't give ***in.***
Don't give in.
Don't let them ***win.***"

As soon as "damn" comes out of Kiersten's mouth, Mrs. Brill is marching onto the stage. Luckily, Kiersten finishes her poem and rushes off the stage before Mrs. Brill reaches her. The audience is in shock. Well, most of the audience. Everyone in our row is giving her a standing ovation.

As we take our seats, Sherry whispers to me, "I didn't get the whole butterfly thing, but the rest of it was so good."

"Yeah, it was," I agree. "It was butterflying excellent."

When Caulder is called onto the stage, he looks nervous. I'm nervous for him. Lake's nervous, too. I wish I knew what he was doing so I could have given him some advice. Lake zooms the camera in and focuses it on Caulder. I take a deep breath, hoping he can get through it without cussing. Mrs. Brill already has her eye on us. Caulder walks to the microphone and says, "I'm Caulder. I'm also doing a slam tonight. It's called 'Suck and Sweet.' "

Here we go again.

"I've had a lot of sucks in life

A lot

My parents died almost four years ago, right after

I turned seven

point of retreat

With every day that goes by, I remember
them ***less*** and ***less***
Like my mom . . .
I remember that she used to ***sing***.
She was ***always*** happy,
always dancing.
Other than what I've seen of her in pictures, I
don't really remember what she looks like.
Or what she ***smells*** like
Or what she ***sounds*** like
And my ***dad***
I remember ***more*** things about him, but only
because I thought he was the most amazing man
in the world.
He was ***smart***.
He knew the answers to ***everything***.
And he was ***strong***.
And he played the ***guitar***.
I used to love lying in bed at night, listening to
the music coming from the living room.
I miss that the ***most***.
His ***music***.

After they died, I went to live with my
grandma and grandpaul.
Don't get me wrong . . . I ***love*** my grandparents.
But I loved my ***home*** even more.
It ***reminded*** me of them.
Of my mom and dad.
My brother had just started college
the year they died.
He knew how much I wanted to be home.
He knew how much it ***meant*** to me,
so he made it ***happen***.
I was only seven at the time, so I let him do it.
I let him give up his ***entire life*** just so
I could be home.
Just so I wouldn't be so ***sad***.
If I could do it all over again, I would have
never let him take me.
He deserved a shot, too. A ***shot*** at being ***young***.
But sometimes when you're seven, the
world isn't in ***3-D***.
So,
I owe ***a lot*** to my brother.
A lot of ***thank yous***

A lot of ***I'm sorrys***
A lot of ***I love yous***
I owe a ***lot*** to you, Will
For making the ***sucks*** in my life a little less ***suck-***
ier
And my ***sweet***?
My ***sweet*** is right ***now***."

I wonder if a person can cry too much. If so, I'm definitely reaching my quota this month. I stand up and make my way past Sherry and David and out into the aisle. When Caulder walks down the steps to the stage, I pick him up and give him the biggest damn hug I've ever given him.

"I love you, Caulder."

WE DON'T STAY for the awards. The kids are excited to be spending the evening with Sherry and David, so they're all in a hurry to leave. Kiersten and Caulder don't seem to care who won, which makes me a little proud. After all, I've been drilling Allan Wolf's quote into Kiersten's head every time I give her advice about poetry: *The points are not the point; the point is poetry.*

After David and Sherry drive away with the boys, Lake and I walk to the car, and I open the door for her.

"Where are we eating? I'm hungry," she says.

I don't answer. I shut her door and walk around to the driver's side. I reach into the backseat and grab two sacks off the floor and hand one to her. "We don't have time to stop and eat. I made us grilled cheese."

She grins when she opens her sack and pulls out her sandwich and soda. I can tell by the look on her face that she remembers. I was hoping she would.

"Do I actually have to eat it?" she says, crinkling up her nose. "How long has it been sitting in your car?"

I laugh. "Two hours, tops. It's more for show, bear with me." I take the sandwich out of her hands and drop it back into the sack. We have a pretty long drive," I say. "I know a game we can play; it's called Would You Rather. Have you ever played it before?"

She smiles at me and nods. "Just once, with this really hot guy. But it was a long time ago. Maybe you should go first, to refresh my memory."

"Okay. But there's something I need to do." I open the glove box and pull out the blindfold. "Our destination is sort of a surprise, so I need you to put this on."

"You're blindfolding me? Seriously?" She rolls her eyes and leans forward.

I wrap it around her head and adjust it over her eyes. "There. Don't peek." I put the car in drive and pull out of the parking lot, then ask the first question. "Okay. Would you rather I looked like Hugh Jackman or George Clooney?"

"Johnny Depp," she says.

That answer was a little too fast for my comfort. "What the *hell*, Lake? You're supposed to say Will! You're supposed to say you want me to look like me!"

"But you weren't one of the options," she says.

"Neither was Johnny Depp!"

She laughs. "My turn. Would you rather have constant, uncontrollable belching, or would you rather have to bark every time you heard the word 'the'?"

"Bark as in like a dog?"

"Yeah."

"Uncontrollable belching," I say.

"Oh, gross." She wrinkles up her nose. "I could live with your barking, but I don't know about the constant belching."

"In that case, I change my answer. My turn again.

Would you rather be abducted by aliens or have to go on tour with Nickelback?"

"I'd rather be abducted by the Avett Brothers."

"Wasn't an option."

She laughs. "Fine, aliens. Would you rather be an old, rich man with only one year left to live? Or a young, poor, sad man with fifty years left to live?"

"I'd rather be Johnny Depp."

She laughs. "You suck at this," she teases.

I reach over and interlock fingers with her. She's leaning back in the seat, laughing, without a clue in the world where we're headed. She's about to be pissed—but hopefully only for a little while. I drive around a bit longer while we continue our game. I could honestly play this game all night with her, but we eventually pull up to our destination, and I hop out of the car. I open her door and help her stand up. "Hold my hands. I'll lead."

"You're making me nervous, Will. Why do you always have to be so secretive when it comes to our dates?"

"I'm not secretive, I just love surprising you. A little bit farther, and I'll let you take off your blindfold." We walk inside, and I position her exactly where I want her.

I can't help but smile, knowing how she'll react once I take off her blindfold. "I'm about to take it off, but before I do, just remember how much you love me, okay?"

"I can't make any promises," she says.

I reach behind her and untie the blindfold. She opens her eyes and looks around. Yep, she's pissed. "What the *hell*, Will! You brought me on a date to your *house* again? Why do you always do this?"

I laugh. "I'm sorry." I throw the blindfold on the coffee table and put my arms around her. "It's just that some things don't need to be done on a stage. Some things need to be private. This is one of them."

"*What* is one of them?" She looks nervous.

I kiss her on the forehead. "Sit down, I'll be right back." I motion for her to sit on the couch. I go to my bedroom and reach into the closet and pull out her surprise. I stick it in my pocket and walk back to the living room. I turn on the stereo and set "I & Love & You" on repeat; it's her favorite song.

"You better tell me now, before I start crying again . . . does this have anything to do with my mom? Because you said the stars were the last thing."

"They *were* the last thing, I promise." I sit beside her on the couch and take her hand in mine, looking her straight in the eyes. "Lake, I have something to say, and I want you to hear me out without interrupting me, okay?"

"I'm not the one who interrupts," she says defensively.

"See? Right there. Don't do that."

She laughs. "Fine. Talk."

Something just doesn't feel right. I don't like how we're so formally seated. It's not us. I grab her leg and arm and pull her onto my lap. She straddles me, wrapping her legs around my back. She hangs her hands loosely around my neck and looks me in the eyes. I go to speak, but I'm cut off.

"Will?"

"You're interrupting me, Lake."

She gives me a half smile and brings her hands to my face. "I love you," she says. "Thank you for taking care of me."

She's sidetracking me, but it's nice. I slowly slide my hands up her arms and rest them on her shoulders. "You would do the same for me, Lake. It's what we do."

She smiles. A tear makes its way down her cheek, and

she doesn't even try to hold it back. "Yep," she says. "It's what we do."

I take her hands in mine and bring her palms to my lips and kiss them. "Lake, you mean the world to me. You brought so much to my life . . . right when I needed it the most. I wish you could know how hopeless I was before I met you, so you would realize just how much you've changed me."

"I *do* know, Will. I was hopeless, too."

"You're interrupting again."

She grins and shakes her head. "I don't care."

I laugh and push her down onto the couch and climb on top of her, pressing my hands into the couch on either side of her head to hold myself up. "Do you have any idea how much you frustrate me sometimes?"

"Is that a rhetorical question? Because you just told me to stop interrupting you, so I'm not sure if you want me to answer it."

"Oh my God, you're *impossible*, Lake! I can't even get two sentences out!"

She laughs and grabs the collar of my shirt. "I'm listening," she whispers. "Promise."

I want to believe her, but as soon as I begin to speak

again, she crushes her lips to mine. For a moment, I forget what my whole point is. I'm consumed by the taste of her mouth and the feel of her hands making their way up my back. I lower my body onto hers and let her sidetrack me some more. After several minutes of intense sidetracking, I'm somehow able to tear myself away from her grasp and sit back up on the couch.

"Dammit, Lake! Are you gonna let me do this or not?" I take her hands and pull her up to a sitting position, then I get off the couch and kneel on the floor in front of her.

Until this moment, I don't think she had any clue what tonight was about. She looks at me with a mixture of emotions in her expression. Fear, hope, excitement, apprehension. I'm sharing those exact same emotions. I hold her hands in mine and take a deep breath. "I told you the stars were the last gift from your mother, and technically, they were."

"Wait, *technically*?" she says. She realizes she's interrupting me again when I glare at her. "Oh yeah. Sorry." She puts her finger to her mouth, indicating she isn't going to say anything else.

"Yes, *technically*. I said the stars were the last thing she gave us, and they were. But she gave me one star that isn't in the vase. She wanted me to give it to you when I was ready. When you were ready. So . . . I hope you're ready."

I put my hand in my pocket and pull out the star. I place it in her hand for her to open. When she does, the ring slides out and into her palm. When she sees her mother's wedding ring, her hand goes up to her mouth, and she sucks in a deep breath. I take the ring and hold her left hand.

"I know we're young, Lake. We've got an entire lifetime ahead of us to do things like get married. But sometimes things in people's lives don't happen in chronological order, like they should. Especially in our lives. Our chronological order got mixed up a long time ago."

She holds out her ring finger. Her hand is shaking . . . but so are mine. I slide the ring onto her finger. It's a perfect fit. She wipes my tears away with her free hand and kisses me on the forehead. Her lips come a little too close to mine, so I have to pause and kiss them. She puts her hand on the back of my head and closes her lips over mine as she slides off the couch and into my lap. I lose my balance and we fall back. She doesn't let go of my head, and our lips never separate while she continues to give me the absolute best kiss she's ever given me.

"I love you, Will," she mutters into my mouth. "I love you, I love you, I love you."

I gently pull her face away from mine. "I'm not finished yet." I laugh. "Stop butterflying interrupting me!" I roll her over onto her back and prop myself up on my elbow beside her.

She starts kicking her legs up and down in a fit. "Hurry up and ask me already, I'm *dying* here!"

I shake my head and laugh. "That's just it, Lake. I'm not asking you to marry me . . ."

Before I can get the rest of my sentence out, a look of horror washes across her face. I immediately put my finger to her lips. "I know how you liked to be *asked* and not *told.* But I'm not asking you to marry me." I roll on top of her and lean in as close as I can while still looking her in the eyes. I lower my voice to a whisper. "I'm *telling* you to marry me, Lake . . . because I can't live without you."

She starts crying again . . . and laughing. She's

laughing and crying and kissing me all at the same time. We both are.

"I was so wrong," she says between kisses. "Sometimes a girl *loves* to be told."

"ARE YOU KNOCKED up?" Eddie asks Lake.

"No, Eddie. That would be you."

We're all sitting in the living room. Lake couldn't wait to tell Eddie, so she called immediately to tell her the news. Eddie and Gavin were here within the hour.

"Don't get me wrong, I'm super excited for you. I just don't get it. Why so sudden? March second is only two weeks away."

Lake looks at me and winks. She's snuggled up next to me, sitting on her feet. I lean in and kiss her lips. Like I said, I can't help it.

Lake turns back to Eddie and answers her. "Why would I want a traditional wedding, Eddie? Nothing about our lives is traditional. None of our parents would be there. You and Gavin would be our only guests. Will's grandparents probably wouldn't even show up . . . his grandmother hates me."

"Oh, I forgot to tell you," I say. "My grandmother actually likes you. A lot. It's me she wasn't happy with."

"Really?" Lake says. "How do you know?"

"She told me."

"Huh." She smiles. "That's nice to know."

"See?" Eddie says. "They'll show up. So will Sherry and David. That's nine people right there."

Lake rolls her eyes at Eddie. "Nine people? You expect us to pay for an entire wedding for nine people?"

Eddie sighs and falls onto Gavin's lap in a defeated slump. "I guess you're right. It's just that I was looking forward to planning a big wedding someday."

"You can still plan your own," Lake says. She looks at Gavin. "How many more minutes until you propose, Gavin?"

He doesn't skip a beat. "About three hundred thousand or so."

"See, Eddie? Besides, I need you to do my hair and makeup," Lake says. "We need witnesses, too. You and Gavin can come, and Kel and Caulder will be there."

Eddie smiles. She seems a little more excited now that she knows she's invited.

I was hesitant at first about Lake's plan, too. But after I heard her logic, and especially after I heard how much money it would save us not having a wedding, I was easily convinced. The date of the marriage was a given.

"What about the houses? Which one will you guys live in?" Gavin says.

We've been talking about it for two weeks, even before tonight's proposal. After she stayed here, we both knew it would be impossible to live in separate houses again. We came up with the plan about a week ago, but now seems like the perfect time to share it.

"That's one of the reasons we wanted you guys to come over," I say. "I had about three years left on my mortgage, and no less than two weeks after Julia passed away, the title came in the mail. She paid it off before she died. She paid the rent on Lake's house through September; that's when the lease is up. So now we'll have an empty house with six months of prepaid rent. We know you guys are looking for a place before the baby comes, so we're offering you Lake's. Until September, anyway . . . then you'll have to sign your own lease."

Neither one of them says anything. They just look at us in shock. Gavin shakes his head and starts to protest.

Eddie slaps her hand over his mouth and turns to me. "We'll take it! We'll take it, we'll take it, we'll take it!" She starts clapping and jumps up and hugs Lake, then hugs me. "Oh my God, you guys are the best friends ever! Aren't they, Gavin?"

He smiles, obviously not wanting to appear desperate, but I know how much they need a place of their own. Eddie's excitement eventually outweighs Gavin's modesty, and he can no longer contain himself. He hugs Lake, then hugs me, then hugs Eddie, then hugs me again. When they finally calm down and sit back down on the couch, Gavin's smile fades.

"Do you know what this means?" he says to Eddie. "Kiersten's about to be *our* parallel neighbor."

18.

FRIDAY, MARCH 2

It's worth all the ***aches,***
All the ***tears,***
the ***mistakes*** *...*
The heart of a man and a woman in love?
It's worth ***all*** *the pain in the* ***world.***

I'VE SPENT THE LAST TWO WEEKS GIVING HER EVERY opportunity to opt out of doing things this way. Lake insists she doesn't want a traditional wedding, but I don't want her to regret her decision someday. Most girls spend years planning out the exact details of their wedding. Then again, Lake's not most girls.

I take a deep breath, not really understanding why I'm so jittery. I'm sort of glad it's so informal. I couldn't imagine how shot my nerves would be if we had more of an audience. My hands won't stop sweating, so I wipe them on my jeans. Lake insisted I wear jeans, said she didn't want to see me in a tux. I'm not sure what dress she picked out, but she didn't want to wear a wedding dress. She didn't see the point in buying a dress to only wear once.

We aren't doing the traditional aisle walk, either. I'm pretty sure she and Eddie are down the hall in the courthouse public restroom doing her makeup right now. It all seems so surreal, marrying the love of your life in the same building where you register your car. But honestly, it wouldn't matter where we got married, I'd be just as excited . . . and just as nervous.

When the doors open, there isn't any music. No flower girls or ring bearers. Just Eddie, who comes in and sits in a chair next to Kel. The judge walks in right after Eddie and hands me a form and a pen. "You forgot to date this," he says.

I press the form down on the podium in front of me and date it. *March 2.* That's our day. Lake's and my day. I hand the paper back to him, and the door to the courtroom opens again. When I turn around, Lake's walking in, smiling. As soon as I lay eyes on her, a wave of relief washes over me, and I'm immediately calm. She has that effect on me.

She looks beautiful. She's wearing blue jeans, too. I laugh when I notice the shirt she has on. She's wearing that damn ugly shirt I love to hate. If I could have handpicked what she would wear on our wedding day, it would be exactly this.

When she walks up to me, I wrap my arms around her, pick her up, and spin her around. When I plant her feet back on the floor, she whispers in my ear. "Two more hours."

She isn't referring to the marriage, she's referring to the honeymoon. I grab her face and kiss her. Everyone else in the room fades into the distance as we kiss . . . but only for a second.

"Eh-hem." The officiant is standing in front of us, unamused. "We haven't quite gotten to the kissing of the bride yet," he says.

I laugh and take Lake's hand as we position ourselves in front of him. When he begins reading his wedding service, Lake touches her hand to my cheek and pulls my gaze toward hers, away from the officiant. I take her hands in mine and pull them up between us. I'm pretty sure the officiant is still talking, and that I should be paying attention, but I can't think of anything else I'd rather be paying attention to. Lake smiles at me, and I can see she isn't paying attention to anything around us, either. It's just me and her right now. I know it isn't time yet, but I go ahead and kiss her anyway. I don't hear a single word of the wedding sermon as we continue to kiss. In less than a minute, this woman is about to become my wife. *My life.*

Lake laughs and says "I do" without pulling away from my mouth. I didn't even realize we had gotten to that part. She closes her eyes again and gets right back into rhythm with me. I know weddings are important to some people, but I have to fight back the urge to pick her up and carry her out of here before it's over. After a few more seconds, she starts giggling again and says, "He does."

I realize she just said my line, so I separate my lips

from hers and look at the officiant. "She's right, I do." I turn back to her and resume where we left off.

"Well, then, congratulations. I now pronounce you husband and wife. You may *continue* kissing your bride."

And so I do.

"AFTER YOU, Mrs. Cooper," I say as we exit the elevator.

She smiles. "I like that. It has a nice ring to it."

"I'm glad you think so, because it's a little late to change your mind now."

When the elevator doors close behind us, I pull the key out of my pocket and check the room number again. "It's this way," I say, pointing to the right. I take her hand in mine and start down the hallway. I'm forced to an abrupt stop, however, when she jerks me back.

"Wait," she says. "You're supposed to carry me over the threshold. That's what husbands do."

Before I can bend down and take her in my arms the traditional way, she puts her arms on my shoulders and jumps up, wrapping her legs around my waist. I have to grab hold of her thighs before she slips. Her lips are right in proximity to mine, so they briefly get kissed. She grins and runs her hands through the back of my hair, forcing my mouth onto hers again. I try to grip her legs with one hand and her waist with the other, but I feel like she's slipping, so I take two quick steps until she's propped up against a hotel room door. It's not our door, but it'll do the job. As soon as her back hits the door, she moans. I remember the bruises from a few weeks ago. "Are you okay? Did I just hurt your back?"

She grins. "No. That was a good sound."

The intensity in her eyes is magnetic. I'm unable to break our stare as I stand there, holding her up against the door. I grab her under the thighs and hoist her even higher, pressing my body against hers for more leverage. "Five more minutes," I say.

I grin and lean in to kiss her again, but she's suddenly farther away. As soon as I realize that the door we're leaning against is opening up behind her, I do my best to catch her. Instead, I fall to the ground with her, and we both end up in a heap on the floor of someone's hotel room. She still has her arms around my neck, and she's laughing until she looks up and sees a man and two children staring down at us. The man doesn't look very pleased.

"Run," I whisper. Lake and I crawl out of the hotel room and pull ourselves up. I take her hand in mine, and we run down the hallway until we find our room. I slide the key into the reader, but before I open the door, she slips in front of me and faces me.

"Three more minutes," she says. She reaches behind her and pulls down on the handle, swinging the door open. "Now carry me over the threshold, husband."

I bend down and grab her behind the knees and pick her up, throwing her over my shoulder. She squeals, and I push the door all the way open with her feet. I take a step over the threshold with my wife.

The door slams behind us, and I ease her down onto the bed.

"I smell chocolate. And flowers," she says. "Good job, husband."

I lift her leg up and slide her boot off. "Thank you, wife." I lift her other leg up and slide that boot off, too. "I also remembered the fruit. And the robes."

She winks at me and rolls over, scooting up onto the bed. When she gets settled, she leans forward and grabs my hand, pulling me toward her. "Come here, husband," she whispers.

I start to make my way up the bed but pause when I come face-to-face with her shirt. "I wish you'd take this ugly thing off," I say.

"You're the one who hates it so much. *You* take it off."

And so I do. I start from the bottom this time and press my lips against her skin where her stomach meets the top of her pants, causing her to squirm. She's ticklish there. Good to know. I unbutton the next button and slowly move my lips up another inch to her belly button. I kiss it. She lets out another moan, but it doesn't worry me this time. I continue kissing every inch of her until the ugly shirt is off and lying on the floor. When my lips find their way back to hers, I pause to ask her one last time. "Wife? Are you sure you're ready to *not* call retreat? Right now?"

She wraps her legs around me and pulls me closer. "I'm butterflying positive," she says.

And so we don't.

acknowledgments

To condense into a paragraph all of the people that deserve a thank you would be impossible. Therefore, I'm just going to have to write dozens of more books in order to fit you all in. For now, I want to recognize my girls of FP: my role models, my confidants, my sounding boards, my friends, my 21. I love each and every one of you and couldn't thank you enough for letting me slip through in that last second. You've changed my life.

about the author

Colleen Hoover is the *New York Times* bestselling author of two novels: *Slammed* and *Point of Retreat.* She lives in Texas with her husband and their three boys. Find out more at www.colleenhoover.com

Follow her on Twitter @colleenhoover and on Facebook.

Read on to see how the story started

Slammed

COLLEEN HOOVER

1.

I'm as nowhere as I can be,
Could you add some somewhere to me?

—THE AVETT BROTHERS, "SALINA"

KEL AND I LOAD THE LAST TWO BOXES INTO THE U-HAUL. I slide the door down and pull the latch shut, locking up eighteen years of memories, all of which include my dad.

It's been six months since he passed away. Long enough that my nine-year-old brother, Kel, doesn't cry every time we talk about him, but recent enough that we're being forced to accept the financial aftermath that comes to a newly single-parented household. A household that can't afford to remain in Texas and in the only home I've ever known.

"Lake, stop being such a downer," my mom says, handing me the keys to the house. "I think you'll love Michigan."

She never calls me by the name she legally gave me. She and my dad argued for nine months over what I would be named. She loved the name Layla, after the Eric Clapton song. Dad loved the name Kennedy, after a Kennedy. “It doesn’t matter which Kennedy,” he would say. “I love them all!”

I was almost three days old before the hospital forced them to decide. They agreed to take the first three letters of both names and compromised on Layken, but neither of them has ever once referred to me as such.

I mimic my mother’s tone, “Mom, stop being such an *upper*! I’m going to *hate* Michigan.”

My mother has always had an ability to deliver an entire lecture with a single glance. I get the glance.

I walk up the porch steps and head inside the house to make a walk-through before the final turn of the key. All of the rooms are eerily empty. It doesn’t seem as though I’m walking through the house where I’ve lived since the day I was born. These last six months have been a whirlwind of emotions, all of them bad. Moving out of this home was inevitable—I realize that. I just expected it to happen after the *end* of my senior year.

I’m standing in what is no longer our kitchen when I catch a glimpse of a purple plastic hair clip under the cabinet in the space where the refrigerator once stood. I pick it up, wipe the dust off of it, and run it back and forth between my fingers.

“It’ll grow back,” Dad said.

I was five years old, and my mother had left her trimming scissors on the bathroom counter. Apparently, I had done what most kids of that age do. I cut my own hair.

"Mommy's going to be so mad at me," I cried. I thought that if I cut my hair, it would immediately grow back, and no one would notice. I cut a pretty wide chunk out of my bangs and sat in front of the mirror for probably an hour, waiting for the hair to grow back. I picked the straight brown strands up off the floor and held them in my hand, contemplating how I could secure them back to my head, when I began to cry.

When Dad walked into the bathroom and saw what I had done, he just laughed and scooped me up, then positioned me on the countertop. "Mommy's not going to notice, Lake," he promised as he removed something out of the bathroom cabinet. "I just happen to have a piece of magic right here." He opened up his palm and revealed the purple clip. "As long as you have this in your hair, Mommy will never know." He brushed the remaining strands of hair across and secured the clip in place. He then turned me around to face the mirror. "See? Good as new!"

I looked at our reflection in the mirror and felt like the luckiest girl in the world. I didn't know of any other dad who had magic clips.

I wore that clip in my hair every day for two months, and my mother never once mentioned it. Now that I look back on it, I realize he probably told her what I had done. But when I was five, I believed in his magic.

I look more like my mother than like him. Mom and I are both of average height. After having two kids, she can't really fit into my jeans, but we're pretty good at sharing everything else. We both have brown hair that, depending on the weather, is either straight or wavy. Her eyes are a deeper emerald than mine, although it could be that the paleness of her skin just makes them more prominent.

I favor my dad in all the ways that count. We had the same dry sense of humor, the same personality, the same love of music, the same laugh. Kel is a different story. He takes after our dad physically with his dirty-blond hair and soft features. He's on the small side for nine years old, but his personality makes up for what he lacks in size.

I walk to the sink and turn it on, rubbing my thumb over the thirteen years of grime collected on the hair clip. Kel walks backward into the kitchen just as I'm drying my hands on my jeans. He's a strange kid, but I couldn't love him more. He has a game he likes to play that he calls "backward day," in which he spends most of the time walking everywhere backward, talking backward, and even requesting dessert first. I guess with such a big age difference between him and me and no other siblings, he has to find a way to entertain himself somehow.

"Hurry to says Mom Layken!" he says, backward.

I place the hair clip in the pocket of my jeans and head back out the door, locking up my home for the very last time.